THE MADHOUSE

THE MADHOUSE

A FANTASY CORRESPONDING TO TRUTH

for Christine —

Nagy szeretettel —

from

Beauxdraps x

JASON ELLIOT

Beauxdraps

First published in Great Britain in 2019 by Beauxdraps Publishing

Copyright © Jason Elliot 2019

Jason Elliot asserts the moral right to be
identified as the author of this work in accordance
with the Copyright, Designs and Patents Act 1988

A catalogue record for this book is available from the British Library

ISBN 978 1 9161105 0 2

Every man specially that one what outside is hungry for
truth and secret of happiness always one thing forget.
Is problem not possible to ecsape but thing what nobody tell like smallest writing in document of
insurance. Any body what wish more than any other
thing for real life and not false, wish that all of his
act has purpose, wish that ~~this is the experience surely~~
~~experience~~ life can be satiafsy and not empty wish
also to —
└to have some love feeling for such dear mother of
wife always not understand that if wish to change, then
cannot stay same. Maybe rich may be poor but not make
any different is same difficult for shah or gondabshur
For one thousand year could drink from fountain of zam
zam or got marry to Queen Bilkis or learned how is
possible to breathe underneath water but problem is
same because nothing can chnge on inside from ~~the~~
what on outside. ~~One should not be surprised this is~~
~~answer is~~ Real man or woman from time of born should
ask that question: what is life porpose and how he can
disccover how can live every day with meaning and
satisfy how can discover what is true each time. Will
get hapinnes from such answer discovered but like
every one did became expert to hide from that question
like fat woman who never admit that thing what every
other one can see when her trouser get each day more
tighter and she did even prefer special mirror what
hide truth.

[s.256]

A page of the original manuscript (see pages 162–163).

Editor's Preface

Occasionally a scholar is favoured by the unexpected discovery of a work of no academic significance but one of such unusual character as to call out for a greater audience, as well as to present almost unique challenges to translator and interpreter alike. Such is the enigmatic text referred to only as a *safar nameh* (meaning 'travel diary' in Persian) by its author, a native of the scarcely explored border territories between Azerbaijan and Daghestan, considered locally to comprise the heartland of the Caucasus.

In 2015 the University of Sordomuto's ethnographic unit was deployed to that spectacular natural conformation of mountain, forest and valley that forms the homeland of such little-known peoples as the Lezgin, Tsakhur and Tabassaran. Among such populations the roots of identity and tradition are deeply felt. Powerful tides from Animist, Christian and Islamic sources have for centuries mingled inextricably here (and for the most part peacefully) to shape those traits so characteristic of mountain populaces: hardiness, pride and spiritual independence.

In the remotest reaches of this dramatic landscape, where fieldwork is both blessed and bedevilled by the hospitality and curiosity of locals wishing sincerely to assist their foreign guests, news of an outsider's presence spreads at bewildering speed. At times the spontaneous appearance of meals, gifts and more invitations from well-wishers than can ever be accepted is almost overwhelming, and the volume of impromptu visits from strangers seeking the attention of foreign 'doctors' must be judiciously managed!

It was on one such occasion that a bundle of papers was presented to me in person by an English-speaking local who, having heard that I was conducting research for a book of ethnographic studies, claimed to have written a book himself on the subject of his own 'travels' – a *safar nameh* in which, the author hopefully proposed, Western audiences might take an interest.

We conversed for as long as my obligations allowed and I undertook to read the visitor's manuscript in my spare time. Finding it at first impenetrable, I put it aside. A much later reading brought unforeseen rewards as well as many questions, but only long after the author had failed to return to collect his enigmatic opus. We would never meet again. Thus was raised the distant prospect of publication.

The original manuscript, which must be considered unique, is unsigned, untitled and hand-typed in English with frequent handwritten annotations (mostly poetic couplets) in both Russian and Persian (*see frontispiece*). So idiosyncratic is the author's manner of expression in English that a direct transcription was considered impracticable, rendering the final text almost a work of translation. In this task we have shared the dilemma of the distiller, who must drive pure spirit away from the unwanted substrate, while preserving the flavours and sensory characteristics of its origin. To assign a title to the result is inevitably problematic; we have chosen *The Madhouse* in order to convey the dramatic dimension of the narrative, but the name cannot be considered all-embracing. It is often argued that a translation should not sound like a translation, and that the characteristics for which a writer is loved are in fact his imperfections. Every effort has been made (in the Heideggerian spirit of 'unswerving, yet erring') to transmit the authenticity of the narrator's imperfect voice, its earnest didacticism and – even at its most disturbing moments – the distinctive humour that is woven like a dark filament throughout.

There is scant evidence in the manuscript to reliably situate either the author or his strange story; the grammatical conundrums on every page render stylometric analysis impossible. In person his grasp of English suggested a period of life abroad in an English-speaking environment; other than brief mention of his father's posting to the Yemen in some minor official context, no other country was mentioned. Although the narrator claims early on not to speak perfectly the language of his captors, he identifies neither his original nor his adopted home. It would be presumptuous to suppose that the omission, like so many others, is accidental.

Other than commonplace references to the well-known cities of the Caucasus and central Asia – a 'kindly dervish' is from Baku, a former lover is from Tabriz, Abkhazian curses are chosen for their explicitness, memory is likened to the meandering tributaries of the Amu Darya – geographical identifiers are obstinately imprecise. Of the story's heroic triumvirate, one speaks 'a broken Daghestani dialect' and another 'sounds' South American. The beautiful nurse with poisonous saliva is merely suspected of possessing Kazakh blood. Only the habitual mendacity of the English and the distinctive anatomy of Ukrainian women are singled out as specifically national traits. A single identifiable historical event – that of Pushkin's encounter with the dead body of the murdered diplomat Griboedev in 1829 – is mentioned in the entire text.

Many more references, borrowings and colloquial idioms go entirely unacknowledged. No effort is made to explain the proverbial imagery of 'cat-dancing', 'breaking walnuts with one's tail' or 'pulling out the salt'. Where I have discovered or been alerted to literary sources, indications are given in footnotes, rather than a glossary, for convenience. Others must remain wilfully obscure.*

Our task here is to introduce *The Madhouse*, not to interpret it.

---

* See Balbettio & Ciancia, *Indigenous felicific indices associated with otiose bisection of keratino-melanate filaments*, Sordomuto University Press.

I wish only to suggest that three avenues of interpretation are probably open to the reader, who ultimately must furnish his own keys to the puzzle. If we take, firstly, the physical setting and characters of *The Madhouse* as faithful descriptions, we are soon obliged to admit not only to significant shortcomings from the narrative point of view – a frustratingly Oriental indifference to fix events in space and time being the least of these – but also to their obvious lack of credibility. Are descriptions of underground cities or Jackal-headed torturers to be taken in their literal sense? We might easily conclude that the author's purpose was to earnestly record experiences in the manner of a confession, best understood as an autobiographical record of what at times must be considered to border on pathology, in line with an outlandish French Surrealist or one of the more bizarre episodes of the Persian novelist Sadeq Hedayat's *Boof-e Koor* [*The Blind Owl*].

Such an interpretation may be the most straightforward and risks the least, but takes no account of what must be considered one of many hints along the way:

> Everything pointed to the fact that we had been set apart from the ordinary world, where the language of things was straightforward and things meant what they appeared to mean, and where they had no hidden significance. *But in here, everything seemed to have another meaning. Everything related to something more than our experience itself.* [My italics]

This may refer to the narrator's experience of the 'parallel' conditions of existence within his new surroundings; it may echo the idea of a second, *psychological* existence that arises in the individual who has embarked on inner search; it may also alert the perspicacious reader to a fundamental feature of the narrative itself. Guided by such clues, we may accept that the fantastic portions of *The Madhouse* depict imaginary conceptions and impossible scenarios which are nonetheless purposefully deployed.

Thus opens a second way, wherein the story may be understood not merely as a flight of Oriental fancy, but an allegorical one, which strives for universality beyond that of the existential *angst* and fantasies of the artist alone. This very issue is raised pointedly by the narrator himself during the period of his subterranean explorations:

> If on the other hand I was simply hallucinating, what was the significance and purpose of these private, yet strangely coherent, mental adventures?

What indeed? The problem of meaning remains above all, and the crucial challenge of deciding what is real and what illusory is as much the reader's as it is that of the narrator's. As his friend and fellow would-be escapologist reminds him:

> Out there ... it's what you appear to be that matters. In here it is what you *are*.

Perhaps this too is an exhortation directed at the reader's powers of interpretation. A third avenue (and challenge) thus opens, perhaps most problematically: to take to heart the author's own description of the document as a *safar nameh* or 'traveller's diary'.* This asks the most of us, as it implies the existence of a meta-narrative which begs to be interpreted psychologically, vindicating the author's own description of his work as *isharati* or 'allusive'; thus interpreted,

---

* I owe the genesis of this intriguing idea to the suggestion of my learned colleague Dr Nader Roshanfekr, who points out that the trilateral Arabic root *s-f-r* (from which the Persian *safar* is derived) embraces the allied meanings of 'discovery' and 'disclosure' as well as 'unfolding' (as of a journey) and 'unveiling'; and that the esoteric exegeses of certain schools recognize in the term *safar* an allusion not only to travel and exploration of the *afaq* or worldly 'horizons' but also of the psychological expanses of the *anfus* or 'selves'; that is, within the (potentially evolving) consciousness of the individual. We offer this suggestion to the discerning reader.

The Madhouse must be re-cast not merely as a symbolic tale, but as something which reaches beyond the social or moral generalities of fable.

Could it be, then, that *The Madhouse* and all its characters is an exploration of the psychology of a single man, corresponding to the realities of psychological experience? Many things are resolved if this leap of faith be made, and the severity of shortcomings in both narrative structure and character development are much reduced thereby. The narrator himself, interpreted thus, represents *the* Protean individual who has experienced first-hand the forceful 'capture' of incarnation within the sensible world, and who has chosen the path of psychological self-discovery, finding the task longer and more challenging than popular notions of 'self-help' might have us suppose. The main characters he encounters – unresolved and even tragic at first glance, but later transformed by their experiences – call to mind the universality of human transformation. Others, together with their strengths and weaknesses, may likewise be understood psychologically, as timeless components of human nature – some to be befriended and others shunned.

However we choose to interpret it, *The Madhouse* is in essence a simple tale; of reluctant captivity, longing and the quest for something beyond the reach of the ordinary self. It is, like its interpretation, full of uncertainty, and a comfortable resolution – as in life – is at no stage guaranteed. Perhaps too as the reader steps into these pages, his journey echoes that of the story's own protagonist; an unsuspecting soul in search of liberation from both past and future, his fate teetering on the ever-renewing crux of the present moment.

Prof. Don de Beauxdraps
University of Kurzsichtig, 2019

R . T . F . E . P

You who are lounging in this house full of dreams and fancies
Just get up, pack your things, and leave. No need to say a word

Rumi, *Divan-e Kabir*, 2219

I

Chapter 1

M Y BELOVED GRANDFATHER, may his noble soul rest in peace, used to say strange things. The Sun, he said, moved around the Earth. Time, he said, did not exist. The human mind, he said, was little more than a calculating machine, useful for yoghurt recipes or inventing devious methods to kill ever greater numbers of people, but incapable of understanding the real meaning of anything.

Among all these strange sayings was his favourite: that in life, there are two rivers. Both begin their journeys far away from their destination, the Ocean. The first, moving by gradual stages from separation towards unity, reaches its final home, flows into it and becomes one with it. The second wanders, divides and branches, slowly exhausting itself in the course of its long passage, and little by little trickles into the earth and disappears, leaving no trace. Every human being, he would say, had both these rivers within him, and the most important task in life was to distinguish, each and every day, between one and the other.

Those were his mysterious words. Mysterious, at least, to me. What was I to make of their meaning when first I heard them in my early youth, and life seemed to be running as smoothly as the conscience of an arms trader or serial adulterer from the provinces? I knew what the words meant, but in those days, I freely admit, I understood nothing.

You could put it all another way and say that to know about those famous Agdashian pomegranates from south of the Turianchay is one thing, and to taste them another; or that a man who has attained a spiritual practice no longer has any need of theory; or that if he longs to experience the kind of love that is uncorrupted by existence, or even to drown in Love's Ocean, he must first give up philosophizing about it.

Forgive my impertinence, but these days does anyone know that such an Ocean even exists, let alone how to make his own way towards it without stumbling into a desert as dry as the Taklamakan?* Even when great truth hits someone over the head, like Vasily Vasilyevitch's peculiar flying meatball, he can make no sense of it because he's never acquired the taste for it, and will either choke to death right there at the bus stop where he's been innocently waiting, or be discreetly recommended by his closest friends for a lengthy period of sedation. Truth, like poison, should be administered in small doses over a long period, but where are the Mithradates† of truth in the modern world, patiently inoculating people against fantasy and illusion? As for modernity, so-called: could the Prince of Slander‡ Himself ever have foreseen his own luck at the state of things? Even his less ingenious opponents, the Archangels, must surely know

---

* Occupying nearly 400,000 square kilometres of the Tarim basin in China's westernmost province of Xinxiang (formerly Chinese Turkestan) and bordered by the Kunlun mountain range to the south, the Pamirs to the west and the Tien-Shan to the north, the Taklamakan is one of the world's largest and driest deserts.

† Mithradates VI 'Eupator Dionysus' (134–63BC), polyglot emperor of Greek and Persian ancestry and thorn in the side of Roman conquest in Asia, whose pioneering investigations into immunity from multiple poisons give us 'Mithradate', the universal antidote (hence *mithradatism*).

‡ That is, the Devil.

that the rate at which mice are turned into real men has no more improved under the glorious influence of modernity than has the fate of turkeys at Christmas. The so-called modern man is just as careless and brutal as he's ever been, and shows no sign of being liberated from the very thing that ruins it all: himself. The world is his mirror, and look at the state of it.

I admit I am jumping ahead. I always have. I have always wanted to be free of the laws of the Earth, to fly before I could walk, and a lot of useless flapping that has caused me. It has always seemed to me that to live well, happily and to reproduce one's species is something any vegetable can do. But a *man*? I wanted to live and to know I was alive, the way you do when you feel ice-cold water on the back of your head after a night of heavy drinking, or when you have to smuggle something large and awkwardly shaped across a border at night.

The devious manipulation of sheep, otherwise known as politics, never caught my imagination. Nor had I any patience for philosophy, the senile chattering of men who couldn't decide whether snow was cold or the sky was really blue. Science might have suited me; I was particularly interested in theories of evolution and toxicology. Had I not fallen on my head as a small child, damaging the part of my brain (or so I told myself) that computes numbers, I might have singlehandedly resurrected the lost works of an al-Khwarazm° or an Ulugh-Beg.† But these

---

° The pioneering ninth-century Arab mathematician from whose name the term 'algorithm' derives (not, as sometimes believed, from the Greek *arithmos*, 'number').

† Mirza Muhammad Taraghay bin Shahrukh (1394–1449), Timurid ruler, mathematician, poet and astronomer, who founded the famous observatory of Samarqand. His star catalogues, along with other astronomical calculations, were not superseded in the West until the nineteenth century.

days a scientist is not supposed to detect intelligence in the miracle of the cosmos, or beauty in a bird of paradise, though he's always quick to be excited by beauty in his own theories. The infinite genius of Nature, who Herself supervised his very creation from the moment his mother's thighs first began to tingle at the sight of her kindly uncle, leaves him cold. A scientist will lecture an eagle on the laws of flight, or thrust the latest formula for a painkiller into the hands of Christ himself in the act of healing the sick. You see what I am getting at. As for religion, or what passes for it, that was spoiled for me by religious people; in particular, by cold-hearted zealots stuffed full of sermons, their piety in public matched only by their lack of charity in private.

I was attracted to soldiering: the idea of risking one's life, a gift given on trust and already at risk, seemed to me both logical and fair. I tried it for a while, in the days when there was still some honour left to it all, until I saw what men could do to others when the ordinary rules are lifted. I lost my appetite. I learned that the dead are safe from torture, and that the deepest wounds can be invisible and remain unhealed for life. But I was glad to have been shown at close hand how thin and easily torn the veil between life and death, and to have understood that to be near to death is, strangely enough, to be close to life.

What interested me was love: the heart is its organ. It seemed to me a higher form of soldiering. Not the *idea* of love; not the meek and sentimental cliché which is not love at all, but the love that is fearless and inspires and, if need be, annihilates. Not the worldly love of a Casanova, but of an Arjuna* or Majnoon,†

---

* Warrior-Hero of the Hindu *Bhagavad Gita*.

† Lit. 'possessed' or 'maddened' (by love), lover of Layla in the Persian epic romance *Layla va Majnun*. Compare Rumi in his *Mathnawi*: 'Love comes with a knife, not some shy question, and not with fears for its reputation . . . love is a madman.'

by which I might be transformed, like a moth in an irresistible flame.

I was a fool, of course, to suppose it was possible to live a life built on love in a world so preoccupied with the dues of Caesar, and sooner or later took my place in the ordinary scheme of things. But the world, for all its glittering distractions is, let's face it, a thankless old hag who leads you nowhere except to more distractions. Like everyone else I wasted much time on what is useless and irrelevant to the needs and pattern of the soul before discovering that it is simpler to be what one really is than to compare oneself endlessly to others. It has been said that death is sufficient as an admonisher to men,* and any fool can see that the harvest of man's life does not amount to much.† Make no mistake: as a man sows . . . you know the rest.‡ God knows if I, your friend in longing, left it too late, but I can tell you how it started.

To establish myself in the world, nothing seemed more important than to own a house. My father had given up his own, having understood that no man can serve two masters, and had long since chosen between the perfection of life and the per- fection of his soul, and lived accordingly. As much as I loved them, I was appalled in my youth by my parents' indifference to worldly gain. They were too humble to share the secret of their happy condition, which I took for poverty, not realizing that it was infinite wealth. Then came the day that my wish, after much struggle was granted. Although it was far from the

---

* A *Hadith* or saying of the Prophet Mohammed.

† Compare the poet Hafez, *Ghazal 75*: 'The harvest of this workshop of space and time does not amount to much' [Editor's translation].

‡ The author assumes familiarity with St Paul's exhortation in his famous Epistle [Galatians 6:7].

country of my birth,* I at last found myself alone in my new home. Now that the dream had come true, I was as happy as I'd ever been.

Why wouldn't I be? I had a signed contract in my hand and wanted nothing more than to get into the place that now belonged to me. There was nothing to stop me: I had the keys. The previous owner had already given them to me, and told me to wait another day or two before I actually moved in, but I didn't feel like waiting. It was my house now and I could go there when it suited me. I accept that you could say this was my first mistake, and that it led to everything else, but it was a genuinely innocent one.

There is a kind of happiness which allows you to forget who you are. To know it once is enough, and the echo of it lasts a lifetime. I remember just how it was, like a child's first vision of a glittering *haft-seen*.† The whole house was filled with sunlight and I wandered from room to room like someone in love – love, as I thought of it then – knowing it was mine to do what I wanted with and that no one could take it away. That night, I slept like a baby, and in the morning woke up with the sun on my face, feeling happier than ever. It was a quiet morning and I remember lying in that delicious no man's land between sleep and waking, relishing the warmth, too comfortable to move. A human ear of corn, you could say, ripening happily in the sunshine, paying just not quite enough attention to the sound of scything in the distance.

I don't remember the name, which was something like Mr Ahmad or Hamed, but I remember the voice that was calling

---

* Neither the country of the author's birth nor that of his acquired home is ever named.

† Persian term for the symbolic decorations associated with the New Year's holiday *Nowruz*.

it out and which woke me up. It had a nasal, whining quality to it, and sounded just how the rag-and-bone men on Tbilisi *prospekt*° used to sound. It brought me unexpectedly to my senses. It was a mystery to me how a stranger could get into the house uninvited, so although I was surprised, I told myself it must be the police thinking the house was empty but been told there was a light on, or the property agent needing to give me some extra document, or the previous owner who'd just remembered the secret stash of gambling money he'd hidden from his wife. And since I'd never been afraid of the police or any kind of official I simply let whoever it was come upstairs. Of course, I asked who it was, but as I was lying in bed as naked as a Belarussian whore, I couldn't stop him from coming upstairs. I watched as he came to the door of the bedroom and looked in, smiling nervously. Then he knocked on the door. I remember thinking what an idiotic thing it was to knock on someone's door after you've already gone inside his house, like trying to put the seeds back into a watermelon after you've spat them onto someone's carpet.

When he introduced himself I realized he wasn't a policeman at all, but some kind of doctor. He even wore a white coat, as if he was in a hospital. He was a small man with a thick black beard and dark, sparkling eyes. To me he looked like a rat, and I half-expected to see a long tail coming out from under his coat. After I'd got over my surprise I asked him what I needed a doctor for because I wasn't ill. I asked in a polite way, because even if he did look like a rat I didn't yet have a reason to hate him.

He called me again by the name I've forgotten so I asked him who he meant, and explained that that wasn't my name. His ratty eyes blinked a few times and he read out the address from a document in his hand and asked if I was the owner of the

---

° Russian term for a broad avenue; but the city remains unspecified.

house. I was certainly the owner, I told him, but added that I'd only bought the house the day before. I could see he was beginning to doubt what was true and what wasn't, and he took a step or two into the room, saying that by means of the document he was entitled to enter the house. Then as he read out a passage from one of the pages he took another few steps towards me.

The language he spoke was not my own, and I admit that some of the words were unfamiliar to me. I was, after all, a guest in his country. But I do know that wherever you go, officials will use complicated words to conceal the truth. Now, this doctor could see that I wasn't completely stupid and he was getting nervous. As the saying goes, when the enemy's strategy is exhausted, he rings on the bell of friendship. His manner grew more gentle. He said everything was for my benefit, and that I needn't be concerned, and that if there was any mistake in the official document he was waving about, it could all be sorted out later.

I could see he'd already decided I was guilty, and that this was all for show, because I know about rats and I know that once they smell blood they'd rather die before giving up. I just knew that he could smell mine. As he got closer to me he even offered to show me the pages of the document, and was all lovey-dovey and coy smiles, just like a Tabrizi* woman I used to know whenever we'd been apart for a spell. But he didn't share her natural gifts, and he was close enough already for my liking.

Apart from my clothes in a heap and the mattress I was sleeping on there was nothing in the room but a sturdy, old-fashioned telephone. I'd no idea whether it was connected or not. I reached for it and said I'd be happy to look at the paperwork but that I needed to make a call before anything else, and

---

* A native of Tabriz, the largest city of northwest Iran.

lifted the receiver. The rat doctor laughed nervously and came right up to me and with great skill managed to get a handcuff on my wrist. He didn't get the other on because I have always had quick reactions, picked up the telephone and hit him as hard as I could on the side of his head.

He fell over, got up and staggered out, clutching his ear and swearing loudly. Then I heard him shouting to someone else to be careful because I had a history of violence. How quickly a Heaven can turn into a Hell! I didn't even have time to get into my clothes. I'd barely got up when a few seconds later another white-coated figure appeared at the door, but this time much bigger and stronger-looking and keen for a bit of thuggery. I could see this wasn't the moment to start exchanging our favourite jokes about regional ethnic minorities.*

Standing in the doorway and blocking out the light like a Soviet battleship, he claimed he didn't want to hurt me, which struck me as a presumptuous sort of thing to say. Now that I had properly woken up, I felt just the opposite, and hurt is exactly what I wanted to cause to him. Who were these people to come into my house and create havoc? I pushed hard against him to get out of the door but his hand closed over my wrist with a grip of iron, so I threw my knee as hard I could between his legs. He wasn't expecting that, screamed like a pig at slaughter and collapsed, and my happiness was almost fully restored.

There was only one thing to do: to run and get downstairs and get outside and get as far away as possible and get help. I had never needed it more in my whole life. I was not only naked but on my own and very afraid. I couldn't run to a neighbour: I didn't have any. I had no money, no possessions, no way of proving who I was or wasn't, and no plan. What else was there

---

* The text deploys derisory colloquial terms for Jews, Gypsies and Khazars.

to do but run for it? Vaguely, I pictured a public telephone, and a link to help from afar. But who would help me?

I got as far as the front door. Then I saw another man coming up onto the porch, also looking for some ∂ava-∂ava* and built for it too. He had the frame and the big bloated face of a wrestling champion, and when he pushed his way inside like a wrecking-ball I knew I didn't have a chance. His hand came up like a guided missile, and a sudden white flash filled my vision. I even heard the crashing sound inside my head travelling from front to back, just like a long, slow freight train coming off its tracks, and was surprised that with all that noise there was no pain. Then a sort of curtain came down, closing out the light, closing out all feeling, closing out all hope, and I felt myself floating down to earth like a leaf, and there was nothing I could say or do, because that was the end of the story.

The truth, of course, is that it wasn't the end but the begin-ning. I couldn't tell you where or how far they took me, or how long I slept. It really makes no difference whether it was for a day or a year, because after they took me my ordinary life simply stopped, like a clock that's been stopped by a bomb blast. I knew that life would never be quite the same again. I didn't know just how upside down everything would be from now on, but I already had a sense, don't ask me how, that none of the usual measures would apply any more.

I just remember one strange detail. I was in a new place I didn't recognize, where a man and a woman were looking at me. They must have been a doctor and a nurse because they were also wearing white coats, but they looked like professionals, not like the bandits who'd kidnapped me from my own home. They were looking at me and talking, not realizing that I could hear every word they were saying. And they couldn't know,

---

* In Azeri, a violent form of competitive bare-knuckle streetfighting.

because all they saw of me was my body, laid out like a dead person on a stretcher, while I wasn't even in my body. I've read about it happening, but you can imagine my surprise at finding myself hovering near the ceiling of the room feeling perfectly fine, seeing those doctors and hearing them talk as if I wasn't there, and seeing even my own body, limp and looking pretty miserable, with what looked like a big black eye coming on and a stream of dried blood down my front. It was the first time I realized without any doubt that your self and your body are not the same thing at all, and that they can exist separately from each other, at least for a short while.

The doctor shone a light in my eye to check my reflexes. I wanted to tell him to be careful because that was my body he was poking around, but of course I couldn't. I just had to watch. Then he touched my face where that big *svolloch*° had hit me, and turned to the woman doctor next to him and chuckled, saying, *That's going to hurt in the morning*, as if I was just a piece of meat. I was astonished at his confidence, his lack of human feeling. The woman doctor had a clipboard and was writing down some details. I could see her profile and her long black hair, the narrowness of her waist and the lovely flare of her hips, and felt embarrassed that she was seeing me in that condition. It was even worse when she began manhandling me to get a sort of pair of pyjamas on me, and I realized she was looking at me in a very specific way. Not me, but my body. I wanted to tell her that they weren't the same thing, and decided that if I ever had the chance, I'd ask her if she'd like to meet somewhere, after all this had blown over. I was fairly sure from those lovely eyes and high cheekbones she had Kazakh blood, and you know what Kazakh women are like. The more I looked at her, the more gorgeous she seemed.

° 'Bastard', in Russian.

13

Then almost by way of punishment, I felt myself having to return to my body, like a *jinn** who has to get back into his bottle after having granted someone a wish. It even gave me some sympathy for *jinns*; it was a horrible experience. I suddenly felt heavy and helpless, and I could feel someone – it was that cold-hearted doctor – pulling roughly on my cheek as if I was a dog. I could actually feel pain again, which I hadn't felt at all while I was floating about on the ceiling trying to get a better look down the front of that lovely nurse's coat. Then instead of that tantalizing sight, all I could see was a hazy version of the doctor's face, grinning at me but not in a kind way at all, and saying as he kept pulling on my cheek:

'Congratulations, you're in the madhouse now.'

That's when I knew, as I say, that none of the usual measures would apply any more, and that nothing would ever be quite the same. I couldn't speak. I was too upset for words in any case. From that moment I had only one wish, which was the same night and day, and which for the first time in my life – if you can call it life – became stronger than any other. And it was only from then on that I first began to fathom the strange words of my dear and very venerable grandfather.

---

* More conventionally, *genie*, but we have preserved the Eastern transliteration.

14

Chapter 2

AFTER THAT, there were times when I couldn't quite tell if I was alive or dead. For a while I must have simply looked like a corpse. Sometimes an hour could seem like all day, sometimes a few moments. Time didn't make much sense at all. I realized the instrument you measure time with is a delicate one and can break completely if you smash it around enough. It isn't the only invisible thing that you take entirely for granted in normal life. I once met an Abkhasian soldier whose sense of gravity had gone wrong after he was injured in the head, and he used to think he was floating and couldn't get his feet back on the ground. It was no good lecturing him solemnly about gravity, or torturing him by telling him he made no sense. That's what he felt was happening to him, and that was his experience of what was real.

They'd put me on some kind of drug which made me feel a stranger to myself, unable to distinguish night or day. I couldn't even tell the difference between what was happening outside myself and what I was imagining, the way the horizon between the sea and the sky loses its definition when you look at it from a long way off. It isn't until you're in that kind of state* that you

---

* осознание, which has the related meanings of perception, or awareness.

realize consciousness is a delicate thing. If you want to build the wall of a house, you need big stones at the bottom, and small ones at the top, where everything is more delicate. Consciousness is more or less the same. If the walls are strong enough, the house will stand up even to storms and flooding. But if you've only ever lived in a comfortable house, you can't imagine what it's like to huddle in a smashed-up ruin. I could look but I didn't see; I could hear but I wasn't listening. I was just waiting for the builder to come back and repair the work that had been damaged, because, at least in my part of the world, a master always wishes for the work that he loves to be complete.

I didn't eat. Some sort of chemical soup was giving me life through a tube, which kept my body going but didn't do much for my mind. But little by little the pieces began to fall into place, like a big family coming back together again, after every different member has been travelling in a foreign country. And like most big family reunions, it's not long before you experience pain.

It was bearable if I didn't move, but the effort of even small movements reminded me that every part of your body is connected to the rest. My eye hurt the most. Next came the whole of my face. My chest felt as though a horse had trampled over it, making every breath a struggle. My legs hurt too, and when I stood up my knees were inexplicably painful, as if I'd been praying on a rocky mountainside like some poor hermit trying to fend off visions of scantily dressed Palestinian women.

Then came a different kind of pain, a more persistent kind, like the brash cousin who everyone else in the family has to listen to. This was the pain of feeling that I was a prisoner, a wrongful prisoner, that my identity had been mixed up with someone else's, and that I must at any price reveal the crime and find out who was responsible for this assault on my rights. Not to mention my dignity. I'd never had a feeling as strong as this before, and I wanted desperately to share it with someone.

16

The problem was I couldn't think. My ability to think was the slowest of all to return, like a really long-lost son coming back after a drawn-out adventure. I was still so confused about everything and the problem seems to have been my memory. You can still have strong thoughts without memory, but the results are different, as your neighbour will remind you when you forget it's his wife's cleavage you're staring at. But when parts of your memory are taken away, you realize how much you needed it for everything, like a map of your own country. You need it not just for big expeditions but even for shopping. If you can't even remember where the baker is, you just wander about without a plan, getting more and more hungry. What I mean is that during those first awful days, that's more or less what I was: a beggar searching for bread, trying to understand what had happened, and how it had happened, and how this Hell had begun.

I said I was a prisoner, but the strange thing is that my room felt familiar. A real prisoner finds himself in an alien place, deprived of all the things he knows and loves. And the pain of being separated from all that is comfortable and familiar to him sustains his sense of affliction and, unless he's lost all hope, fuels his determination to return to the life he knows from before. That's the whole point of prison, which is supposed to be a punishment. But when I stood up for the first time and tried to make sense of the room I was in, I saw such an unexpectedly personal and familiar thing that all my brooding about being a prisoner was turned on its head. It was the *gelim** I'd bought years before from a kindly dervish in Baku, a thing that had lived with me ever since the beady-eyed old fellow had rolled it up and wrapped it in newspaper and string. It evoked a feeling

---

* More conventionally, *kilim*, a flat-surfaced, tapestry-woven carpet, predominantly produced in Turkey and Iran.

17

of intimacy so much at odds with the black thoughts swirling around in my head that I was completely baffled. Who would go to the trouble of capturing someone and putting him in prison, only to make him feel more at home?

I walked very slowly to the cupboard, and found my clothes and shoes. I walked to the table, and saw several framed photographs which, like the *gelim*, had been with me for years. I looked at them for a long time, and because my memory was still so damaged, remembered the details of the people and things connected to them only gradually, like someone following a path in thick fog. I reached for one of the pictures and felt a sharp pain in the bend of my arm, and looked down to see the needle marks on the vein where they'd put the tranquillizer. Then I went back to trying to gather up my own memories, piecing them together like a photograph of a woman you've torn up after discovering she was more than just good friends with your own brother.

There's a proverb that says your first three days in prison are the longest in your life. I can vouch for that. You are gripped by a feeling of the impossible, that your situation can't be happening to you and that the whole thing is a dream. You cannot believe it because you have no way to measure it; the whole experience is too far outside your ordinary life. It's a feeling of sickness, just like a child's terrible feeling of separation at going to school for the first time, when he can't swallow food and his stomach is as tight as a fist. Your mind tells you it can't be happening. You would give anything just to return home. It's not a bad dream but a nightmare. You can wake up from a bad dream. But a nightmare keeps going no matter how much you scream or cry, and you just get used to it because it doesn't stop and you have no other choice. I know I am going on about it. I do know.

It turns out it's not such a difficult thing to take a man and throw him into a new reality such that he doubts his own identity and even his own name. I even doubted my own name the first few days I was in that room. In a theatre, the line between what is real and what is illusion is deliberately distorted for the story that's being told. But after you get out into the street, your sense of what is real is restored and you know the show has ended.

It was the other way around here. Having woken up, I was even more confused, especially by my surroundings. At first it seemed like a kindness that someone had gone to the trouble of putting the things that were precious and familiar to me in the room. Then I was suspicious. I didn't want to be comforted. I wanted justice – violently, if necessary. I wanted to break the heads of the criminals who'd put me in here against my will. But why, why would anyone give comfort to someone whose life they'd just ruined? It was like one of those American films where they shoot someone violently to bits, race over to the bullet-riddled body, and then with a look of tender concern, call urgently for the medics.

Of all the things that should have been familiar, you'd think that my own reflection in the mirror would have been the one. But I was looking at the face of a stranger, who answered my questions with nothing but silence. I've always found mirrors a bit disconcerting, especially after a few drinks, when I wonder who the other fellow is, looking at me like that. This was a thousand times more frightening. I didn't *know* the person I was looking at. Had I become a stranger to myself, now that normal life had been taken away from me? Or was I such a stranger to myself in normal life, and simply hadn't known it?

I refused to go out. I didn't speak. I suppose that was my own stupid idea of a protest. I was hoping that when they discovered the terrible mistake the authorities had made, the director of the place would come on behalf of all the others and kiss my feet until I decided to forgive him. But the visit never came. I grew tired of silence.

They left me alone, perhaps to allow me to carry out my own private war, leaving me to exhaust myself. I wondered all the while why they would bother to kidnap me just to leave me on my own in a room with my own things. Perhaps they, whoever they were, knew that a prisoner is like a cat who hears scratching under the floorboards and, being a cat, has to respond to the instinct to investigate.

I decided that I would watch and observe every possible detail before taking any action. I took stock of things. There was nothing in the room to suggest that it was in fact a prison, or any kind of ordinary institution. I was in the bedroom of an old grand house, which a century or more earlier must have belonged to an important family. It was spacious and had perhaps once been elegant. There was a bold plaster cornice around the ceiling and high wooden wainscot around the wooden floor, which was dark with age. There was a small empty fireplace with a narrow mantelpiece above it, and everything had been painted over many times. The window was tall and curtained but the original panes had been removed and replaced with the kind that are impossible to open. The glass was thick and green and inside it was a net of thin wire reinforcement. Beyond it were several thick metal bars. Not a breath of air escaped from around the sides. I admit that seemed a bit strange.

Beyond the glass, at only an arm's length, was a brick wall which obscured whatever the original view might have been, though it was impossible to say whether this was to prevent people looking in or looking out. Apart from this unusual feature there was nothing out of the ordinary about the room itself. It looked like a room in a country hotel, except for the fact that nearly all my own clothes were in the cupboard. This suggested the possibility of an extended stay. For that very reason it was a long time before I got changed, feeling that if I did, I was sending out a signal of consent.

Three times a day I was brought food, along with a pill which I never took. Every morning, afternoon and evening I would hear the jangle of keys turning inside the locks of the door, a sound I came to know so well it was like a brand on my skin. Then the door would open and one of those Mudaks* would come in carrying a tray, put the food on the table and collect whatever was left over from his previous visit, and all without a single glance in my direction. The Mudaks wore blue tunics like the dim-witted orderlies in hospitals who push wheelchairs around while they gawp at the nurses. I called them Mudaks, forgive me, because the part of their brain responsible for humour had been removed at birth. At least that's how they behaved. They never smiled or looked at me. They did most of their tasks in pairs, and whenever one came to the room there was always another waiting silently outside the door like a bodyguard just waiting for an excuse to commit violence. They all had black eyes and black hair, cut short like a boot-brush, and strongly Asiatic features like Mongolian warriors. They never said a word. The food, however, was surprisingly good, and it was helping me get my strength back. But why give me such good food on top of such an awful crime?

I didn't know anything back then. For much of the day I took to listening to the sounds made by pipes inside the walls. It may seem like a strange way to spend one's day, but I never got bored of it. Captivity changes what you take an interest in. It felt like I was discovering what was happening in other parts of the house, and even though the walls were thickly plastered, a glass pressed against one of them allowed me to hear all sorts of different sounds, like a boy who's made a radio and is listening to those first faint and tantalizing signals. There was the

----

* A strictly masculine term of extreme offence in Russian suggesting both stubbornness and ignorance.

sound of flowing water, and the sound of it stopping, either by a valve (suddenly) or by a tap closed by hand (slowly). Sometimes a piece of metal or something solid banged against a pipe. Once or twice I could tell that someone had hit a pipe with something really heavy and the sound seemed to transmit the violence of their mood. Long before I saw any other life in the place, I already knew it was there, just from listening to all these sounds. Of course I stopped when the Mudaks brought in food, and watched them silently just in case they showed any sign of human emotion. And I've nothing against Mongolians but I was always glad, and especially at mealtimes, that I hadn't been born there.

Then it all changed, on the day of the alarm, because everything changes eventually. It was almost fun to watch because it was the first time I saw those expressionless faces look almost worried. One of them stood guard by the door like one of Timur's° personal sentries, and the other came in to clear away breakfast and put some lunch on the table. My memory must have been better by then because I remember it was salmon for lunch, and I'd asked him whether he'd caught it himself. Had he used a fly to catch it? I asked. Or had he just charmed it out of the water with his natural charisma? I enjoyed teasing them like that, though they never said anything.

Then the alarm went off. Not just any alarm, but a siren to separate the dead from their souls, or at the very least to signal a nuclear onslaught. The Mudaks froze, while I wondered for a brief moment whether I'd touched something and actually set off the alarm myself. I admit that part wasn't funny. What was funny was seeing them fixed to the spot in surprise, like rabbits

---

° Timur (1336–1405), the West's Tamerlaine, legendary founder of the Timurid Dynasty and in his own lifetime the military conqueror of most of south, west and central Asia.

– or lizards, more like, with their cruel black eyes – caught in a searchlight. They looked at me, they looked at each other, they looked around, and then fled like devils from holy incense. They even left the tray with the dirty plates on the table. And they also left the door open.

Chapter 3

I CREPT OUT AS SLOWLY AS I COULD, half expecting to be slaughtered on sight, like one of Ashurbanipal's unlucky captive lions.° I was careful to leave the door open and unlocked in case I had to run back. Now I could see that I was on the upper floor of a large building, on one side of a square which overlooked a large atrium. There were about a dozen other doors like mine, giving onto a balcony with walls of latticed marble. If this was a prison, it was an unlikely one. I seemed to be in an enormous old-fashioned house. There was some comfort in this; it gave the place a vague sense of familiarity. Not that I'd ever lived in such an enormous place, but everyone has heard about grand old houses, and I felt as though I'd seen the place as if in a dream or in the memory of another life.

I jumped in fright as I saw my first other normal-looking human being: a man in smart business clothes, hurrying past me as he struggled to get inside his jacket, as if he was late for an investors' meeting. He didn't even look at me and disappeared on the far side of the square.

° Ashurbanipal, king of the Assyrian Empire 668-627BC, famously portrayed in combat with lions (sometimes mortally wounded in advance for the purpose) in palace reliefs of the period.

The sight of him gave me the confidence to move to the edge of the balcony and look down into the atrium. Below me everyone was racing around like stage hands between the acts of a play when all the scenery and furniture has to change. For a moment I even thought it might actually be a theatre. The Mudaks were all running to and fro, making me think that perhaps they had brains after all, each of them carrying armfuls of books or clothes or a chair or a carpet. The alarm was driving everyone into a frenzy. I couldn't make out any purpose to all the running around, but after a few minutes I realized they were cleaning the place up, like teenagers who've thrown a party and whose parents are coming back home early.

Beyond the far corner of the balcony was a staircase with wide steps and a small landing at the halfway point. I went down slowly, surprised to see how well-crafted the original structure must have been. The steps and banisters were made from a dark polished wood and the handrail, which looked as if it might be ebony, was broad and as smooth as a mirror. I stopped in fright once again as some others ran past me, in such a hurry that they paid no attention. I decided to stay on the landing, where there was a good view of the main space below, but from where I could get back quickly to my room if necessary.

At the far end of the atrium two men were struggling to right an overturned sofa, and several others were lifting the central carpet so that someone else could clean underneath. Another man was carrying a painting towards the hook on the wall where it had been hanging before, and another was returning a plant to a small table, after which he began dusting off the leaves with a cloth. Four or five of the Mudaks were cleaning the floor and walls with brushes and sponges, but instead of their usual somnambulance they were really throwing themselves into the task. From time to time a small man, who looked as though he wouldn't come up to my waist, stepped boldly up to them and pointed out the spots they'd missed or needed to clean, then walked over to point out the defects in someone else's efforts. Perhaps he was a kind of foreman.

As the place began to transform in front of my eyes, I could see the whole area was in fact a large entrance room. On one side, opposite a grand fireplace, was an arch and a hallway and a large black front door. I was excited to see it because it was so close it looked as though I'd have no difficulty reaching it and running outside when no one else was looking. Seeing how easy my escape might be lifted much of those bitter and desperate feelings I'd been experiencing alone in my room.

The whole thing seemed mad. If the place was so easy to escape from, I had to wonder what the purpose of keeping people inside really was. If they could come and go it certainly wasn't a prison. I already knew it couldn't be a prison. But it wasn't an ordinary madhouse either, because it was obvious that the people I could see, including the Mudaks, were acting with some kind of purpose towards definite ends.

Just as I had that thought, the alarm stopped. It was a huge relief, which signalled another transformation among the people I was watching. They put away their tools and rags, straightened out their clothes and hair and made quite sure they looked clean and smart. I nearly laughed. Then the Mudaks all walked to one side of the room like the staff in an old-fashioned household when the master has returned from the capital. Others sat down on various chairs as if they were doing nothing more than watching blossom falling on a tranquil spring day. Two men in smart clothes sat at a table and began to play a civilized game of chess, in the very spot where moments earlier the pieces had been scattered across the floor.

Less than a minute after that, I understood the reason for the transformation. The man I had earlier seen struggling to get into his suit was walking, calmly now, towards the hallway door with a dutiful-looking middle-aged woman by his side. They opened it and went in and I could see that beyond it was another black front door. Above this door was a pair of lights in metal housings, just like the lights above the door in aircraft which parachutists jump from, one red and one green. The red one was on at that moment but the green one lit up a few seconds later, and as the door opened the two of them stepped beyond the threshold.

I couldn't see what happened next because the door swung shut for about another minute, after which the diplomatic-looking couple stepped back into the hall and moved politely aside for another couple, who were very obviously the honoured guests of the occasion. Looking at them I had a sudden feeling of familiarity which seemed to be impossible, until I remembered the strange interlude of the doctor and nurse who examined me when I was unconscious. It all came back to me at the sight of them: the doctor's cold-hearted confidence, the way he'd spoken to me when he thought I couldn't hear, and the tall nurse with her strong chest and the curve of whose hips seemed to be calling out to my hands. What's more I could see the Oriental-looking features of her face now and she was even more beautiful than I remembered. I couldn't wait to see the looks of embarrassment after the conversation that we'd soon have, and after that, who knows, that sultry-looking nurse might even take me up on an offer to meet, after the slight problem of my identity had been properly sorted out.

Then the two of them came up the entrance steps and into the main room, and seeing such a tranquil and ordered scene broke into smiles like Ali Baba setting eyes on his cave-full of treasure. The residents looked up from whatever they were doing and smiled back in the most genteel way, and one of the smartly dressed men who was playing chess even lifted his hat with a polite nod, as innocently as a neighbour wanting to borrow a cup of sugar. Then the happy pair advanced to the line of staff, who mumbled greetings with their eyes turned down. I knew

27

then that there was definitely some serious cat-dancing° going on, and that the Mudaks and the residents were in it together by way of some kind of deal that I didn't fully understand.

After their little tour, they crossed the room towards another room which I couldn't see. Just before they reached it, the little man who'd been giving orders ran up to them, and sank into a theatrical bow so low that he nearly kissed his own foot. When he stood up, they had already walked past and were talking to someone else, and it's just as well they didn't see the obscene gesture he delivered when he realized he'd been overlooked.

I wasn't quite sure what to do. I crept down a few more steps, and could see that some of the residents were looking at me, which was disconcerting at first because it seemed likely some-one would point me out as a stranger. But the odd thing is that they were looking *through* me, like goldfish staring out from their bowls with the same lack of expression in their eyes, before their attention turned somewhere else.

I reached the grand stone fireplace, which wouldn't have looked out of place in a castle, and could see from there into the adjoining room. Within it, there was a smaller room which must have been an office, because the door wasn't closed and I could see books and papers and the corner of a desk. As I was watching, the man who'd let them in walked out of the office and passed me. It was clearly the same man I'd seen earlier running past my bedroom and I felt a momentary kinship with him, even though he did look like a bank manager. I apologized for interrupting him and asked whether he thought it would be possible for me to speak to the doctor.

A pair of large and owl-like eyes turned suddenly onto me, as if their owner had seen a ghost. The dome of his head, as if

---

* In both Azeri and Persian, '*gorbe raqsani*': the equivalent of 'monkey business'.

it contained some detecting instrument which my speaking had set off, leaned unexpectedly towards me, displaying a silvery halo of closely shaven hair. He was silent as if he was thinking about the question, then smiled and opened his mouth as if he was nervous about the reply, which was causing more effort than normal to make. Then his mouth got wider and wider and for a moment I thought he was about to be sick over me, until I heard the muscles of his throat trying to work, but without the benefit of a voice behind them. Then he closed his mouth and smiled again as if nothing was the matter, and then tried again to speak.

It was agony to watch. His mouth got wider and wider but all that came out of it was the tortured sound of his throat contracting, like a man who's seen a dead body for the first time but has nothing in his stomach to release, or as if a chicken bone had lodged there and he was trying desperately to get it out in his own special but not very effective way. Instinctively I wanted to hit him on the back, but he wouldn't have it. Once again he stopped the whole effort and was very quiet, as if he knew that this time it would all work. Then he tried to speak very suddenly, as if to catch his own voice before it disappeared, the way some dogs can catch a rat and kill it with a single bite. But the dog wasn't fast enough. All that came out was the chicken-bone choking sound. It was too unsettling to watch any longer, so I thanked him and walked towards the office myself. I looked back once, and saw that he was still trying to speak, this time not to another person but just to the empty fireplace, and with about the same rate of success as he'd had with me.

As I walked closer, I could see that the office had once been a library, perhaps from the time when the house had been a home and in the days when the master of a house actually did some studying. The door was still open and I could see one of the residents inside talking with the doctor, and behind him I could make out the same dark wood as the stairs and the same quality of workmanship, even though the shelves themselves were largely bare. I couldn't hear the words being exchanged but I could see that the resident was agreeing with something the doctor was telling him. Then the conversation finished and he came to the door and opened it more fully. On the far side I could see the nurse standing by the window, the shape of her body silhouetted by the sunlight streaming in from the window behind her, and once again the sight seemed like a familiar thing to me and I felt my desire strengthen like new wood being added to a fire.

In my former life I was no stranger to the opposite sex, and at that moment I felt my confidence returning. So I smiled the smile which I knew women found sympathetic, and went towards the office. She saw me coming, I think, because a moment later her eyes met mine and lingered there out of recognition, surprised perhaps that I was recovered now and wanted to talk to her. I wanted her to know that I could not only speak but also make sense, that I understood the situation and above all wanted to explain the problem of my mistaken identity and take the first steps towards resolving the error. I admit that already I was looking beyond that conversation to the one that I hoped would take place in the outside world, after the whole thing had been cleared up, and when we could laugh about it and enjoy the intimacy of those who have been through a difficult situation and come out of it as friends, or better.

When I came to the door, I put out my hand to shake hers. I saw her hand come up in turn. Her expression wasn't quite as friendly as I'd hoped, but she would come around. All they had to do was check the documents against my name, which I could verify in any number of ways with a few phone calls. As I entered I could see the doctor sitting at his big desk like a dictator, just looking at me in grim silence. I admit that didn't bode too well. I noticed lots of piles of paper on the desk, and thought of teachers who always forget to read their students' work. I could joke with him afterwards about that. Anyway, I was three or four steps from the nurse when I saw her expression getting more and more intense, but it still wasn't the expression I was hoping for. I'd almost reached her when she snapped her fingers.

The sudden weight on my arm and neck made me think that a wall had fallen on me. I was on the floor in less than a second, and could just make out two of the Mudaks clambering about on top of me, having jumped out from behind the door at the nurse's signal. I was astonished by their strength. At another time I would have made a go of it, but I wasn't feeling fit and with one knee digging brutally into my back and an arm twisted to breaking point I was in no position to resist. Then a third and fourth Mudak joined the fun and grabbed my feet in order to drag me out.

I tried to speak, but my beloved nurse wasn't in the mood. I wanted only to explain, and to tell her in a calm voice that I was just trying to introduce myself, but my effort was dampened by one of the Mudaks, who put his knee firmly in my face as if he was trying to push it through the cracks in the floor, the way you push meat for *kofte*° into a mincer. I did manage to catch her saying that I was trouble just as they'd thought, and out of one eye I could see the doctor writing something down and saying that sexual perverts were all the same. Then he nodded his head without even looking up and the Mudaks dragged me out. As I felt the floor sliding under me I looked back to see him stand up and put his arms around his shocked companion to comfort her. She rested her head on his shoulder and closed her eyes, and their heads rubbed together like two doves on a

---

° Meatball, popular throughout the Middle East and Balkans, made from ground meat, usually beef or lamb, mixed with onions and spices and cooked in a liquid sauce.

branch. That was too much for me. I shouted some unpleasant names about the two of them and kept going until a foot found its way back onto my face. Then I felt myself being yanked up and thrown into the entrance room where I staggered about for a bit until I found a nice comfy place to spit out the blood in my mouth.

Of course I wanted to run back to the office and make them understand. Of course I wanted that doctor to know I wasn't a pervert and that he'd hurt me without any good reason. Six or seven Mudaks, all of them staring down at me with their brutal features, persuaded me to stay on the floor. I understood then that they could see but they didn't feel, as if all their original capacity for normal thought or emotion had been diverted into physical power, without having to flow anywhere near their brains.

When they were satisfied that I was no longer any threat, they just walked away at the same instant, the way a whole flock of birds flies from a tree. A few of the residents drew near, just to look at my body like a thing of curiosity. A few others walked past, looking down their noses as if I'd committed an offence against the nobility of their families. I pulled myself into a chair and stayed there until my breath came back, feeling my hope draining away like bathwater. Then I wanted to cry like a baby because I felt a pain coming up from somewhere inside me I didn't know existed. I managed not to give in to it, and just put my head in my hands and asked out loud what kind of a place this was, and whether someone could tell me where the Hell I was. I wasn't expecting an answer of course, so you can imagine my surprise when I heard a voice say:

'You're in the ground-floor atrium, on the south side of the east wing.'

Just as Heaven can turn to Hell in an instant, the reverse is equally possible. I looked up to see a tall man with a kindly oval face, a greying beard and round gold-rimmed glasses, wearing a doctor's white coat with a pen and a stethoscope sticking out of the top pocket.

'Thank God for that,' I said. It wasn't exactly the Angel Gabriel, but it would do. He touched my cheek gently.

'Nothing broken,' he said, with a smile. 'I haven't seen you before.'

'There's been a mistake,' I said, but before I could really explain he spoke again.

'Yes, there has,' he said, in a solemn tone of agreement, 'a terrible mistake.'

'I tried to tell the other doctor,' I added, 'but they attacked me.'

'Doctors,' he scoffed ironically. Then he looked over to the office and said in a quieter voice, 'They won't be here for long.'

'Can you speak to them for me?'

'That won't be necessary,' he said. I felt reassured. He was perhaps their supervisor. But something in me wanted to be sure.

'Why isn't it necessary?'

'Because *I* am a doctor. Put your tongue out please.'

He held it down with a wooden spatula from his pocket and then looked with his special torch into my ear. He felt my neck as he looked up to the ceiling. Then he put his cold stethoscope on my chest and told me to breathe. I didn't say anything because I thought he might have been confused, or perhaps because it was a sort of standard procedure in that place to confirm that no one had a particular affliction, which he knew specifically how to check for. Then he finished and looked at me with a serious expression, and I could see that he was looking not exactly into my eye but slightly above it.

'I'm sorry to tell you this,' he said, but then he didn't tell me anything.

'What are you sorry to tell me?'

'I'm sorry to tell you that there's nothing to be done,' he said, hooking his stethoscope onto his neck. When a doctor tells you such a thing, you're bound to think the worst. Immediately I imagined I'd finally understood the situation. I must have developed some unusual medical condition which had required me to be isolated with others who'd been unlucky enough to be struck with the same thing. That explained why they had brought me to this place and even taken the trouble to bring my things with me. I hadn't committed any crime; it was just that they couldn't explain because it was somehow special or secret, like having been exposed to some experimental biological weapon. That explained why the windows were sealed and the door had some kind of air-lock on it.

I had to know the truth. I would never find peace, however awful the diagnosis, unless I knew exactly what it was that he could do nothing about, and for a moment I felt the relief of one who learns of his inevitable and inescapable fate, and makes peace with it.

'There is a distinct thumping noise coming from inside your chest,' he said, with a solemn look.

'And?'

'It's like a drum. It doesn't stop.'

'What does it mean?'

'What does it mean?' he repeated, with a note of irritation. 'It doesn't mean anything. It's just a sound. How can a sound *mean* anything?'

'What does it mean in terms of a diagnosis?'

'It means,' he said, now with a tone of resignation, 'that in the short term you can be helped, but in the long term there is nothing else to do. There is no known cure for having a human heart, and no one is likely to ever discover one.'

This threw me.

'What's your advice?' I asked.

'My advice is to enjoy as many birthdays as you can,' he replied.

'Why birthdays, in particular?'

'Because medical science has definitively proved the statistical connection between the number of birthdays you celebrate and the age you eventually reach. My own paper correlating age and mortality demonstrates this conclusively.'

He felt inside one of his pockets and took out a sandwich which looked as though it was already half-eaten, then looked inside it and closed it again.

'Take one of these in the morning,' he said, handing it to me, 'and come and see me again tomorrow.'

'But how does any of this help me?' I asked, pushing the sandwich back towards him. I was genuinely confused.

'If you don't want my help,' he said defensively, 'I won't give it to you.'

'I am just trying to understand.'

'Some people don't know *how* to be helped,' he went on. 'Remember that! And what thanks do *I* get?' Then he turned his head to the office again and said: 'Look. I told you so.'

I looked round. The doctor and the nurse were crossing the atrium and heading for the entrance. The same couple, Mr Chicken Bone and the other woman, who was wearing a woollen skirt and top, were walking beside them. The incredible thing is that Chicken Bone was still trying to talk and the doctor was just smiling at him, as if to say he was making great progress with his little problem. Then they all went out of the atrium door and waited by the second black door, and once again I saw the green light turn on and then the red light and then the green one again. It was impossible to see who was controlling the actual operation of the door and I was upset that I wasn't closer so as to see things in better detail, but the Mudaks were all over the place and I simply didn't dare.

Then Chicken Bone and his girlfriend came back and even then he was still trying to speak, which I admit made my heart go out to him. Then they walked to the centre of the atrium

and looked upwards towards the roof where the frosted windows let in a grey light that filled the space below. The other
doctor, or whatever he was, had walked away, but I saw him
from a distance on the far side of the room, just standing still in
the shadows and looking at me with his slightly staring eyes. A
single finger was raised to his lips in a gesture of silence.

Then I heard a sound which I thought might be another
alarm; more like the wailing of a police siren this time, echoing
downwards from somewhere high up in the room. I looked up
and saw that little man, smiling malevolently from the balcony
which he'd climbed onto like a monkey, and realized the wailing
sound was coming from him. He was waving one arm in the air
in a gesture of victory and with the other one pulling down his
trousers. Then he pissed onto the heads of everyone standing
below. I was astonished to see that not only did they not run
away but didn't even show any signs of minding, and Chicken
Bone and his partner just stood there looking up, the way farmers
do in India at the end of a hot summer, when they stand outside
just to feel and smell the beautiful first rains of the year.

Until then, I'd had some kind of hope. Now I felt a sick sort
of panic. I'd hoped that there was some kind of normality in that
place around which life was organized. I accepted that there
might be some people who were never going to heat any water,*
but not that the whole place was deranged. I'd seen some signs
of normal behaviour in preparation for the doctor's arrival, but
now that he and the misguided nurse had left, taking with them
any hopes of deliverance that I might have had, this was too
much, on top of too much.

The whole place was reverting before my eyes to an appall-
ing state of chaos. I heard a blood-curdling scream and turned,
half-expecting to see a man with an axe embedded in his head.

---

* i.e., who didn't 'amount to much' or 'make the grade' (Azeri).

But it was one of the other residents, who as soon as he'd walked past me reverted to an amicable conversation with himself. Then he'd scream again as if his fingernails were being pulled out, and just as suddenly, revert once again to a friendly chat with his invisible friend. It was even worse to watch than Mr Chicken Bone. As I stumbled back towards the stairs, a man jumped into the empty fireplace and sat there like a frog. He didn't have arms but hands like pincers which came straight out of his shoulders and nipped at whoever came near. I passed another man who was pressing his cheek against a window as if he enjoyed the feeling of the glass. Then suddenly he would hurl his head against it as hard as he could. What did I know then of this kind of madness? At the foot of the stairs I saw a woman with a smile so large that it took up half her face. Her teeth were abnormally large and prevented her from closing her mouth, and although she was obviously in great pain, her enormous smile persisted.

You know those films where a person is trapped in a kind of house of horrors, banging against one awful thing like a decaying mummy and then being thrown into the arms of another one. That's how it was, only the feeling wasn't one of blind fear, but something more awful, a pitiful kind of revulsion. You think I'm joking, but I am describing something real. It only got worse as I went up the stairs, where I saw another woman coming down, tall and slender and wearing a full-length fur coat of great elegance. But she looked like she was drunk, and her feet fell heavily at each step and she had to steady herself against the wall, muttering curses in French. Long ago she might have been beautiful, but all that was feminine had long since abandoned her and left behind a thing half-destroyed. Her hair was a yellowish grey and unbrushed, and her features incised with deep lines around her mouth and cheeks, as if the portions of her face had been badly fitted together by a careless joiner. As she lurched onto the landing I saw that she wore nothing under her coat, and that her free hand was sawing pathetically between her legs. She fell against me, and I instinctively recoiled, feeling her hand fumbling hastily across me in an awful mockery of intimacy.

Then at the top of the stairs I saw the little man again, whose smile left his face as soon as he caught sight of me. Unlike most of the others he looked me straight in the eye, jumped down deftly from the balcony and kept himself as far from me as he could, slinking down the stairs past me like a guilty dog. He never took his eyes off me, but once he'd got to a safe distance he stuck his tongue out and then fled downwards as fast as his little legs could carry him.

From the balcony I threw a final glance down into the atrium. I'd only seen the most violently deranged ones until now, but that clearly wasn't the whole story. My attention was caught by an abnormally tall man with long straw-coloured hair tied in a ponytail, pacing the perimeter of the room in slow, loping steps. From a basket over his shoulder he was gathering handfuls of seeds and throwing them into the centre of the room, in exactly the same gesture as a farmer in planting season, except that both the basket and the seeds existed only in his imagination. He had a gaunt, saintly looking face, untroubled by the madness around him, and smiled as he scattered his invisible seeds, his head slightly cocked as if attuned to some angelic chorus inaudible to the rest of us.

There were several other quieter characters I hadn't noticed earlier. One man was sitting at a table and had picked up a newspaper to read, but after a few seconds of studying the print his gaze would lift from the page and dart all over the room, as if he were following the flight of an insect. Another had the habit of walking a few paces and then stopping as if he'd dropped something. Then he would turn back and, just as he stooped down to pick it up, his mind would change and he'd carry on just as before, until the whole thing was repeated a few seconds later.

In the centre of the room stood a man wearing an army jacket and sunglasses, with the look of a Guevara about him. He held a thin cigar at waist level, turning his body every few moments to the events around him with an admiring smile on his face, in the manner of a general talking to his men and confident of their adoration. No one looked at him. The nearest other person to him was the drunken woman in the fur, who had found the sofa and was now sprawled along it, with the man in the smart jacket and white hat helping her at her side. At least I thought he was helping her, but then I realized he was just getting into a better position to clamp his mouth onto her breast.

I looked away in disgust and at that moment saw a woman enter the atrium from the far side. The sight of her was totally unexpected. She was young and slender, and her golden hair was tied in a scarf like a peasant girl's, though I could tell she was no peasant just by the natural intelligence of her face and bearing. She was carrying a tray with a plate and a glass, and walked purposefully in a straight line across the room. It occurred to me then that perhaps she worked in the house's kitchen where that delicious food was prepared each day, and that the kitchen must obviously be staffed by normal people of whom she was one, because deranged people obviously couldn't cook properly. If I got to the kitchen I would be bound to meet normal people and could talk to them, and even her, and I felt stupid for not having come to such a simple conclusion earlier. Once again that day my hopes soared, as if my heart itself were at the end of a string which some devil or angel was using as a plaything. Then she looked up at the balcony where I was standing and she saw me, and she stopped.

I didn't know it, because I hadn't yet met Vasily, but there are different kinds of future. There is a future caused by the past, which emerges naturally from everything that has gone before, like one of those Agdashian pomegranates ripening on the branch of a tree. It is relatively predictable by mathematics.

There is also another kind of future which calls to us here in the present: this is the fruit already conceived, which causes the tree to come into existence. It defies one's ordinary thinking because you have to look at time in a different way, but if you've ever felt the touch of that sort of thing, it's unmistakable. You feel it in your life like a force, and if you practise you can sometimes hear it, though the mind alone isn't much help here, just as my grandfather supposed. The point is that when that woman looked up at me, I *heard* the future, and knew I was joined to her by something that *had* to happen, even if I had no idea at the time what I was really hearing. These things don't depend on time. You could say they reach us through the spaces between time, which open up when you're not expecting them and which anyone who's played a few games of *shashonbush* can probably understand. Later on I argued a lot with Vasily about just this issue.

In the sense of time itself, all this only took a moment, because I looked away almost as soon as I saw her, hurried back to my room, shut the door and tried as hard as I could not to cry.

Chapter 4

A MAN ISN'T SO DIFFERENT from a child. He may have more experience, more complicated ways of expressing himself and greater means to carry out his wishes, but both man and child wish for someone who can tell them the basics about what is real and true and certain. A child believes his parents know the answer to everything including the secret of life. Later on things change. He discovers that his parents don't know that milk comes from cows or that snow is cold, and that no one who really ought to actually knows the answer to anything. That's how I felt. I wanted more than anything for someone to come and explain the Hell I had walked into and how I could get out of it.

Whenever I thought of making a plan, my thoughts would race back to all the horrible things I'd seen. Whenever I tried to think about anything, in fact, I realized the scenes from that mayhem had lodged in my mind's eye like so many poisoned arrows, and even on a good day some of these memories would jump out at me like thieves from the shadows. It came to me that to get out of this mental torture I had to build up my own thinking just as you'd build a house, with a foundation I could be sure of. The foundation, it seemed to me, was to have an aim. Without an aim, everything was pretty much the same and the mind had no way to order things. With an aim, your decisions and actions fall into some kind of arrangement and begin to make sense in terms of what you're trying to achieve. That much I knew was true. Even those feelings of panic and loss couldn't defy that simple truth; and if I could build on that foundation then gradually I'd be able to make sense of everything, only in a new way appropriate to my new surroundings.

The other thing that seemed important was to think logically, even if the world around me had gone mad. Some things hadn't changed and were unlikely to change. The laws of the natural world must still be true. Gravity still existed. If I cut myself, I would still bleed. I still had to eat, and exercise, and learn everything I could about the place, even if I didn't necessarily understand it. These two small things sound simple, I know, but they went a long way to preventing my own feelings of hopelessness in those early days. You may know that in real prisons – I mean prisons in the ordinary world – the suicides always come in the first few days. And a normal prison is almost a reasonable place compared to the nightmare I'd found myself in.

I had good days and bad days. I knew it was a good day when I looked in the mirror and remembered that's who I was and that my patience and determination would be rewarded. On the bad days I didn't recognize myself and everything seemed to spin downwards in panic, and I would wonder whether my whole life up to that point had been a fiction and a mirage. Evenings were worst, like a death. When I saw the light outside the house beginning to fade, I sometimes felt as though I was bleeding to death, and the end of the day felt like the end of my own life, and the feeling of being a captive was a thousand times worse. You know that for two lovers, discovering the pleasure of each other for the first time, a day passes as swiftly as a minute, time is as gentle as a *nasim** in springtime and all else is sweet.

---

* 'Breeze', in Persian.

But when you are walking on fire each moment seems to last a lifetime.

A normal clock can never measure such a difference. If such a clock existed in the world it could measure real time, that is, the experience of it inside a man. It would not only distinguish between the time spent by lovers and by those being tortured, but could measure the true duration of a person's life. From the outside two men might appear to live the same length of time. But by that truer measure one might have lived a year and the other a thousand years, so different was the way they lived; the one allowing time to flow past him like a river, and the other making every moment count and squeezing from it the very essence of life.

My lists were useful, and helped me to regain some kind of calm in that inner turmoil. They helped me to remember who I was and what I was, like a rough map of my own self that I could use to get my bearings. They were quite simple at first: ten places I had been to and explored, ten books I had read, ten people who I knew and cared for, ten foods that I enjoyed. Then I threw these away, because they seemed unreal and unsatisfying, and drew up ten more which were different.

The second lists were more of a challenge: ten things I loved and ten I hated, ten things of which I was ashamed of having done and ten of which I was proud, ten things I had seen that were beautiful, ten things inside myself that I admired and ten others that I wished sincerely to overcome. The result wasn't the same at all. I had to search much more deeply for the answers and each time I delved more deeply I found myself more at peace, like a diver who has left the turmoil of the waves above him for gentler currents below. I know they sound as though they might be easy to compile, but to do the job honestly, I struggled to find ten things for each list. So I changed the number to five.

One evening, after I had tired of them, I was experimenting with a glass on the walls to find out the best spot for listening to the pipes, and challenging myself to guess the origin of the various sounds I could hear. Then I heard a new sound. It wasn't regular, but it was persistent. You'd be surprised what you can read into a sound, which even when very simple acquires a unique character of its own. This one made me think at first of the sound you hear when hot water travels down cold pipes and makes them tick irregularly. But it was too deliberate, and sounded more like the pecking of a bird that's discovered a new food and is getting used to it in stages. Then I discovered that the sound persisted even when I lifted my ear from the glass, and that it was inside the room as much as it was inside the wall. It was coming from the door. So I went to the door feeling like a fool and listened for a while and finally said hello, having no idea what to expect because it was not the place to make easy predictions about things.

'Hello,' said a voice, in a matter-of-fact tone. It was a woman's voice. I was so surprised I didn't say anything for what seemed like a long time. I was surprised not only to hear the voice of a woman, but surprised that I knew exactly who it was. Nevertheless, I asked:

'Who are you?

'You know who I am,' came the reply, and that surprised me more than everything else, because it was true.

'You're the woman I saw carrying the tray on the day the doctor came.'

'Yes,' she said, 'I am.'

Pressing my ear against the door, I could smell the paint and see the tiny brush marks on its surface. Then there was another long silence, but inside my head a thousand thoughts and hopes were dancing the *kosa kosa** at twice the normal speed. Perhaps she was in the same situation as I was, and had been brought

---

* A traditional ritual Caucasian dance.

here by mistake, and she'd come to me in the hope that I might help with her escape. Perhaps there were others like her and she was their representative and was contacting me to organize an escape committee. Perhaps she was the captive young wife of a mad resident and wanted desperately to get away from him, and had come to me in secret. She was certainly beautiful. We might easily fall in love and try to escape. I had all these thoughts and many others; the only thought that did not occur to me was that she might herself be as mad as the other residents I'd seen.

'What do you want?' I asked, after what seemed like an unbearably long time.

'I want to help you.'

'Help me do what?'

'Help you to be free.'

Such words. Such simple words. To be free is a special thing for a man, and only those who are qualified should really talk about the subject. I chuckled out loud, because you can't give freedom to another person the way you'd give them *shashlik* in a restaurant.

'Free?'

'Yes.'

'Why?'

'Because you don't belong in here.'

Then I could feel my heart beginning to beat properly, asking myself how she could know what I knew, and how it was that she seemed to be reading my mind, not in a trivial way but in a way that laid bare my most private wishes. I was already secretly full of hope that someone else actually understood that I really didn't belong in that Hell, and felt as though I'd finally met someone who understood. How could she smell my thoughts with such uncanny accuracy, such that her words went straight to their target without the slightest deviation?

'Where do I belong, then?' I asked.

'You don't belong in a cave.'

That was another surprise. I couldn't tell how she was using the word, but I guessed she was thinking of it in as many senses as was I, and I was thrilled. Had she dwelled on freedom and its meanings more than I had, such that she was able to prescribe it to others? I was humbled, too. And ever more curious.

'How would I get out from such a cave?'

'Well,' she said with a note of playfulness, 'you have to open the door first,' and I felt sure that she was smiling as she said it.

'They lock the door,' I replied. 'It's always locked.'

'No it isn't,' she said, 'they just turn the keys in the locks to make you think that.'

That too was another revelation, and an unlikely one, unless our conversation had been entirely metaphorical. There was silence after that, and doubts began to creep into my thoughts. Could the whole thing be a trick? Could all those mad residents actually be on the other side of the door, waiting for a gullible newcomer to fall for their cruel trick and to start pulling on the door handle, when they would fall about laughing as his cries and curses grew more and more desperate? Maybe that's what they all did for their evening's entertainment – going from room to room among all the new residents in order to humiliate them and crush their spirits even further.

My heart was beating like a Novorosyskian pile-driver. I was sure the door would be locked. Every day I heard at least three distinct rattles from the Mudaks' keys, and it was impossible to believe – oh, to hell with what was impossible.

I pulled the handle. The door opened.

There was no one outside. No sound and no movement. Just the occasional distant shout, of ecstasy or despair I couldn't tell. I wondered briefly if I'd imagined the conversation. But I knew it was real not only because the door to my room was now open, but because I could smell perfume in the air. The woman who had shared her secret with me might have run away, but the night couldn't fully conceal the trace of her on the air, even if she herself was a mystery. I savoured it as if it had been her touch.

I wasn't free, of course. I had simply managed to open the door of my room. I inspected the empty spaces where there had once been locks, and closed and opened the door a few times experimentally. I wondered if everyone made the same dis-covery, or whether the Mudaks themselves knew the function of locks, or whether they even cared. But I did feel I'd made an important step towards my aim, and now at least I could start exploring properly instead of listening to pipes in walls. I'd made a real discovery and it belonged to me and no-one else, and that at least was one thing that they couldn't take away.

It then occurred to me that if she'd helped me this far, the woman I longed to meet might know other things about how to escape. She'd said I had to open the door first. That meant a beginning; perhaps she knew a lot more. I admit my feelings towards her were not free of longing of a specific kind. I was grateful to her but my gratitude was mixed thoroughly with desire. But what did I know then? Until a man is free, the truth always presents itself firmly upside down. The more I thought about that woman and how she might help me towards freedom, the more I became her slave.

I wandered to the far side of the balcony, where I could see light coming from the lower part of the building. There was no one about, so I crept downstairs, astonished at the contrast with the last time I'd been in the same place, battling my way past lunatics amid all that noise and chaos. It was as quiet now as the deserted stage of a cancelled opera. At the foot of the stairs I looked across the atrium beyond the shadows of the furniture and could make out the door of the office where I'd given the Mudaks the pleasure of stepping on my face. At the sight of the door I thought of how the visiting doctor had been duped collectively by the residents. That made him stupider than them, which was a strange thought because it meant that they were using a superior form of reasoning to outwit him. I didn't yet understand the purpose of the deception, but there must have been a reasoning to it. And if there was a reasoning to it, it meant the mad people knew how to deceive the sane ones, and that meant they knew what sane people considered what was mad and what wasn't.

As I was struggling with that troublesome thought, I heard a muffled shout and the sound of smashing crockery. It came from behind a large door on the far side of the adjoining room. I picked my way through the shadows and was soon close enough to hear what sounded like a dinner party in progress. At the door itself I could just make out the delicate marquetry along its frame, where interlocking patterns of squares and triangles were picked out in light wood and their borders defined by an intermediary shade. It was once again obvious how much care had gone into the original details of the building, and how little they could be appreciated by its present occupants. I knelt down and put my eye to the keyhole.

About thirty people were sitting at a long table, feasting. The table, draped in a long white cloth, was covered with plates and platters and glasses of several different shapes, sparkling under the light of an enormous chandelier with at least a dozen gold arms dripping with bright crystal spears and prisms. At the far end of the room, heavy blood-red curtains hung in front of a pair of tall windows, drawn back by thick braid cords, even though it was dark outside. All this was evidence of both wealth and old-world elegance long since vanished, but whatever the history of the place, I doubt if its former owners could have imagined the scene I was now witnessing.

In the centre of the table was a naked man. At first glance it seemed he was a sort of living statue and an object of perverse fascination for the diners, but after a few minutes I glimpsed him deliberately changing position, as if he was an artist's model or an athlete wanting to show off his muscles. There was no indication of either pleasure or pain on his face. He stood, he crouched, he knelt indifferently, varying his position each time at some unknown signal and paying no attention to his surroundings. At the far end of the table was a character I recognized: it was the little man, who by now I understood was a prize trouble-maker. He was standing with one foot on a chair and the other on the edge of the table, like a man about to get into a boat. Each time the man on the table changed position, he would shout and point and say something derisory that I couldn't catch, but which made everyone else laugh and point in turn, and then throw food at their immobile target. The naked man made no effort to resist or retaliate, like a castle waiting for a siege to be called off, even though by now every kind of food and sauce was dripping off him. In the intervals between food-throwing, every-one carried on eating and drinking as if he wasn't there, until the whole thing started again, fired up by the little man's enthusi-astic ridiculing, and new salvoes of food would be unleashed onto their apparently helpless victim.

Having seen enough of this repulsive ritual, I stood up and turned to head back to my room. Then the sanctity of my aim returned unexpectedly to me, as if a voice were asking what I had to be afraid of by going inside the dining room, if my goal was really to find out everything I could about the place. The truth was I felt intimidated. Yet it was wrong, said the same voice, to be afraid of mad people, and besides I might be able to influence some of those who weren't too far gone to help me in some way. I took a step towards my room, because joining a food-throwing party among lunatics wasn't my idea of pleas-ure, and my wish to be true to the aim I had promised myself protested yet again; so it was there in the shadows that the battle was waged, between what I wanted and what I wished, and perhaps you know better than I that this is where life really begins.

The result, when I threw open the door in a manner to suggest that I was unafraid, was electrically swift. Every head turned towards me and in an instant the room fell silent, like a scene of enchantment from a book of fairy tales. Such was the effect that I could even see mouths open in surprise, and wine glasses in mid-air as if suspended in the hands of puppets.

'Don't look at me,' I said loftily, disguising my anxiety, 'look at yourselves.'

The silence continued. I walked to an empty chair, ignoring the feel of food underfoot, and sat down. I was wondering how long the spell of stillness would last when a piercing burst of laughter erupted at the far end of the table. It was the little man, shrieking with animal-like abandon, and that was the spark that set the others off, because then the whole room erupted in hysterics. Then, as if a great joke had run its course, it settled down again and, if you'd glimpsed the scene at just that moment, you would have suspected nothing but a large dinner party in a rather grand setting.

I was surprised when the man sitting next to me greeted me enthusiastically and found me a plate and glass, apologizing for the mess on the table and saying that it wasn't always like that. He shook my hand and said his name was Fidel. He looked and sounded South American, and I recognized him. It was the swarthy-looking man I'd seen standing alone in the middle of the atrium on the day of the doctor's arrival. I guessed he was older than me, but by how much it didn't occur to me to calculate. When you are young, the age of other people is fairly meaningless; anyone outside your immediate age is either very old or very young, and your age is the right age, the only age, to be.

He had short hair which was still black and a carefully trimmed, week-old beard on his face. He wore a fisherman's jacket with lots of pockets and a military-style shirt, which hugged the contours of his powerful-looking frame. His hands were unexpectedly beautiful. Their backs were smooth and square, the fingers strong and elegant, like those of a champion boxer. I couldn't see his eyes because he was wearing sunglasses, as he had been the first time I saw him, and I was too polite to ask why he wore sunglasses inside and at dinnertime.

'How long you been here?' he asked, not looking at me as he spoke, which gave an air of stealth to our conversation.

'I can't be sure,' I answered, truthfully. 'Not long, because all this is new to me. But I don't know exactly.'

'I remember that feeling,' he said.

'What feeling?'

'When they mess with your head,' he said, waving his fork in front of his forehead. 'Them. The ones who did that to your eye.'

I'd forgotten about my eye, which still had a dark purple crescent underneath it after its embrace with the knee of a well-intentioned Mudak.

'Did you talk?' he asked.

'Did I what?'

'Did you talk? Did you tell them anything?'

'Anything in particular?'

'Any details, locations, anything they can use.'

'No, I didn't,' I said, reluctant to expose my bafflement. 'I wanted to, but I didn't.'

'You're a good man,' he said. 'I need men like you. I'm sorry they were hard on you.'

Then we heard the wild, shrill laughter of the little man again, igniting a new round of mockery. Suddenly the air was thick with missiles of food hurtling towards their helpless target. Someone even threw a glass of wine into the naked man's face.

Fidel, who I suspected of not wanting to seem passive, picked up a sausage and threw it in the expected way, then looked at me as if to say his heart wasn't really in it but that he had to play along. Then he asked me whether I had a plan. My expression must have told him I had no idea what he meant.

'A plan,' he said, through his teeth, while keeping his eyes on the merriment across the table. 'A plan to get out of here.'

'No. I don't have a plan. Do you?'

'I have a plan,' he said, 'but I can't do it alone.'

That caught my attention. I hadn't expected to be discussing an escape plan during a food-throwing ritual presided over by a midget, but who was I to argue? I had to pursue every line and every hope.

'Once a month,' he said. 'That's our chance.'

'What happens once a month?'

'The doctor comes once a month. More or less. That's the only time to get out. When they get in, we get out.' He made a chopping motion with his hand. 'Surprise is the key. Once we've got the attention of the guards and we get into the doorway,' he drove his hand forward, 'we'll be out of here.'

A small sausage fell nearby. He picked it up and swallowed it.

'Did you ever try to explore anywhere else?' I asked. 'I mean to see if there's a way to get out by a wall, or a window, or by tunnelling?'

'Not interested. Infra-red cameras. Vibration sensors. Proximity alarms. They can see us and hear us coming from anywhere else. Front door is the only way.'

What he said seemed perfectly credible, and I'd no reason to doubt it. He was the one who'd done the research and knew the territory. I admit to being vaguely troubled by a theatrical quality to his delivery and the contrived manner of his expressions, as if he felt the need to copy the mannerisms he'd seen other people making in films, or else wanted deeply to be in a film himself. But there might be many different reasons. A streak of self-conscious vanity was not the worst fault in a man, especially if it was offset by a different strength.

'Meal's going to end soon,' said Fidel. 'Let's talk about it more tomorrow.'

I was wondering what the signal for the meal to end would be when four or five Mudaks came in from the kitchen side of the room and began clearing the table and sweeping up the food from the floor. They paid no attention to the others. Some of them finished their food and stood up and left and others stayed behind, but to the Mudaks it didn't seem to make any difference, and they took the plates away whether their owners were still eating or not.

On the other side of the table not far from us was a tall, dignified-looking elderly lady with red hair. I had earlier noticed that she spoke incessantly whether anyone was listening to her or not. Even the most fascinating story in the world is made unbearable by such a habit, and I felt a twinge of sympathy for whoever had been sitting next to her. It had been much too noisy at the table to hear anything she was saying earlier, but now that things were settling down I could just hear her cheerful nattering when one of the Mudaks came up and took her plate. There was still food on it, so she patted his hand with hers, as gently as you might pat a child's head at bedtime, and smiled to show that she meant it as a friendly gesture. But it had come too late. With unbelievable speed the other Mudaks raced to her from every side of the room. Two of them held her arms behind her chair and the other two forced her head repeatedly against the table, where it crashed against her plate until blood was pouring from her face. It was an awful spectacle to see such violence committed against an innocent old woman, but none of the others paid any attention. We'd hardly had the chance to intervene: it had only taken a few seconds. But the pitiful sound of her wailing made further conversation impossible, and looking over at the poor crone, who was now trying to stop the flow of blood from her nose, we both lost our appetite.

'War is hell,' said Fidel quietly, though I couldn't see his eyes as he said it.

'Were you a soldier?' I asked.

'I did my duty for my country,' he said, though I wasn't quite sure what duty exactly, or what country. 'Can't talk about it – mostly special services.'

'I was in the army,' I said. 'Do you mean special forces?'

'Exactly. Black missions. Covert insertions, exertions, that kind of thing. You understand.'

Then he turned his head away from the spectacle across the table, and held his head up as if he was hearing a voice that no one else could hear, nodding almost imperceptibly to himself with what I assumed, had I actually been able to see his eyes, was very probably a faraway look.

Chapter 5

MY GREATEST FEAR during the period that followed wasn't that I'd be trapped in that place forever, or that the Mudaks would once again exercise their tender methods of care on me, or even that I'd never be able to win over the affections of that shapely but misguided nurse. It was simply that I'd get used to the place, and that one day the madness and people around me would seem normal, and that I would say to myself: this is life, this is just how it is, and there's nothing I can do about it.

I was aware that the process had already begun, which is why I mention it. In those parts of the house which I now knew, I no longer tiptoed like a fugitive, terrified of what might be waiting around the next corner, but moved confidently and without much thought; and if I saw one of the characters whose behaviour had not long ago seemed so disturbing, I hardly paid any attention. Such is the miracle of the human being. Perhaps that's the reason Man is said to have been fashioned from clay, which can be shaped equally into a beautiful vessel worthy of a museum, or can line a river bed where fish with monstrous-looking faces live. People think of this as a strength, but it seemed to me a dangerous weakness. I'd heard but never really believed that one can adapt to any situation, but now I realized it was possible to adjust even to a house of deranged people based on deranged rules, tyrannized by deranged automatons and goaded by a deranged midget. Would such a place ever really seem normal to me? How could I prevent it becoming so? A drunken man, long since accustomed to intoxication, will consider his state perfectly normal; just try telling an old sop that life is actually possible without alcohol. He'll laugh and think you're a fool.

The terrible sight of the old woman's face being pounded into the table was haunting me; not just because of the brutality of the act, but because no one had paid the slightest attention to it. Was I too capable of becoming indifferent to such a sight? Perhaps their failure to recognize the wrongness of things was a form of protection, of self-concealment against the awful arbitrariness of the place itself. There didn't seem to be any rules at all, and if there were any, there was no one to ask what they might be. Perhaps there had been rules once, just as there had once been locks in the doors, but they'd all been forgotten. I'd seen people punished for the most innocent things, and outrageous behaviour going on without any sort of intervention. What if I lost my moral bearings in the place? I prayed that it would never happen, and that nothing there would ever seem normal to me; if it began to seem normal, then it meant that I was losing my direction, and with it the sense of purpose that I hoped would propel me towards freedom.

But you cannot stop a thing becoming normal. Even the weather in Batumi seems normal to the people who live there.[*] I could feel normality creeping into me like a poison. One night I dreamed that the poison really had entered me. I pushed my tongue against a tooth to clean my mouth, but the tooth worked loose and fell out. The same thing happened to the tooth next to it, until I'd run my tongue over all my teeth and one by one

---

[*] Annual rainfall in excess of 100 inches makes this Georgian port the wettest city in the entire Caucasus region.

pushed them out, and my mouth filled with blood. I spat them all into a cloth and showed them to a peasant woman sitting on her doorstep. As soon as she saw them she began wailing and beating her face with her hands and saying that the teeth were an omen of death. I saw her eyes fill with tears as she predicted that her son would never return from the journey he had made. I know it was a dream, but I felt her pain as if it were my own; and what is stranger is that I actually felt the truth of what she had foretold.

I was lonely as a phoenix in a bamboo tree.* My room, which contained all the reminders of my earlier life, was the loneliest place of all. For long periods I sat listening to the muffled sounds of the house, wondering who was making them and who else was in the building. From somewhere closer came the sound of water, dripping within the walls or roof. It must have come from a leaky pipe, and night and day it ticked like a clock. Sometimes I was aware that I had stopped noticing the sound of ticking, and was convinced the sound itself had actually stopped, but it was always there. Was this the sound of my life dripping away? It felt like it. It felt like a quiet but distinct form of torture. Sometimes I wondered if it was an accident, or whether each of the rooms was designed to have the same dripping sound, each a quiet source of torture for their inhabitants.

I had two lives now. One in the world that I knew and had come from, and the other in here. One which was comfortable and familiar, and based on the memories of all that had gone before in my life. I knew *that* life was my *real* life. There, in the world outside, I had always been able to rely on my identity and, within reason, the results of my own actions. I had no doubt, in that other life, about who I was.

But in here the rules had changed. Here everything was

---

* The reference is obscure.

strange and unpredictable. At times it was unbearable. Even the most basic rules of time and space were distorted. Nothing seemed certain. Worse, perhaps, the place was populated by characters who astonished and frightened me. Sometimes they were terrifying, sometimes absurd or pitiful. My daily life was now in the hands of all these strange people.

I should mention my impressions of them. Much later on, when I knew more about the place and the fact that my experience there needed to be interpreted, I understood them quite differently. But for now I took them for what they seemed to be: mad people. Mad, in the sense that they didn't seem to have any connection with reality, or reference to any norms beyond their own.

The Mudaks were the most obvious candidates for my loathing. They seemed to be in contact with one another telepathically, which meant that they were in a sense everywhere, and couldn't be taken on singly. They couldn't be reasoned with, they never spoke, nor appeared to have the slightest intellectual life, perhaps precisely because their brain was a collective one, shared out between them all and leaving very little left over for the appreciation of logic or metaphysics. But it was nevertheless a brain. They performed their main tasks of cooking and cleaning and regulating things without emotion, but they did calculate situations with great precision, which showed they had some way of measuring what was going on around them and reacting to it. They were the least interesting of all the residents, because you couldn't talk to them or reason with them. That also made them the most dangerous.

The others varied greatly, from the eccentric to the severely deranged. How had characters with such different kinds of affliction all been assigned to the same place? (I understood so little then). For the most part they could be observed, if you took the time, and to some extent predicted. They paid no attention to me or anyone else and showed no sign of noticing anything that happened in their surroundings, and their behaviour was almost always repetitive, as if they had learned only one thing in life.

Some seemed content to live out the passion of their madness without caring whether anyone else was listening or not. There was one man like this who I saw nearly every day. He spoke to no one except himself, in a low, furtive mutter, a sort of running commentary on everyone he saw and the threat they posed to him. To avoid actual contact with anyone else, he would flatten himself against the walls and behind doors, and darted stealthily from one patch of shadow to another. He was entertaining to watch, creeping around like a cat-burglar, checking the way ahead to make sure it was clear and looking behind himself to make sure no one was following. Yet he didn't seem to understand that he could be seen by everyone else.

There were others who were talkative and desperate to claim the attention of others. There was an old and bent woman, a real Baba Yaga,* who talked all the time in Italian and made quite sure we could hear her. She had a fierce look in her eye when she tilted her head sideways and upwards towards you, and seemed to do nothing but wander around recounting out loud the conversations she'd had with others. When she repeated her own side of the conversation, she'd pronounce the words in a reasoned and even tone, but the other person's tone of voice would be ridiculed in a ruthless parody. The result, if you believed it, was that she came away blameless, while everyone was either a thief or a liar, a cheat, unreliable, a dreamer or a coward or a slut.

Another, like an actor who only has a few chosen lines to say and feels he has to say them with great feeling, walked around

---

* The best-known and most terrifying witch of Eastern Slavic and Russian folklore.

uttering only maxims, slogans and truisms, which no one ever listened to. A few others like him seemed to be acting out a characteristic they wanted to be known for, but which was obviously only skin deep. I often wondered what these characters were really like underneath.

There were others who didn't care who noticed them or not, like the Chicken-Bone man who was always on the point of saying something and was obviously trying to speak but was never quite able to make it happen. He would even try to talk to a wall. The strange doctor with the glasses and bewildered scowl didn't seem to care whether anyone listened to him or not. He once loomed up to me for no apparent reason, and said: 'This is too much.'

'What is?' I asked, but he wasn't trying to have a conversation. He just kept talking.

'Too much! Too much to expect *anyone* to put up with! After what I've done, I deserve an acknowledgement. And until I get it . . . I have *every* right to be angry. All the effort . . . the sheer *ingratitude* . . .' Then he wandered away in mid-sentence, wagging his finger in the empty air and then shouting something rude before searching for someone else to bother, scowling and muttering to himself. Perhaps he had once been a psychotherapist.

Some of them even had temporary followings of their own, who they managed to hypnotize. Their devotees would crowd around, like theologians around a patriarch or an ayatollah, laughing when they were supposed to laugh and crying when they were supposed to cry. Then without warning they would suddenly disperse and disappear or attach themselves to another resident who happened to be passing.

Perhaps the strangest thing of all was that there were also residents whom the friends I later made could themselves see, but who were never visible to me, and vice versa. They were simply never there when I was out of my room, which meant for me they were only stories and might as well not have existed.

Yet the others could describe them and their mannerisms in great detail.

✢

After I'd discovered that I could leave my room whenever I wanted, I never had another visit from the Mudaks. How they found out that I'd left my room I have no idea. It was hard to guess how much they really knew and understood, and how much they were simply acting according to whatever instructions had been drummed into them. I doubted whether they had the brains to appreciate the implication of turning keys in empty locks; it seemed more likely that they were following a set of rules which were, at least in the case of the room I'd been put in, obsolete. I say brains, but I'd decided they actually shared a brain between themselves. It was this that enabled them to act with such speed and ferocity at precisely the same instant, as if they all received the same message at the same moment.

They certainly knew how to work. When I was next in the dining room, at breakfast the following morning, I was amazed that the place was back in perfect order. There was no trace of food on the floor, which had been polished, and the white table-cloth, laid with platters and carefully arranged silver, looked brand new. One of those black-hearted* Mudaks was even cleaning the carved white marble of the fireplace with manic affection.

A few residents were breakfasting quietly. There was an elderly man with white hair and a yellow jacket, muttering benignly to himself, and a woman nearby who sat at the table doing nothing at all, staring vacantly at the wall opposite. Mr Chicken Bone and his lady friend were there too. He looked at

---

* From Persian, meaning 'cold-hearted'.

me and made the effort to greet me but the same ghastly choking sounds came out of his mouth. His companion, the plump and inoffensive middle-aged woman, put a comforting hand on his arm and suggested that things would be better soon, but I think we all knew what was true and that wasn't it.

I decided to sit next to the big window at the end of the room, not far from the fireplace where the Mudak was doing his polishing. I could see that the glass here was just as thick as it was in my bedroom. Beyond it was the same featureless brick wall, except that at its base I could see a much older and imperfect stone path made from large flagstones, which I imagined must have belonged to the original house before it was enclosed by the modern brickwork. I ran my finger along the frame of the window to feel for any trace of a current of air, finding none. Then I saw a single leaf, dancing wildly in a breeze beyond the glass, and wanted more than anything to be where it was, in the open air, connected by the air itself to the rest of the world and every other breathing thing. I put my hand against the glass without being aware of it and moments later realized the Mudak, who was now sweeping near the fireplace with a small brush, was watching me whenever he looked up. I didn't want any trouble and lowered my hand, but I was curious all the same, and threw a small piece of bread onto the floor behind him where he'd just cleaned. Then when he next looked up I caught his eye and pointed to the piece of bread. He swept it up and moved on, so I threw another piece behind him, and pointed it out again. He looked around, and looked at me, and it was obvious I was the culprit.

My calculation was that if he did attack me, I would circle him at the last moment, trip him off balance and throw him into the window, smashing it open. I could hear my heart again. There were a few moments of what was more or less a standoff, until I made a helpless gesture to indicate I'd dropped the bread by mistake, and then, surprising my own self, made a sweeping motion to suggest that he really ought to get on with his job. To my huge relief he turned away and kept working. My heart was pounding, but I felt I'd won a tiny victory, the way you do when someone else has to leave the heat of the *banya*˚ before you do.

I wanted to find Fidel and continue our discussion but had no idea how to. So I decided that with the paper napkins I had taken from the dining room and a pencil I had stolen from the pocket of the mad doctor, I would continue to explore the house and draw a plan of it. I went first to my room and, outside the door, paused without really knowing why. Then I realized: in the air was the faintest trace of perfume. I recognized it. She wasn't in my room – that would have been too much to hope for – but she must have come looking for me and then left. I walked the square of the balcony, and saw that there were three corridors leading off that I hadn't noticed before. I peered along them in turn. They were extraordinarily long, and for the first time I had a sense of the proper size of the house: it was enormous. At the far end of the third corridor I could make out the shape of a person, so far away I couldn't distinguish the face. But I knew it was her.

The moment I saw her, whether by coincidence or because she somehow sensed it, she disappeared the way a cat disappears if you try to follow it, allowing me to glimpse her from time to time but cleverly managing to keep up the same distance. I ran as far as the end of the corridor, passing more doors than seemed believable, and for the first time I had a twinge of worry about how to find my way back. At the far end, two more long corridors formed a T, but there she was, still a long distance away, at the far end of the left one. I ran after her again, and then she disappeared into a stairwell to one side, which went down to a lower floor and yet another long corridor. All this was fun, in a

---

˚ Russian for Sauna or steam-bath.

way, but I had no wish to get lost, and decided to stop and find my way back to my room. Then I noticed that halfway along the corridor, what looked like natural light was pouring in from one side. Then I came to a glass wall which gave onto a small outside square resembling a garden. It wasn't completely outside; there was a translucent glass roof above it but it still gave the impression of being beyond the building. There was a narrow path of old stone leading from the door, and dark green hedges, about the height of a man, laid out in a maze. High above each corner of the square was a carved stone shield. I was looking at them when I noticed that in the centre of the maze was a white face, staring at me.

I ran in and tried to get to the centre as quickly as I could. The hedges were too high for me to see her, but I could hear her running. The path that I thought would take me to the centre didn't seem to be working, so I lost patience, and when I heard her nearby, pushed my arm through the hedge and nearly caught hold of her. I heard an unexpectedly distressed cry of surprise. She pulled herself free like a wild animal and ran off. I got to the centre and saw the square plinth on which she must have been standing when I'd seen her earlier, and where long ago a statue must have stood.

When I found my way back to the entrance she was sitting on a small stone bench with a faint smile on her face. I sat down next to her. She said nothing.

'This place is bigger than I thought,' I said, after a long silence.

Her hair was the colour of straw and tied with a piece of blood-red cloth into a bunch at the back of her head. Her neck was long and slender. I could see from the rise and fall of her chest that her breathing hadn't yet come back to normal.

'I hope I didn't hurt you,' I said, but she didn't reply.

'Nothing here is what it seems,' was what she said, after another long silence.

'Is that true for you, too?'

'Even you are not what you seem.'

It's not quite enough to say I was intoxicated by her beauty. Beauty alone can't cause that degree of intoxication, and for some people doesn't have much effect at all. It wasn't the beauty of the woman beside me that was making me feel like such a moth in the presence of a candle, but the combination of her beauty with her character, her bearing, her strangeness and the inexplicable affinity between our way of expressing ourselves – well, nothing new there, to anyone who has fallen over himself in love. How else can silences seem as loud as crashing waterfalls, and glances as powerful as meteorites? The circumstances of our meeting made everything much more heady. The fact that we were both prisoners in that place, and realized we didn't belong there was like a meeting of two people in a foreign city in a time of war, when danger and uncertainty have such a magnifying effect on intimacy.

'What's your name?' I asked.

'Ask me no questions and I'll tell you no lies.'*

'Then I'll ask many, many questions,' I said, 'and if the answer to every one of them is a lie, I will at least know what isn't true. Then I'll begin to see what is true by elimination, like the sculptor who reveals his creation by taking away everything that isn't a part of it.'

I could tell she wasn't expecting that.

'A sculpture,' she said, swallowing.

'Yes. I will reveal you. You will be my work of art.'

'What will you do with your work of art?'

'I will put life in it.'

'You cannot put life inside a stone.'

'That was exactly the task of the real philosophers when they wished to make gold.'

---

* In Azeri, 'the word hides from the word'.

'My name is Petra.'

'Why are you here?'

'I was betrayed.'

'Where are your parents?'

'I have no parents.'

After that it was difficult to make the kind of conversation you do on a happy country picnic, so I shut up.

We sat for a while in silence, and it seemed to me that we'd already reached the limit of what might be achieved with words. There was nothing more to say. I couldn't really guess what was in her mind but I sensed it was a mixture of great happiness and great sadness. Then she turned towards me. For the first time, I looked into her eyes and observed the strange beauty contained in them. Around the ebony centre, like rays emitted from a darkened sun, a thousand narrow fragments of emerald and turquoise tumbled across an amber sky. There was a jewel-like intensity to the colours, the like of which I'd never seen. But theirs was not a harmonious radiation. Her eyes possessed a fractured beauty, utterly disordered and lacking the promise of resolution. This was disconcerting, but at the time added to my sense of intrigue. This is now, and that was then.

'Close your eyes,' she said with great tenderness.

I closed them, not knowing what to expect next because of the intensity of the moment. There was a faint sound made by the movement of her clothes and then silence, so I asked when I could open my eyes and there was no reply. I waited a minute or so, happily, but when I couldn't wait any longer I saw that she'd gone. She'd run away.

I already knew this was a kind of game, and after all this time it's easy to see, like someone who bangs against their furniture for years before discovering he can wear glasses instead. But it was a game I wanted to play because it was the most exciting one I'd discovered until then. I also had the feeling that the game had been designed for me in every detail, and that if I didn't play it wouldn't be right.

There's a story of a man who sees a scorpion drowning in a river. He lifts up the scorpion in a handful of water to carry it to the other side, but the water drains out before he gets there, so the scorpion bites him and he drops it back in the river. But instead of letting it die he sticks to the plan and carries it to the far side. Some people watching the scene said he was a fool to carry a scorpion in the first place, and much more of a fool to carry it a second time after it had bitten him. Some others disagreed and said it was a saintly thing to do, especially after it had bitten him. When the man heard what they were saying he told them he wasn't as saintly or as stupid as any of them had supposed. The scorpion was a scorpion and did what was in the nature of scorpions to do. He was a man and had done what was in his nature to do.

I was alone now in a part of the house that was entirely unfamiliar, and far from certain of the route back. The passages and doors I had passed looked much the same and there were no signs or indications of any kind to follow. It took me a long time just to be sure I'd found the same staircase that I'd originally come down. At that moment it seemed quite possible that if I did get lost, I'd be as helpless as a man in a desert and just as unlikely to find anyone to help me. I did get up to the floor above, but then things got confusing, because now there seemed to be passages which I hadn't noticed before. I pushed on a few doors to see if I might find someone to help but they were all closed. Then I pushed on another and it simply disappeared.

I had the distinct feeling that I had entered a place which could not possibly exist. At the same time it was indisputably real. I knew it wasn't possible because as soon as I went in, I found myself in an enormous space and I was walking downhill not on a normal floor but on the floor of the sea. I was walking in a perfectly normal way, but when I looked up I could see the waves on the surface of the water and the blue of the sky beyond them and was astonished and happy to find that I could breathe underwater. At a small distance away in the corner of a green meadow – I was in a meadow – I could see a big tree underneath which Petra was sitting patiently, having arranged things for a picnic. I went to her but we decided not to stay there because of the noise coming from some roadworks nearby. So we walked together up a gentle hill and on the far side in the next valley was a racetrack where a crowd had gathered to see a car race. It was a glorious summer's day and everyone was happy. I walked down and met some former school friends while Petra waited. Then I understood that my friends were waiting to drive their cars in the race and that that was their skill in life; they assumed I was going to do the same thing, but I didn't tell them that none of it interested me. When the race began and the crowds began to cheer, I walked alone to the far side of the valley and began to climb. It was a place of great natural beauty and a few families and their children were quietly walking along the trails there. The higher I got, the steeper the slope became. The other walkers began to thin out, realizing it was getting dangerous and not a good place for conversation or sightseeing. Then I could see that the top of the hill wasn't far away, and on it there were some men and women in white sports gear playing tennis in the sunshine like millionaires. I could just tell they were leading a life of utter contentment and leisure. But the slope then became so steep that even the grass I was holding on to was coming out of the ground in tufts, and the hill had become a wall that was impossible to go up any further. Just before I fell, I managed to get out of the door and back into the corridor.

It all seemed so real I was sweating like a Karakalpakian *crut*,° and the relief of feeling solid ground again was indescrib-

---

° A type of dried goat's cheese known for its pungent suppuration in hot weather.

able. But the encounter had made me so curious I went back up to the door to see if I could get in again, but it wouldn't open. I pushed hard, and then kicked it harder and harder, but it wouldn't budge. 'These rooms,' I said to myself, 'are entrances to different worlds which do not exist in time.' I had no real reason to suppose any of this. 'That's why there are so many long passages, because there are so many possible things which are waiting to happen but so few ever do.' At that moment the thought seemed obvious but later it made less and less sense to me.

I walked for a long way after that, and managed to find my way back to my room without getting lost even though what was most on my mind was the vividness of the faces of my school friends, whom I hadn't seen since I was a teenager. Then I began to wonder if there was any way to prove that anything that had happened to me wasn't simply my imagination. Mad people will tell you something is real when it obviously isn't; but I knew that if I started to describe the events of the day someone might justifiably accuse me of being mad, and what proof would I have otherwise? Ordinary life, where everyone more or less agreed what was real, was much simpler.

I was thinking along this theme when I reached my door. I turned on the light, realizing it was evening and that I must have been on the lower floor for almost the whole day, and saw a slight movement from my bed. Somebody's fingers then crept over the top of the sheets and quickly drew them over some locks of blonde hair. Then I could see the scissor-like movement of a pair of legs.

There was no need to guess the identity of my visitor: it was someone who knew where my room was, where the bed was, and wanted to get inside it. I turned off the light and for the second time that day I could feel my heart beating in my throat, but for an entirely different reason. I thought of a fairy tale where a princess has given a task to a prince with the promise of a prize. Now the prize had arrived and I had no reason to hesitate because when the oven is hot there's no excuse not to make bread.

I took off my clothes and as gently as possible lifted the sheets and moved underneath them, thrilled by the feeling of warmth. I didn't expect them to be yanked out of my hand. It was all part of the game, I supposed, and yanked them back, pressing my body defiantly against the shape next to me. It was strangely muscular, and larger than I had imagined, and now it was swearing in Russian; and it was a man.

I leapt to the other side of the room faster than a cat you throw water on, and got the light back on. The shape was flailing about like a wild animal in a net, expressing all the ripest fruits from the tree of profanity. I pulled on my clothes, and tore the covers off the bed, finding a fully-dressed man trying to stop the light from reaching his eyes, and gripping a bottle in each hand.

I was shocked and angry and disappointed and asked him who he was, but all he did was raise a finger to his mouth to try and silence me, and pushed his head with his eyes still closed into my pillow. That made me more angry so I pulled the pillow out from under him and demanded he tell me what he was doing there.

Very slowly and with visible effort, he uncurled his arms and head like a snail emerging from its shell, and a single eye, clearly having difficulty with the task of focusing, swivelled in my general direction. He was no longer young, but there was something youthful and utterly unthreatening about his manner that robbed me of the wish to throw him out.

'I'm not doing anything,' he said quietly. He was pitifully drunk, and I could see it took him a great effort to pronounce each word. 'So you shouldn't be angry.'

'Why shouldn't I be angry?'

'Because if I'm not doing anything, you can't be angry about nothing.'

The humour in his reply, whether intended or not, took most of the fire out of my anger. I couldn't fault his logic.

'My body was quite exhausted,' he continued. 'It found this bed and . . . it wanted to sleep.'

Then he started, as if he'd suddenly remembered something.

'You must have a drink . . . rude of me not to offer.' He looked at the bottles in each hand and, unable to decide which one to pass me, held them both out. One of them was in fact a jar of pickled cucumbers, so I took the other, which was vodka, and although it wasn't my habit, swallowed a large gulp. I felt its fiery passage through my chest, which I enjoyed, so I took another.

'It's not a perfect world, is it?' he said enigmatically.

'No, it isn't.'

'You have to eat now,' he said, and struggled hard without success to remove the top of the pickle jar. 'You have to make the devils go out.' I steadied the jar on the bedside table and helped him get the top off.

'The devils?'

'Yes. When you eat, you have to drink something to make the devils come out. Or perhaps it's the other way round,' he frowned. 'I'll show you anyway.'

With huge effort, he managed to direct his fingers onto a pickle in the jar, which he shook off and held up between us.

'First you have to focus on the task,' he said. He was so tired and drunk that his eyes were trying to close as he spoke, but with repeated effort he brought them back to the pickle, which at last he managed to bite in half. Then he handed me the remaining half, and took back the bottle of vodka.

'Next,' he said, swaying wildly, 'comes determination. Nothing,' he shook his head emphatically, 'can happen without determination.' He threw his head backwards with the bottle attached to it, then let out a bear-like growl, as if someone were pulling a bullet from him without anaesthetic. The bottle swung downwards.

'Did you see the devils?' he asked, blinking like an astonished child. 'Did you see them coming out? They run everywhere. It's very important . . . to let them *out* . . .'

Then his voice weakened and his eyes rolled back into their sockets and his head collapsed onto the bed like a stone. I shook him but he was as good as dead. I took some towels and a blanket and made an extra bed on the floor as you might for a stray dog, only I was the dog. I know it might seem like a strange thing to have done. But I felt as though I'd made a friend, and you do things for friends, even in a madhouse. I knew that a friend in that place would be more important than almost anything else. And just then, I was happy.

II

Chapter 6

HIS NAME WAS Vasily Vasilyevitch, and he didn't feel at all well the next morning. He woke up moaning the name of God in his native Russian, and it was obvious he was in pain. On seeing me, he looked around, rubbed his eyes and looked at me again as if surprised that I was still there. Then he asked the same questions that I had asked him the night before: who was I, and what was I doing there? To judge from his deep frown, I could see the answers didn't make much sense to him.

'Coffee,' he said. 'We need coffee.'

Groaning, muttering and swearing in Russian every few seconds, he lurched out of the room and, gripping the banister tightly for support, made his way downstairs. In the dining room the first thing I noticed was the same naked man I'd seen at dinner, only now he was standing on his head at the far end of the room. My friend paid him no attention, but made straight for the pots of coffee on the table. Near the fireplace, two elderly women were engaged in a wrestling match, and on the mantel above them stood the midget, grinning delightedly as he watched the horrible spectacle of two exhausted crones trying to throttle one another. As we helped ourselves to coffee, a spoon began to hammer against a metal tray. It was the midget, signalling the end of a round in the pitiful match he was judging. Vasily winced in pain at the noise, and a string of colourful curses flew from his lips. The sight of the little man made him look uncomfortable.

'Is he dangerous?' he asked.

'I don't think so. Just very annoying.'

'There's one like that where I come from, and he bites.'

The subject of our exchange had been observing us and, still balancing on the mantelpiece, managed to perform his low, theatrical bow.

'Otto at your service.' He had a squeaky, foreign-sounding voice. Then his attention went back to the wrestling match.

'I don't know any of these people,' said Vasily, in a puzzled tone.

'Nor do I,' I said, to reassure him.

A minute later Otto had somehow managed to get behind us without our seeing him. He'd taken a chair and, standing on it as close as he dared to Vasily, began hammering on the metal tray with a spoon as hard as he could.

'King Otto to you!' he yelled at the top of his voice.

Vasily crouched into a spasm of pain at the sound, turned, and lunged at the little man, catapulting himself over his chair and falling into a swearing heap. Otto threw the tray into the air and fled, sniggering in our direction as he reached the safety of the doorway.

I helped Vasily to his feet and we sat down again at the table. He sipped his coffee sullenly for a few minutes, then seemed to be taking in his surroundings in greater detail. He looked at me thoughtfully.

'How do I know you?' he asked.

'You climbed into my bed last night.'

'Strange,' he mused. 'You're not my type. Was I lost?'

'I have no idea.'

'It is my – my habit, to explore,' he said, apologetically. 'Sometimes I get lost.'

'Where were you before you came here?'

'I'm not sure,' he said. 'I've met people like this before – in other places – but they are not the same ones.'

This interested me. It suggested that there were different branches or versions of the house which were nonetheless similar.

'How large do you think this house is?' I asked him.

'House? You call this a house? It is infinite in size.'

'It can't be infinite,' I said. 'If it was infinite, it would use up all the substance of the universe.'

He shot me a look that suggested great tolerance.

'The building is in fact finite, yes, but its limits are beyond our means, as individuals, to measure. Therefore for practical purposes it is infinite.' Then he added: 'But you and I may not in fact occupy the same building at all.'

It was too early in the morning for such a paradox. I felt disappointed to have met another madman. Overlooking the irritated tone of his delivery, I asked what he meant by his last comment. He sipped his coffee indifferently, saying that two individuals, using two systems of reference and measurement, could never share a common scale, and would therefore arrive at entirely different results even for measurement of the same phenomenon.

'Each of us has a different map. You have obviously not been here long enough to understand that.'

Everything in the building, he went on, including any attempt to measure it, was subjective, and in the absence of an encompassing law was bound to be irreconcilable with every other attempt, which was why it was in the nature of the place for nothing to make sense.

'Of course,' he added casually, 'that is not the whole story, but is sufficient as a starting point.'

This made a strange kind of sense, and caught my attention. I was attracted to the gruff familiarity of his tone and indifference to small-talk, as if I were a former and slow-witted pupil of his, testing his patience anew. He had the air of someone who wasn't trying to convince me of anything; he simply knew more than I did, and didn't seem to be bothered whether I understood it or not. Hearing him speak I felt increasingly certain I was learning something entirely new from him, as if all my own ideas were being suddenly challenged. In truth they weren't even my own, and it occurred to me that I hadn't learned anything really new for years. When I pretended to be thinking about something new, I was simply rearranging ideas to no effect, like a pampered bachelor who moves the dirt around a room, thinking he's cleaning the place.

I may not have grasped every detail, but I was already hooked, and insisted he say more. So he went on in the same – to me – oddly matter-of-fact tone, explaining that false subjective measurements, using incorrect geometries, could show that we were in different places when we were in fact in the same place; they might equally show that we were in the same place when in fact we were not. In the outside world, there were systems of measurement to which people have agreed to conform. But in here it was different. People and things were much more different here than in ordinary life. Then he moved on to something about the dynamic and absolute geometric object fields which meant nothing to me.

One thing in particular had caught my attention. I asked if the mere discovery of what he had called an 'encompassing law' would actually alter the nature of a place, and he replied that that's exactly what it would do, and asked irritatedly why I had not listened better to any of his classes on wave-function collapse. I said I had never been to his classes and he scoffed as if I was being a fool again, then began to look at me differently, and then again at his surroundings, as if something was beginning to make sense to him. Then he stood up.

'We need a drink,' he said.

We went upstairs. Vasily looked around for his bottle and, pausing before he drank with a look of self-excuse, took a gulp, and let out a sign of relief. He looked at me for a few moments without saying anything.

'Do you know why we met?' he asked. He spoke again before I could answer. 'Because I came in that door.' He nodded towards it, and took another sip from the bottle. The absurdity of such an obvious statement made me want to laugh, but he was speaking seriously.

'I came here out of all the other possible destinations available to me in this quasi-infinite world – this "house" as you call it. And out of all the other things that might have happened, I came through that door, and met you. Think. All the other possible things which did not take place are as much a part of that outcome as the one thing which did take place. The unrealized outcomes are not nothing, even though they are not actual. What has *not* happened is as important as what *has* happened in determining the result; it is simply invisible.'

'I hadn't thought of it like that,' I said.

'Forgive me, you were not in my lectures.' He took another sip from the bottle. 'You are familiar with the space–time geometry of Minkowski?' I shook my head. 'Reimann? Have you heard of Weyl? Have you heard of Einstein?'

I had heard of Einstein.

'Well. That is something,' he said quietly, 'and he was no genius.'

'What classes did you give?' I asked.

He sighed deeply.

'My classes were for those who sought to reconcile the actual and the potential. I doubt if they themselves knew that. In the ordinary world I had a thousand students. In here, I had three. A man who cleaned compulsively; another who spoke only in clicks; and a woman who every few moments gave the impression of imminent childbirth.'

'I am not sure what you mean by your description of the subject,' I said.

'Are you not?' he asked, with a new note of sadness in his voice. 'Each moment,' he said slowly, 'passes from the present into the past. How to understand this mystery? The present is continuous. We experience it at every moment of life. You could say it *is* life. Yet it is the most difficult and the most subtle to penetrate. It is impossible to put into words.' Shaking his head gently to himself, he looked at the remaining liquid in the bottom of the bottle and twirled it pensively.

'You were a scientist?' I asked.

'A scientist?' He brightened extravagantly. 'I was a priest! A high priest of science – a physicist. An impartial representative of reality!' He said the words with theatrical emphasis. 'You find that absurd? A scientist and a priest in the same job?' He raised the final drop of vodka to his lips.

'Science and religion are different,' I said cautiously.

He leaned close to me, and his voice dropped conspiratorially. 'Science is the most religious thing of all!' Then his voice rose again. 'Is it not so? A religious man is committed to something invisible, no? He is told it is there and that it gives significance to life. If he doesn't agree, he is considered an unbeliever. But what is the doctrine of science? That there is a thing called *reality*. It is invisible; we are told it is what makes life significant. The only ones qualified to undertake its investigation are scientists; and every phenomenon must be reconciled with what they – with their books and theories and experiments – imagine this reality to be. If you do not believe them, you are considered an outcast. Does this not remind you of something?'

'Are you saying –' I began, but he was underway now.

'The idea of a unified explanation for all natural forces and phenomena, a driving force behind it all – the Holy Grail of science – is this not the most religious thing of all? An explanation for everything? You will not be expected to know anything of the special techniques of this discovery – they are hidden from you just as the religious hide behind theology. Instead of incense, you have the clean smell of a laboratory. Instead of fancy robes you have the technician's white coat. But you don't understand any of it, any more than you understand the mystery of the Trinity. The mathematics alone is impossible to penetrate! And the doctrine is unchallengeable, even though there's no proof for any of it. Did any one of these scientists actually *show* you a black hole or an electron?' He made a spinning gesture with the bottle. 'Of course not. What is worse is that science revises its theories all the time. There is even a formula to predict the rate at which its theories are revised. At least the religious ideas stay more or less the same.'

A note of resignation had come into his voice. I felt sad for him.

'Science,' I said, careful again to choose my words, 'has enabled us to view the world more objectively.'

He smiled as if a child had spoken.

'If you want to find out what kind of fish live in the sea, what to do?'

'Make a net and catch some.'

'Exactly. Then?'

'Look at the fish. Measure them. Examine their shape and colour. I don't know – their teeth?'

'Yes, yes, yes. But what are you forgetting?'

'Their bones? Their diet?'

He waved his hand exasperatedly as if he were searching through the pages of a book.

'No, *doorak*,* all is external metric.'

'What then?'

'You are forgetting the *net*! But your net determines what you

---

* In Russian, 'idiot'.

catch, from which you build up your so-called objective view of the universe. That is why no objective knowledge of the world is possible through physics because physics itself is subjective, because it is structured by humans. How to get around that?'

'Then we cannot know physical things? I mean what is real?'

'We can know them relatively.'

'Can there be objective knowledge?

'Objectively speaking, no.'

'What about this place? Does this place exist objectively?'

'Subjectively speaking, yes. But this place is different. It doesn't follow the usual rules. Have you not noticed? How long have you been here?'

'I'm not sure,' I said, because I felt I had been there for ever, and suddenly it seemed impossible that I had been there only a few days.

He chuckled. 'That is one of its characteristics. Time cannot be measured externally here. Have you noticed there are no clocks? Or that your sense of time is continually changing? Time is entirely subjective here.'

That was also interesting to me. I had noticed the same thing and it troubled me but I'd never thought to formulate it in such a way.

'You may also have noticed,' he went on, 'that there is no contact with the outside world, except occasionally.'

I recalled the arrival of the doctors and the strange spectacle of preparation for their arrival that I had observed. Yet these very doctors seemed, as a result, to have a distorted picture of the place on account of the collective deception carried out by the residents.

'A good observation,' he said. 'Perhaps you should have become a scientist. What is the implication of a deception?'

I had never thought of this either, but the answer was suddenly obvious.

'A deception,' I said 'implies a truth.'

'So!' He pulled a short pencil from one of the pockets of his shirt and looked around for a piece of paper. I gave him one of the paper napkins I had taken. 'In this deception,' he drew a 'D' and a pair of intersecting axes, 'lies an indication that we exist in reference to something else' – he now drew an 'E' and at the top of the page began to develop a formula, drawing lines across the axes as it grew in complexity – 'which is non-spatial but nonetheless measurable if we allow that the deception is deliberate and of an order sufficient to modify the collective behaviour of all the residents here. And the direction of the deception enables us to plot thereby the direction of the truth and our position in relation to it.'

He held up the napkin. It was virtually meaningless to me, and he saw that I didn't share his sense of achievement. Then he looked over to the vodka bottle on the table, saw that it was empty, and sighed.

'There are, of course, truths which are easier to calculate.' He held up the bottle and peered at me through it so that I could see it was empty. 'Forgive me if we continue this very interesting conversation a little later,' he said, standing up and momentarily adjusting to his verticality. 'There is something I have to look for.' He walked unsteadily towards the door. I stood up but he motioned for me to stay put.

'Where will you find vodka?' I asked.

'You can find everything you wish here.' He made for the door and then turned back to me. 'That's the other thing about this place. It hears your wishes. Choose your wishes with care!'

☩

Vasily didn't come back during the day, and I was asleep before he returned, but the next morning he was stretched out on the opposite side of my room, on bedding he must have taken from somewhere else. He hadn't asked if he could move into my room. I wasn't sure how the arrangement, or lack of one, would turn out, but decided to go along with it for a short time. I was pleased to have found a friend of obvious intelligence, flattered I suppose that he had chosen to stay with me, despite the complicated interpretation he assigned to our meeting.

I didn't see much of him during the daytime, when we were both out exploring. But in the evenings we would both prefer staying in the room to the bizarre spectacle of dinners downstairs. We played chess instead, or discussed mathematical problems, snacking on slices of cucumber and cheese, and for several days at a time, wedges of meat from a leg of lamb Vasily had somehow procured, while he downed vodka at regular intervals throughout and demonstrated how to allow devils to escape. He didn't sip his vodka, as I attempted to do, but poured it with ritual extravagance into his throat with his head thrown back and his elbow raised to the height of his shoulder, like a guard presenting arms at the gates of the Kremlin. Occasionally when I forgot to let my devils out he would correct me strenuously, demonstrating by his own example the importance of the correct method. But despite this old-fashioned delight in ritual, he had the mind of an inventor, restless and animated by insatiable curiosity. If something puzzled him, he would try to formulate the problem mathematically, which meant that he was always jumping up from the table and scribbling streams of hieroglyphics with his pencil to illustrate the mathematics behind seemingly simple ideas. Our games of chess were seldom finished not only for this reason, but because at different moments in the course of every game the configuration of pieces would remind him of problems relating to his favourite field of enquiry which, wanting to learn more, I would usually encourage him to explain.

I remember the first time this happened. When a long sweep of his bishop eliminated my knight, I joked that I hadn't imagined that his bishop, waiting quietly on the furthest rank, could travel so far so swiftly. He pointed out that from the point of view of my queen the distance it had travelled was much less, and that the change in its position was only relative. I said that it was just a matter of perspective; yes, he agreed, but we could go further, and explained that there was no such thing as an independently existing trajectory but only a trajectory that was relative to a particular observer. What then was the true distance travelled by the bishop?

At this point he jumped up and explained that a single system of coordinates was inadequate to describe both points of view, and illustrated the fact first with a small picture of a train and rays of light and then with some mathematical notations. But there was a problem, he said. If the speed of light was a constant, and light was the medium through which our perception of events took place, then we would have to reconcile the differing systems of coordinates possessing their own perceptions of both time and space with the unvarying speed of light; and this called for a special theory which he began to unfold with great relish. At a certain point my ability to comprehend began to falter and collapse, but he took up the theme the following evening, approaching it from a different angle, and little by little I began to grasp what he meant by the geometrical structure of time, a basic notion by his standards but a difficult one for someone to whom basic arithmetic had always been a challenge.

Our chess games continued, and at different times he would jump from the table and attempt to explain to me some aspect of his theories about time and space and their attendant paradoxes and conundrums. He once showed me the calculations behind how far the centre of the universe had moved in the course of a single evening; at another, how a telepathic message sent to a distant star might result in a reply from the future, seen from the sender's point of view, which was able to influence the past; he proved the idea that an open future was not incompatible with the absolute space–time model of Minkowski, and how non-existent matter in the virtual state could act on material objects in the present.

I was fascinated by his presentations, but he was so often drunk by the time he had finished them that he forgot how or why they had begun, and my later questions would be met with a glazed look of reproof. Sometimes he would have no memory the following day of what he had spoken about with such enthusiasm the evening before. I began to understand that his attachment to vodka limited our friendship. Sometimes when he arrived in my room he was simply too drunk to talk coherently. At others he was perfectly sober but as the evening progressed his intelligence and sincerity grew obscured by a veil of intoxication and his manner became by turns grandiose, comic, incoherent and tragic.

One comment, which seemed to me a combination of all of these, has stayed with me more than any other. He had just delivered a complicated explanation for what he called non-local quantum entanglement, based on an intuition his former wife had expressed during the breakdown of his marriage, years earlier. His wife had been away for a weekend, and he'd succeeded in a long-delayed ambition to seduce an attractive woman in a neighbouring apartment on the pretext of obtaining her recipe for Circassian chicken. Speaking to his wife by telephone the next day, she told him of a horrible nightmare she'd had the night before, in which she had gone into a room and discovered him so engrossed in conversation with another woman that he hadn't even looked up when she entered. The dream had woken her up, hundreds of miles distant, at the precise time that his secret passion had been consummated.

A kind of despair crept up on him as he recounted the story, and then the physics behind it, and by the end of it he looked more dejected than I had ever seen him.

'Does any of it help?' he asked miserably. 'It's all theory, and we are – *here*. What good is a Lorentz Transformation when you need the love of a woman? Our life is here, but we are always somewhere else.'

I wasn't sure what he meant by that, but later on – much later on – when I had myself struggled with the practice of 'being here', it made more sense.° And it helped me to understand how so many people can claim only a handful of memories which are real for them, and for whom the rest of life is a sort of extended haze in which nothing really appears to happen, for the simple reason that we are always, in Vasily's words, 'somewhere else'. It showed that what are supposed to be the big events in life are so often nothing of the sort. It explained the man for whom the most luminous moment in his youth was neither the concert at which he played to his rapturous parents, nor his military graduation, nor his wedding, nor even the birth of his daughter, but the memory of the single sunlit afternoon he spent sucking Easter eggs on the shore of the Caspian Sea with the grand-mother that everybody said was mad and not to be trusted with children. It explained the tycoon who has spent his life doggedly working his way upwards in business, but who secretly loathes everything about it and the people he mixes with, and wants more than anything else to live alone half-naked in an Indian tepee. It explained the man who drools in his sleep not over his devoted wife of twenty years, but a peasant girl he once took on a picnic in his youth, and whose spontaneous laughter at the act of purposelessly rolling a melon down a hill he has never forgot-ten. It is her smile that he sees in his dreams and her laughter that he still hears.† And it helped to explain the woman who despite having lived an interesting life remembers only a single

---

* No other reference is given to expand on this enigmatic claim.

† We have not been able to discover whether these descriptions relate to contemporary events or are deployed illustratively by the author.

event with untarnished vividness: the precise instant when the conception took place of her unborn child, during which fraction of a second the entirety of both her past and future seemed to become visible like a broad panorama, in which she not only saw, but also felt, every experience of her life.

Each has been swept along in a succession of forgotten events, a life hardly his own, towards a destination none has ever given a second thought to, and each day of their lives has been a little pushing-away of the dread that never wholly disappears.

Two themes were particularly dear to my new friend. They meant little to me at the time, perhaps because I'd never had even an elementary grasp of mathematics and had all my life ignored anything that touched on the subject. Whenever I mentioned this, by way of an excuse, Vasily would blame my teachers for not having introduced me to the beauty of numbers. Correctly taught, he said, mathematics was more like music; a glorious and unending symphony limited only by the listener's imagination and an infinitely creative field in which every phenomenon, and even abstract ideas, could be explored.

He was convinced that, somewhere in the building, the past and the future were as visible as the present was to us in normal life. When I argued that his theory was tantamount to time-travel, he asked what was strange about that, since we were in any case constantly travelling in time? There was no doubt theoretically that both past and future existed *now*, but that they were separated from the present by the intervention of time. The problem with the present was that it was continually turning into the past. Did it even exist? If so, for how long? Vasily loved this kind of quandary.

We had many conversations too about how it might be possible to alter the past. He cited forgiveness as an example, demonstrating that forgiveness – not just the idea of forgiveness, but the deliberate, sincere, unreserved act – didn't simply alter one's attitude to the past or one's memory of it (this was my suggestion) but that it actually changed the past.

'You can't reverse time,' I said.

'I didn't say time could be reversed,' he countered. 'I said that the future can act on the past, from the point of view of the present. Think of the things in a person's life that only make sense later in life. They can only make sense when his life is considered as a whole, rather than a progression along a single line in one direction alone. Even a simple thing like a man experiencing his calling cannot be explained by a single dimension of time.'

Time, he proposed, like space, possessed different dimensions, which not only made possible the things that we called 'timeless', but also meant that the future could act on the past. The ordinary flow of time in one direction was insufficient to explain not only a person's experience of timeless meaning, but many other things taken for granted in the natural world: the invisible intelligence of a seed, for example, or that of a tiny butterfly that migrates a thousand miles to the very same place as its fellow butterflies from around the world. Such intelligence was preserved outside of ordinary time. Then Vasily would say something like:

'That doesn't mean we have to resort to extravagant theories of supersymmetry to compensate for Minkovskian reductionism.' And I would say: 'Of course not.'

The main point about the future was that certain things could affect one future out of a number of possible futures, from the most probable to the almost impossible, in a definite direction. So while I couldn't become the President overnight just by thinking about it, making a commitment to statesman-like behaviour increased the likelihood of my becoming a senior politician. Why anyone would become a politician he didn't know, said Vasily, but the point was this: we could not change the movement of the planets, but among the different futures

89

that were available to us as individuals, there were certain free-doms that could be exercised. The useful thing was to become sensitive to this possibility. All the philosophical confusion over ideas about free will derived from people mixing up the scales on which freedom could be exercised, said Vasily.

'How can you know,' I asked him in the course of our session, 'that any idea I have about changing the future or the past isn't simply wishful thinking or imagination? How can you prove it?'

'You can't *prove* anything that is really important.' He looked at me as if I hadn't really understood anything. 'But you might experience it.'

I admit that, at first, all this was too theoretical for me; it sounded like so much word-play and puzzling over pointless riddles. But as time passed I began to feel more comfortable with the ideas we talked about, which until then I had simply never bothered to think through. Later still I realized I had begun to look at past and future not as fixed, abstract things that were equally irrelevant to ordinary life, but as living things, delicate things, only hidden from view. Now time itself was redefining itself to me. Time was not so much a process that happened invisibly to me and everyone else, like gravity, with-out anyone having to do anything, but a thing in its own right, with its own living and purposeful existence, only one that we never normally noticed.

Around this time, Vasily introduced his Paper Dwellers to me. These were the inhabitants of a two-dimensional world, whose visible reality was limited to the length and breadth of a sheet of paper, and to a minuscule extension into the third dimension of thickness. To such beings, said Vasily, our world of solid objects would be unknowable. Taking a paper napkin he unfolded it, held it up and punctured it with the tip of his pencil.

'Enter into the world of our little friends, and tell me what they see.'

'A black circle.'

'Precisely,' he grinned. 'A growing black pool, appearing from nowhere.' Then he began to push the pencil further through the paper. 'And now? It becomes surrounded by a ring of wood, which transforms into a strange and opaque circle. What is this unknowable apparition? They will study its appearance, its rate of growth, analyse its atoms, argue about it and claim to have understood it. And when it has passed through the paper –' he pushed the pencil through the napkin and let it fall to the floor – 'they will say it has disappeared inexplicably and has been annihilated by time.'

Then he picked up the pencil and shook it meaningfully.

'What would happen if you tried to explain to them that their mysterious cross-section was in fact a whole pencil with a purpose of its own, with its own direction, meaning and function? They would start an inquisition, a Holy War! What we know to be a truth would for them be a dangerous fantasy – the invisible dimension of a higher reality. Our truths would be incompatible. Descend into their world and talk about pencils, and you would be locked up.'

Our ordinary sense of time, he explained, resembled for us the near-invisible extension of the third dimension of his Paper Dwellers, the cross-section of an infinitely greater world.

'But as soon as a man realizes that his life *is*, and extends invisibly into both past and future *at this very moment*, his relationship with the whole of life changes.'

'How?' I asked.

'His life becomes more real,' he said, 'a horizon instead of a wall. He can at last feel what is hidden to the ordinary senses. His actions begin to have consequence – a context. He begins to *participate* in the meaning of life instead of viewing it as a mere spectator, through the arrow-slit of the present, behind which he normally sits all day, watching life "pass by". Everything begins to change for him when he begins to realize this. All other

91

worldly excitements and revelations, all the apparent gains and losses of life become – shadows.'

'And such a man,' I said, 'would no longer feel the need to drink himself into oblivion.'

'That is different,' he muttered, after a long pause. 'A personal matter.'

And I hadn't the heart to pursue that.

His other favourite was to calculate probabilities, not by numerical expressions, but in terms of other events. They all seemed very unscientific to me, but probability, said Vasily, was just a way of modelling things, and it was good practice for the mind to have a sense of scale in matters of probability as much as in any other field. There were orders of certainty, like the turning of the Earth, and the movement of the other planets in relation to the Sun, that could be relied on. The speed of light, he said, tended to be fairly predictable.

There was an ascending scale of improbability too. Dice and coloured balls were useful to picture the odds of an outcome on a small scale; the mind could readily grasp such expressions as one-in-five or one-in-ten. The chances of a man being struck by lightning, about one-in-a-million he said, took things higher up the scale of unlikelihood. A man might even drop thousands of feet from an aircraft and, falling through soft branches and landing in deep snow, survive. Such things could, and occasionally did, actually happen. Theoretically improbable events could nonetheless be calculated, relatively. The chances of being bitten by fleas in the precise two-dimensional pattern of the Keplerian polyhedra were small but entirely possible. Sunlight flashing between trees planted alongside a railway, and casting shadows onto a newspaper being read in a passing train, might spell out in Morse code the clue to a crossword puzzle being read at that moment. Two loose roof tiles might fall at the same moment in different cities and kill one's ex-wife and her lover on one's birthday.

Though the odds were definitely against a flying pig, the chances could be calculated, at least relatively; they were considerably higher than the likelihood of a stork giving birth to a donkey, or a minnow climbing a poplar tree. Smaller still were the odds that all the oceans of the world would turn to decent vodka. The planets reversing their direction was not something one would bet on to occur any time soon.

Smaller still was the possibility of a man, while waiting for a bus, being struck by a giant and fragrant meatball containing the sum of all human knowledge (later on, I don't know why, the meatball idea would become a kind of yardstick by which we measured unlikely outcomes, or when one of us was being unrealistically hopeful about something). But all this, he said, paled beside the magnitude of improbability of human life on Earth. It came out as a number – a huge number to the power of something, with enough zeroes to fill a book, and enough books to fill some outrageous space. Was it from here to the Moon? To the Sun? I don't remember. But I remember the gist of the argument that followed it. It made Vasily quite emotional.

'In science,' he began, with more than a touch of sermon, 'the ordinary explanation for life is that after three hundred million years of pointlessness, conditions were favourable on the surface of the planet to produce self-replicating molecules that acquired life. Then over another enormous period of time – da da da,' he walked his fingers with cynical briskness across the surface of the table, 'these molecules happened to organize themselves not only into the miracle of the natural world and all its forms of life, but into people – not just any people, but into a Pythagoras, a Confucius, a Helen of Troy, a Leonardo, a Kolmogorov! Even allowing for cumulative genetic advantages, so called, the sheer improbability of such a theory is so fantastically high that it amounts to belief in the most outlandish fairy tale. Yet this is the very foundation of what "science" tells us about life! That all of it, and the Queen of Sheba, and her pet leopard, *arose.*' He accompanied the word with an extravagant welcoming gesture, as if he was introducing a cabaret. 'And this "science" believes that blind chance was able to create not only life and intelligence and consciousness on Earth but all life, cosmos upon cosmos, galaxy upon galaxy, perhaps universe upon universe. A blinding rain of steaming meatballs, flying on unwavering trajectories into every mouth that ever opened! Now, the religious man, if such a thing exists any longer, believes that God did the whole thing. Poof! A magnesium atom in every molecule of chlorophyll. How convenient! Poof! The ozone layer! Poof! Self-replicating nucleic acids. *Evolution!*' His hands rose in fluttering mockery of a wizard casting a spell. 'But does either the scientist or the religious fanatic have the slightest idea how any of it was possible, or to what purpose, if any, the whole of creation just keeps going? None whatsoever. The first is a negative faith, the second is a positive faith. But both are equally illogical and idiotic from the point of view of common sense.'

I was uncomfortable that a scientist was making fun of science, as if a child were making fun of its parents in front of me. It suggested a betrayal of sorts. But what if he was right about everything? I couldn't know, but it seemed likely my grandfather, who had always said that evolution was a fairy tale invented by the confused, would have heartily approved.

☩

A time came when I didn't see Vasily for what seemed to be several days, though I wasn't sure exactly how long he was gone. Alone again, I realized how much I'd enjoyed his company and that I missed him. I imagined him roaming, in search of answers, among the rooms and corridors he had never before visited, and adding each day to his complicated knowledge of the house. I hadn't yet accepted his notion that the building was infinite or even nearly infinite, reasoning that although it wasn't ordinary, it could hardly be supernatural, and had to exist in space and time like anything else. I knew that strong emotion could alter one's perception of both these dimensions, and also that there were drugs which could be used to distort one's sense of them. This seemed to me the more likely explanation for much of the apparent strangeness of the place.

I must already have fallen under Vasily's influence because I began to wonder how one could devise a scientific, mathematically sound way of testing our findings against themselves, to arrive at a greater objectivity in the absence of an outside measure. From two points of reference you could derive so much more than from a single one. Years earlier, I had been climbing in some high mountains of the Caucasus when a sudden snowstorm had descended out of the sunshine and separated me from my guide. I had soon lost my way and without my warm clothes I began to freeze. Tired and dangerously cold, I could hear an insistent voice telling me to just sit down beside a boulder and to sleep. Then another voice reminded me that this was one of the effects of shock from the cold and that I mustn't sleep at any cost. Anyone with training in the dangers of the outdoors learns how seductive the former voice can be and how to recognize it, and my experience spurred me on until I eventually found my guide. But had I listened to the temptation of falling asleep I would never have survived; and since then I had always trusted my own second voice, which stood apart from my convictions of the moment.

One morning, tidying up the sheets of paper where he had been scribbling mathematical formula, I found the equation by which he had calculated the strong probability of both a basement and an attic to the house. Those scribbled symbols meant nothing to me as usual, but Vasily had seemed so convinced by them that my own intuitive suspicions along the same lines seemed confirmed. I went out to investigate. The hallway was quiet. On the stairs, a man who was muttering both sides of a conversation to himself passed me without looking up. Another was sleeping soundly on the landing.

I reached the bottom of the stairs and headed for the kitchen, which I had never seen. It seemed the best place to look for the entrance to a basement, if there was one. Then I went through the door at the far end of the dining room, down a few stairs, and found myself in a windowless and unlit area lined with cupboards and shelves, beyond which I could see the swinging doors to the kitchen. Through the glass of the door's upper sections I could see about a dozen Mudaks working at various tasks in their habitually sullen manner. At a large central counter several of them were preparing food which reached them from a system of racks passing above their heads on a sort of conveyor. I couldn't tell where it started or where it ended but the thought that it might be somewhere beyond the room itself was exciting. It was the first sight I had of something which suggested a connection beyond the limits of the building, and for a moment I wondered what might happen if I simply entered the kitchen and went to see for myself.

I felt a hand on my shoulder, and jumped in fright. It was Fidel, who had crept up on me in the shadows. He made a calming gesture with both hands and motioned that we leave. So we walked out and when we reached the dining room he turned to me and took off his sunglasses and smiled.

'I didn't mean to scare you,' he said. 'I was looking out for you. You need to train yourself to relax.' We reached the atrium, where he put out a hand in the manner of a bodyguard when he senses danger. Then, after peering from right to left, he guided me forward. We sat down in the alcove.

'We should move soon,' he said, looking straight ahead. 'Did you make a plan?'

'I was thinking we would agree on one together,' I said.

96

'That's good,' he agreed. 'Good man.' He gave a friendly nod of recognition to the man I had seen a few days earlier, naked and standing on his head, in the dining room. Now, on the far side of the atrium, he was again naked, but managing somehow to propel himself on his hands with his legs hooked over his shoulders. He was oblivious to Fidel, who turned his attention to the entrance door on the far side of the atrium.

'We should watch,' he said. But there was nothing to watch. There was no one near the door or any indication that anyone was about to come through it. I tried instead to picture Mr Chicken Bone and his helper greeting the doctor and nurse as they arrived, and their trajectory across the atrium. Our chance would come just as they entered the first door in order to unlock the outer door for the doctors. I asked if he knew of anyone who had tried the same thing before. He shook his head.

'Look at them,' he said sourly, nodding towards the others. 'They don't even know how to look after themselves.'

'Why didn't you ever try it?' I asked.

'I never met a man I could trust to help me.'

I asked what he thought of the idea of creating a diversion, to catch the attention of the guards while I attempted to get into the doorway. He nodded thoughtfully, then looked furtively around as if someone might have seen him. It was obvious that no one was watching us.

'You check the door,' he said. 'I'll watch.'

I walked to the door and studied it. It was black and metal and looked very solid. There was no indication as to how it could be opened. The hinges were hidden by the metal frame and the locking system must have been activated from the far side, which was unreachable. I couldn't see any button or switch nearby, and there was no evidence of a pressure plate or any sensors to detect an opening device. A forced breach from the inside of the house would be impossible. Above it I could see the red and green lights protected by metal grilles. God provides, I thought to myself, but he is really going to need a nudge to open this door for us.

I went back to Fidel. He had no idea either how the outer door was operated or what lay beyond it. We discussed for a few minutes the details of what we would both do as soon as we heard the alarm that signalled the doctor's arrival, and agreed that getting the Mudaks' attention at the right moment was essential.

'We should have hand signals,' he said. This seemed unnecessary to me but I agreed he suggest one for initiating the plan and one to abort it. But the signals he invented bore no resemblance to any others I had seen, least of all the no-nonsense gestures used by the military. For the first he pursed the fingers of one hand and made a pecking motion; for the other he held his fist under his chin.

'Codewords, too,' he said, but that was too much. We could speak freely in any case, and there was nothing to write down that might be intercepted. Much more useful, I said, would be to do some physical training; we might not know what lay beyond the front door, but the chances are we would need to do some running.

We agreed to meet the next day. I had in mind a long empty corridor I had earlier discovered, where we could run and exercise away from anyone else. Fidel appeared looking vaguely military, wearing army boots and trousers, and walked beside me to the beginning of the corridor. I couldn't help notice his arms, which were bare and powerful-looking. There was a black ink tattoo on one of them near his shoulder depicting a snake ascending a ladder, which looked as though it had been copied from an antiquarian book. On top of this image, on a sort of scroll, appeared the words 'THE WAY UP', and underneath it was written 'IS THE WAY DOWN'.

'Let's warm up,' I said. He shrugged and fell into a kind of shuffle beside me. I had assumed from his military manner that he was accustomed to disciplined exertion. But his arms swung like a monkey's, and he kicked his legs out behind him with clown-like awkwardness.* At first I thought this was all an act, but he kept it up the length of the corridor, by which time I realized he had simply never learned to run properly. At the far end, as I was about to run back, he puffed and threw a boxer's jab against the air.

'That's better. I feel good now.'

I had meant to run the corridor a dozen times, but having seen that he couldn't run I suggested we run on the spot to warm up more. I counted out loud so as to synchronize our steps, but he made no effort to keep pace. I stretched my arms, bending from my trunk and counting to a rhythm, but he refused to keep time, puffing and flexing his arms like an animal woken from hibernation. I changed to a simpler routine, but for each separate exercise, he performed his own ineffective variation, humming tunelessly to himself.

'You don't want to do this,' I said. We had not yet broken a sweat.

'I have my own way,' he said, tapping his chest knowingly. 'The really important thing is mental discipline.'

We walked back to the main hall, my mind full of doubts. A man I hadn't seen before was attempting to skate in circles around the room as if it was an ice rink, only he had no skates. His face displayed the full delight of his delusional gliding across the ice. The miserable-looking woman who retraced her steps repeatedly back to the same spot was by the empty fireplace, moving back and forth like a piece of film stuck in a loop. Fidel put on his sunglasses. Our fitness training session was over.

'We need to watch,' he said.

---

* No attempt has been made to reproduce the original colour of the simile 'напоминающая осла с красным перцем в заднице'.

'And pray,' I added, half to myself.

He was still for a moment then turned to me with a smile of one who has shared a sly joke.

'Yeah. Watch and pray,' he said. 'I get it. Watch and pray, for you know not when the master of the house will come.'

'Precisely,' I said, hiding my surprise.

Chapter 7

I WAS GLAD when Vasily returned. My room had seemed a dull and lonely place in his absence, and his return was like family life returning to an empty house. He had somehow managed to acquire a boxful of vodka, several different types of cheese, a loaf of the black bread that I disliked, some vegetables and several jars of pickles.

'I had to go a long way for these,' he said with a look of guile.

'There are other Russians in this place?'

'Plenty. But you have to be Russian to find them!'

He began to slice cucumbers as he hummed to himself; he was always happiest when preparing this ritual preamble to oblivion. People, he mused, had been drinking since the beginning of time, but had never found anything that went so well together as vodka with a piece of salted cucumber. But something was different this time; something was changing the way I spoke to him. I could hear the difference in the smallest details, of which the Devil makes such expert use; the occasional hesitation that betrayed, however minutely, my own unease; the silent, private wandering of my mind while I watched or listened to him; the turns of phrase that didn't correspond at all to what I was really feeling, and the slightly raised pitch of my own voice throughout our conversation. I knew what the cause was: I was keeping the secret of my plan to escape from him, and it was affecting the simplicity of our friendship. And I realized then that you cannot try to be more sincere, or more honest with others – you either are or you aren't; the sincerity, or honesty, is already there, patiently awaiting its own expression, and all you can struggle with is the habit of covering it up.

I felt uncomfortable with this dishonesty. It seemed to be another characteristic of the place that lying was a much more uncomfortable habit than it ever had been in our former existence. The following evening, after we had begun our vodka and *zakuski*,° and were talking about the ordinary things of life (he was recalling, in fact, the difficulty he'd had years before of resisting the charms of a particularly beautiful student of his from Ekaterinburg – not the promiscuous type, he cautioned me, but pure and aloof and blessed with a natural facility for quadratic equations), when the moment seemed to present itself.

'Vasily,' I said. 'I am planning to escape from this place.'

'Excellent,' he said in his declamatory voice, then raised his glass. 'To the health of every man who has in his mind the sincere wish to escape from his surroundings, to improve his —'

'Vasily. A real plan. Soon.'

He chuckled, as a parent might when his child says he wants to be an astronaut.

'Drink,' he smiled.

'You don't believe me,' I said. I suppose I was disappointed that he wasn't more excited, like someone who just heard of a plot to rob a bank and has the chance to be in on it, but does nothing.

'It isn't a matter of belief,' he said with a touch of irritation. Then he regained his poise, and raised his glass, which had been hovering in mid-air. 'To the man who can distinguish between belief, hopefulness and fantasy.'

° A traditional selection of appetizers to accompany vodka-drinking.

I drank, then raised my refilled glass.

'To the man who can distinguish between the time for theory and the time for action,' I said, looking directly at him.

I could see he didn't really approve of my toast, but he drank anyway, and then looked equally intently at me as he bit loudly into a fresh pickle.

'You cannot just think of escaping and it will happen,' he said, slowly and with the benefit of hand gestures, as if he were talking to a deaf person.

'I'm not just thinking about it. I have a concrete plan, which I'm going to act on.'

'It is still impossible,' he said, taking another bite of the pickle.

'Why?'

'Because too many things need to come together before you can escape. This is not the ordinary world, where everything can be reduced to mechanics. If time and space alone were sufficient, it would be easy to escape: you could just walk out of the door. But you cannot, because the circumstances of your *life* have to be correct.'

I admit that there was, in what he was saying, an echo of my ongoing feelings of folly for the plan, of my sense that I was sharing the skin of a bear I hadn't yet killed, and that the whole idea was unrealistic. But I wasn't about to admit it to him.

Vasily wasn't finished, in any case.

'Think!' he went on. 'Everything that has gone before has led you to this point – here. Now everything has to be equally in place to get you out. You cannot ignore some aspect of your life and favour another, as if it had not left a trace on what you are. Maybe you are special – I don't know. But I do know that the pattern of your whole life has to favour your escape before it can happen.'

'My whole life?' I pictured an inverted pyramid, balancing on its tip in the present moment. 'Millions of people,' I countered, 'have had varied and different lives, yet they often end up in the same situation. You and I have had completely different lives, yet we are both in here together.'

'True,' he mused, unflustered by my protest, which annoyed me. 'But only in appearance. What you need to do to get out of here is different from what I need to do.' He sighed deeply. 'We look at everything in the world by appearance, but the real pattern of a person's life is invisible.* Out there,' he pointed to beyond the window, 'it's what you appear to be that matters. In here it is what you *are*. And what you are is a record of everything. Even your secret thoughts, when you think no one is watching you.'

I was about to speak – I was about to thank him, in fact, for expressing his feelings so cogently, but he spoke first.

'Look at this chessboard,' he said, waving a hand over our unfinished game. 'I know the moves. I know in theory I can win. But now look at the restraints, the unexpected reverses, the varying fortune of the enemy and all the time and effort needed before all these things combine in my favour. Mathematics alone can show this. But even if the underlying factors are in favour of your escaping, the physical configuration of both events and opportunities will still have to agree. It is not so simple, my friend.'

I knew there was truth in what he said, but I wasn't obliged to listen to him. He was obsessed by theoretical knowledge. He could not look at a simple event without formulating a theory to compute it. He was paralysed by theory. But I would be sorry to leave him behind.

'If I succeed, I will come back for you,' I said.

'You will need a miracle,' he said. 'And I would wish one for you,' he added amiably, 'but the laws of thermodynamics are particularly stubborn.'

---

* The author has annotated the original text with the opposing Persian words *'zaher'* ('external, apparent') and *'batin'* ('interior, hidden').

'Vasily,' I said. 'It's not an experiment in a nuclear reactor. It's just a house.'

'Even if it was a single atom, it would still be subject to thermodynamic equilibrium,' he said, biting into a strip of cucumber. 'Everything about this place suggests it is a system with its own laws and rules. To escape it, you would affect the entropy of the entire system, yet you are expecting to do so without a change in either work or order from your side. You cannot just think yourself outside of this place,' he repeated. 'To escape it you must first learn about it the hard way.'

'Perhaps,' I suggested, 'the practice is simpler than the theory.'

'On the contrary,' he said, 'the theory is perfectly simple, assuming that we are in a dissipative system which preserves measures for which we can prove ontic probabilities. We only have to calculate an expression of the two relevant entropies and, assuming a state of ignorance *ab initio* on your part, find a valid operator for the ratio of energy to information. I admit that what appears to be a reduced susceptibility to time will have a negative entropic factor that is difficult to calculate, but we can say – roughly – how long it will take you to get out of here.'

'Go on then, *imnik* – calculate it.'

Taking up the challenge, he felt in his pockets for his pencil, then picked it up from the table, looked for a few moments at a blank sheet of paper and began to write. An intricate net of grey symbols, unravelling energetically from the tip of the pencil, soon held the page captive. Like someone attempting to read an alien script, I could make no sense of them. Observing the expression of determination on Vasily's face and the precision of the shapes flowing from the tip of his pencil, I experienced a sense of absurdity at his attempt to calculate something so abstract by means of something as removed from real life as the obscure patterns of pencil dust across a page of paper.

But as I kept watching I had the strange experience of observing my feelings change; a dawning experience, really like a dawn, where everything changes colour slowly and when it's over the night has miraculously given way to day and your surroundings have been utterly transformed. I gradually realized, with the same feeling of magical transmutation, that the existence of these mute hieroglyphs, and the laws and formulas they expressed, drew upon the efforts of countless thinkers who had lived before us, the effect of whose lives and discoveries were touching us now and weaving themselves in turn into the fabric of our own lives, however remotely from their origins. And though I didn't think of it in words, it struck me then that those very atoms of pencil dust were being deployed as the result of men whose lives were both invisible and unknown to us, and yet peculiarly relevant, and that the same thing must hold true for countless other phenomena, which in turn were connected to countless others. Everything, it seemed to me at that moment, was connected to everything else, could we but see it, and as this very thought came to me I realized my feelings of ridicule had been entirely displaced by one of mystery and wonder. For an inexplicable moment, the world seemed a place in which every cause and every effect had some ultimate correspondence, however attenuated, and where every act was both registered and responded to in turn. Neither time nor distance had the slightest effect on this arrangement.

'God sees everything,' I said. I didn't mean to.

But Vasily didn't look up, raising his hand in annoyance to silence me until, several minutes and several pages later, he dropped the pencil and nodded to himself like someone who has finally heard some long-expected piece of news.

'Obviously,' he began, 'to allow for the deformation of infinite-dimensional diffeomorphisms by —'

'Vasily. The simple version, please.'

'Well,' he sighed deeply, 'you are aware that time does not exist here in the ordinary way, so we can express the answer only relatively, in terms of limits.'

'Meaning?'

'I regret I cannot lie as well as an Englishman,' he said, apologetically.

'Get to the point.'

'Meaning that if you work ceaselessly – that is, at every moment that is possible for you, to the extent of fully utilizing the knowledge you have acquired here by deliberate effort – on the problem of how to escape, the event does in fact become possible, but not necessarily probable, within a finite period.'

'A finite period,' I repeated.

'Yes, finite.' He looked at me without expression. 'Your lifetime.'

✢

For the next few evenings, at the edge of sleep, I pictured myself having escaped. I pictured myself breaking out into the fresh air and sunlight and running past those bewildered, cruel, cold-hearted and just plain stupid doctors onto a real street with real trees and real passers-by, until I found a public telephone and could make the call to someone I trusted to come and rescue me as quickly as possible. If anyone chased me I would leap over walls and climb fences the way fleeing criminals do in films, and no one would be fit enough to catch me. Then, after I'd been rescued, I'd begin the process of piecing together the mistake that had led to my unlawful capture, and the only place they would see me again was in a crowded courtroom. First I would find out from the property agents the name of the department that they had sent to my address. I would find out everything about it. I had friends who could make enquiries. Then I would cause hell. And then I would make sure the world got to hear about this place.

There was no reason, after all, to suppose it was impossible to escape. I had been wrongly imprisoned there; the place was not designed for people of normal intelligence, and I would escape after a few days and then I would tell my story. The entire thing might turn out to be an anti-climax, and the rest of the deranged characters I'd met would stay there because they had nothing to do with me and for the very reason that they were unfit for life in the world. Perhaps it was a mistake to read too much into my own captivity. It hadn't happened for any reason other than a stupid error; it wasn't life teaching me a lesson, it wasn't my fate or my karma, or part of any kind of cosmic plan. It was simply one of those unlikely and importune events which occasionally arise in the life of a man, like slipping on a banana skin or mistaking a sleeping cat for a hat, or jumping onto the wrong train by mistake and ending up in a suburb you didn't know existed and which feels like the end of the world. It didn't mean you were going to end up living there.

And yet. The more I told myself such things, the more I was aware of a stubborn feeling which told me it couldn't possibly be so simple to escape. It told me that it would be anything but simple, because life simply wasn't like that. However strange this place was, it was still a part of life, and it was much more likely that the task of escaping would take longer, and be harder than I was pretending, perhaps even harder than anything I'd ever done. I didn't give this feeling a name. I ignored it the way you ignore an unpaid bill when you have no money. But if I'd dared to call it something, I would have called it dread.

✝

The alarm, when it finally sounded, broke into my sleep like a wrecking ball, and sent me tumbling from my bed before I really knew what I was supposed to do about it. I had stayed up late playing chess with Vasily, who despite being half-drunk was on the verge of beating me when I'd claimed to be too tired to go on.

I dressed in a flash, folded my chosen photographs into my pocket and my coat into a pillowcase, and stepped towards the door. Vasily was still snoring on the other side of the room, but I had to say goodbye. I would miss him.

'Vasily,' I said, as a look of recognition came into his eyes. 'It's time for me to leave.'

He looked genuinely annoyed as I shook him gently.

'Can you stop that noise?' he asked. Then he blinked a few times and gave a snort of ridicule. 'You cannot leave,' he nodded his head towards the chessboard. 'We didn't finish the game. Your queen is in terrible danger . . .'

'Vasily. Look for me,' I said, 'and I will look for you.'

A dim look of comprehension began to cross his features. It wasn't the moment to linger for the sake of emotion. The future is hidden for a reason. I pulled myself from the room, went to the balcony and looked down onto a copy of the pandemonium I'd witnessed soon after my arrival.

The Mudaks were running to and fro, hustling various residents from one place to another. The lecherous woman in the fur coat was being roughly bundled into an adjoining room, along with the naked man who had perfected the art of swinging his legs over his shoulders while walking on his hands. The small chess table was being set up near the door, the sofa was being straightened out, and someone was steadying a large reproduction Monet on the wall where a plate of food had earlier been thrown. Someone else was already sweeping the floor in the vicinity of the door, and a woman was on her knees with a metal pan gathering up the dust and debris. All that was missing from the scene was Petra, whom I had first glimpsed from that very spot. But I couldn't afford to think about Petra.

Watching the transformation unfold below me I remembered what Vasily had said about the implication of an untruth, or however he'd put it. By his logic, which I suppose was mine too, the lie implied a truth, and here was a collective lie if ever

I'd seen one. What had not occurred to me the first time I'd witnessed the spectacle, and what I still couldn't figure out, was what the advantage might be, if everyone understood the deception, to maintaining it with such effort. If the inmates were sane enough to act as though they were sane, then why not stay sane, and save themselves the effort of a deception?

I saw Fidel from above, his habitual composure momentarily unbalanced by the untied laces of his boots, which he was trying to tuck in as he walked. Then we met, as agreed, at the bottom of the stairs, and as I looked at him I felt my own confidence and sense of purpose exceed his. I asked him if he was ready. He was ready, he said, but his eyes didn't meet mine for as long as they might have. I crossed the hall, noting the movement of the Mudaks, and made my way to one of the alcoves near the door, where I sat for a few minutes to take things in.

On the far side I was relieved to see that Fidel had chosen his target for a distraction, and that the Oafish-looking seed-scatterer, standing beside him, was already engrossed in whatever shameless tale he was spinning to him, which even from a distance you could tell was a complete fiction. I felt a twinge of pity for the simple-minded Oaf, who was already raising his hands to his mouth in an expression of horror at whatever lies he was being told, because it seemed likely that Fidel had chosen him for his slow reactions and his gullibility and would soon pick a violent fight with him, or smash something over his head. But this violent act would enable me to escape and I privately acknowledged my debt to him by way of a prayer that reminded me of prayers I had told myself as a child, the validity of which always I had always doubted because they were never quite as eloquent as the official ones I had heard. Perhaps the whole world suffered from the same doubt. 'Dear Oaf,' I whispered, in the antique belief that rendering a prayer audible made it stronger, 'thank you for your albeit unwilling part in what I am about to attempt. In the event of a successful diversion caused by the lunatic Fidel inflicting severe pain onto you, I hereby register my gratitude and pray that the remainder of your incarceration here be as painless to you in the future as mine is painful to me now.'

I nodded to Fidel, half-expecting to hear a scream from his witless victim, and moved closer to the door so that I could reach it in a few quick paces, then sat down and tried my best to look nonchalant, while scanning the room for Mudaks. They were still running to and fro and showed no interest in me. The woman who had the habit of retracing her steps had broken miraculously out of her habit and was now dutifully carrying a pile of what looked like encyclopaedias from one side of the hall to the other. She was greeted at the far end by the priest, if that's what he was, in the panama hat, who smiled warmly at her and helped her to lay the volumes on a table where he would no doubt later position himself, and pretend to have been reading them. The poor woman couldn't have known that after her back was turned, her smiling friend would make a vomiting gesture and double up in giggles. Nearby, gripping the window frame with both hands for extra purchase, stood the man who had taken to banging his head hard against the nearest pane of glass and then looking at it reproachfully, as if it might offer him an explanation.

Then I saw Mr Chicken Bone and his dowdy consort walking purposefully across the atrium towards the door, and knew that within a few seconds I'd have to follow them. I looked across to Fidel, oblivious to the other sights in the room, and frustrated to see that he seemed to be recounting the full details of his life story and hadn't yet begun anything resembling a diversion. In desperation I yelled his name and he turned to me with a startled look, while I replicated his idiotic hand gesture, pecking the air frantically with my pursed fingers. I hadn't yet decided, because I was reluctant to lose faith in my own judgement, whether Fidel was in fact a very cool-blooded operator indeed, cutting things as fine as could be, or was in fact a psychopath like the rest of them.

The Chicken Bone duo arrived at the door and stood underneath it, looking up expectantly at the red light. Nothing else really existed for me over the next few moments. Then the red light went out and the green one lit up and something from inside released the door, which swung open. I couldn't risk waiting any longer. I looked over at Fidel for the last time. He hadn't acted yet; with a strange timeliness, he looked at me without expression, as if he couldn't see me. Perhaps he was about to start a magnificent diversion. I doubted that now, but I couldn't wait.

The Chicken Bones stepped inside, and the door began to close behind them, but just before it did, I jumped forward quickly towards that sturdy woollen skirt that was disappearing into the darkness beyond the door. As the door closed, my body was pushed against hers and she gave a sudden gasp, like a corpse risen from the dead by a lightning bolt, and tried to turn towards me. The space was much smaller than I had expected and, lit only by a dim bulb overhead, much darker. It was like being trapped inside a lift. I had imagined that the outer door would open almost instantaneously but there was no sound or movement from the opposite end. Then Mr Chicken Bone noticed me and with a hand-wringing gesture of panic began a sustained chorus of finest quality choking noises.

'Don't be afraid,' I told them, 'I won't hurt anyone.' Then I added, 'Unless I have to. Just do what you normally do and you'll never see me again.'

But there was nothing normal about what happened next. While Mr Chicken Bone kept up his tortured choking sounds, his companion began panting and convulsing as if she was about to have a seizure. For a few seconds I imagined this was from the unexpected shock of my intervention. Then she braced her arms against the opposing walls and at first I thought she was somehow trying to escape from the confines of the tiny space, but then she pushed herself against me, facing backwards, with such force that I was pinned against the closed door. She began to moan and writhe and between gasps was saying something about her husband being on an oil tanker, or that it was his job to sail them, I can't remember which. I ducked under her arm and squeezed next to Mr Chicken Bone.

'How does the door open?' I grabbed him by his tie. 'Tell me how the door opens!' What was I thinking? I already knew he couldn't speak, and the closest he came to telling me anything was another round of awful choking sounds, only more agitated than ever. Mrs Chicken Bone was trying feverishly to wrap her body around mine, and pushing her away only increased her ardour, so I was forced to fight her off with one hand while I ran the other desperately over the interior, in search of a handle or lever or switch. There was nothing. I banged against the far end several times with my shoulder, but it didn't move.

I wasn't sure how long I could keep up the effort while squeezed into such a small space with a man who was chok-ing convulsively and a woman behaving like an octopus looking for a mate. I asked them both again how the door opened, but they were both incapable of speech. Then Mr Chicken Bone collapsed on the floor from terror. I gave a few final kicks to the end of the space, but there was no movement. I had failed and knew I had failed, and heard Vasily's words going round and around in my head: *your lifetime.*

From that hellish interlude I escaped back into the main room. It was uncannily peaceful. I looked around for Fidel, who was standing in the same spot as before, talking to the Oaf, who was still under the spell of his storytelling.

There was no sign of any of the Mudaks. A few characters were quietly minding their own business at the periphery of the room. I had the strange feeling as if nothing had really hap-pened, and for a moment it seemed that that was the end of the event. Perhaps that was simply another of the surreal things that could easily happen here, without changing anything. I looked at Fidel and held up my hands to him to ask what had happened and saw in reply a troubled look appear on his face.

Then the image of him was jerked out of my vision, as the Mudaks began leaping onto me in turn from behind. I registered again their unnatural strength as my arms were forced behind my back and I sank helplessly to the ground. They drove their knees into my back and legs and whatever was exposed they kicked without mercy. Coloured lights ran across my vision like bright streamers. I felt no pain from the blows but was aware of the crunching sound each time a foot connected with my head, as if a crust of dry bread were being snapped inside my skull.

At one moment I could just make out Fidel, wincing as he looked on. It was obvious he had never budged from his comfortable distance from danger, and that he'd made no attempt whatsoever to cause a diversion. At least my instincts that I shouldn't have trusted him were now being rewarded, but it wasn't quite the reward I would have chosen.

The worst sight came a few moments later, as I was being dragged away from the door by a team of Mudaks, each one grabbing whatever part of me they could in an excruciating grip. From the far side of the hall a flash of green caught my eye, and I glimpsed the light above the door, from which Mr and Mrs Chicken Bone were stepping calmly into the room, followed by the white-gowned doctor and his gorgeous-looking assistant.

Is it any surprise that this was too much for me? That everything was now going on exactly as it should have, in its own mad way, after I had been taken out of the picture? That the Chicken Bone duo, both of them deranged by normal standards, had managed not only to sabotage and obstruct my precious efforts to escape but were once again masquerading as paragons of civility and restraint towards the only people who could actually help me, and were probably at that very moment explaining that a madman had been causing trouble in the doorway but that everything was fine now. How eminently sensible and calm the depraved Mrs Oil Tanker looked now, with her skirt neatly straightened over her thighs instead of wrenched upwards so hopefully around her waist! And how terribly courageous of the pathologically incapable Chicken Bone himself, who minutes ago was quivering like a jelly in terror on the floor, to now stride confidently beside the authorities, a champion of the disadvantaged and living proof of the power of rehabilitation!

Imagine the puzzlement, then, of the Mudaks, whose prize maniac at that moment suddenly stopped struggling and went as limp as butter in their hands, sending them tripping over themselves in surprise. I admit there was no real logic to this last-ditch effort, and I should have known it would end badly. But how is one to overcome the logic of a lifetime for a logic which inverts every aspect of reality? You assume that normal people will help you if you ask for help.

For a few seconds I lay entirely motionless, letting the puzzled Mudaks wonder whether they had killed me, then jumped up and burst through the line of bodies with a scream of anguish that shocked even them. I sprinted across the open space, unable to move fast enough and feeling as though someone had turned down the switch controlling the rightful speed of things, so that I seemed to be wading rather than running, and the turn of the doctor's head in my direction seemed to take for ever. How long does a thing really take, anyway? A human day spans the entire lifetime of a gnat; to lovers in each other's arms a day passes as swiftly as a breath. Whose breath, then, endures the length of a human day, or lifetime? Is not the measure of time a matter of reciprocating scales, rather than those mute and inflexible calibrations of minutes and seconds? Every man has in his life a few short experiences which leave their mark disproportionately on the whole of his life, and periods of years which seem to disappear without trace. How long has each really lasted? This whole discussion seemed to be unfolding in great detail, with arguments on both sides, in the time it took that doctor to turn his head towards me, and to behold a bloodstained lunatic racing towards him.

His darling companion, that achingly beautiful woman I had once so naively hoped to charm, moved cautiously behind him. I heard myself shouting for help, saw the look of fear on the doctor's face as I neared him, saw even my own hands gripping his neatly ironed doctor's gown and heard my own voice, as if from afar, screaming a disappointingly clichéd succession of pleas:

'I am not supposed to be here! You have to believe me!
Help me, please! These people are all mad . . . !'

You always doubt the authenticity of such desperate statements when you hear of them, perhaps because they're so inadequate and seem to border on the comic. But then perhaps you have no idea what desperation is. The truth is that anguish of that magnitude cannot be expressed in words, and all that's left is the kind of pointless truisms that sound so pathetic and absurd from the outside. They even sounded pathetic and absurd to me at the time, but that's what came out. It isn't your ambition at such moments to emulate the eloquence of Shakespeare or the reasoning of Aristotle: you have become an animal, driven by an uncomplicated flame of rage that has burned through everything else, and at that moment if a thousand knives cut you to pieces, you would feel not a pinprick. But in the meantime, the doctor was lurching backwards, trying to beat my hands off him as you'd try to beat away the embrace of a leper, making me even more upset, if that was really possible, when he turned his head and said over his shoulder to that vicious piece of skirt hiding behind him: 'He's *completely* mad!'

Within a few seconds I was once again pinned to the ground, listening to the familiar crunching sound of old bread, surprised again too that I felt no pain, except the kind of pain one might feel leaning into the wind at the edge of a cliff, in the grip of a wonderful terror exceeding any ordinary emotion, indifferent to life or death, because in a strange way there doesn't seem to be much between them at such moments. I could see that a number of the Mudaks were breathing hard from all their exertions, and I felt a moment of satisfaction. Then I saw the doctor's face loom over me.

'Moron,' I said, with what was left of my strength.

'Punish him,' he said.

Then he disappeared and in his place, unexpectedly, I saw the cruelly seductive features of his gorgeous companion. She was definitely Kazakh. I longed to hear her speak. Her eyes looked lovelier than ever now, as dark as they were intense and charged with purpose. She leaned over my captive face, close enough for me to feel the warmth of her breath and her hair dangling against me, and for a second I thought she was about to kiss me. Then in a strangely intimate refinement of her feelings towards me, she pursed her lips and released a stream of saliva, which fell first into one eye and then, as she carefully adjusted her aim, into the other. I saw then, as she wanted me to see, the slight but distinct smile that spread across her face.

'It was love at first sight for me, too,' I said, thinking back to the moment I had seen her lovely shape from my vantage point near the ceiling on the day of my arrival. Then the image came to me – why that one I don't know – of the gleaming, ice-bound peak of a mountain I had seen in the Pamirs one glorious summer morning years before. And I wondered what time it was there, and whether the same peak was still gleaming in the same sunshine, though I couldn't remember what time it was, or even whether it was summer or not.

Then I was aware of the surroundings racing by, at the edge of consciousness, as I was escorted from the atrium and from one room to another until we stopped for a moment in another large room where I had the sensation of the world beginning to float up above me, as if it were painted on a curtain that was now being lifted above my head. Then I realized it must have been me who was sinking. The Mudaks were dragging me down a ramp into a pit or cellar from which the light from the upper room was steadily excluded until I could make out nothing of the surroundings. What was strange was that most cellars were colder than the houses above them, but this one was warmer. At the bottom of the slope they dropped me roughly, and walked back in the direction we had all just made our happy way, upwards towards the light and warmth above which resembled so much the view from a deep forest clearing open towards the sky. They didn't even look back. I could for a few moments make out their silhouettes as they emerged into the room overhead, disappeared briefly from sight, then reappeared as they lined up behind the long and heavy trapdoors they were lifting, which now slammed shut above me with a final and obliterating echo.

Chapter 8

I DON'T MEAN TO SOUND as though I've always known this, because at the time my thinking was very much in opposites, and everything was good or bad and I was either for or against every action. But I know it now: even to the things we naturally fear and run from, there is a purpose much deeper than we ordinarily suppose. To darkness and shadow there is a purpose no less profound than that of light and brilliance, and no less important to life itself; and both darkness and light are joined by a mystery.

I say mystery because the very thing that makes them both possible is invisible, and is the thing that no one sees. No one actually notices the turning of the planet that creates and regulates night and day and turns one into the other. But without darkness there could be no such thing as light – it would mean nothing at all, and couldn't exist – and without shadow you would not have such a thing as brilliance, and without the dying of each dusk there could never be the birth that is carried on every dawn; and each owes its possibility, its meaning, and its wholeness to the other.

The same is true of pain, which after all is a form of darkness. For most men pain becomes over time either a shroud or a weapon, which shuts out or opposes life until bitterness and pity do the rest. But for another kind of person pain is the only medicine strong enough to break open the kernel of the self to reveal the fruit by which one is made whole.

I admit this was hidden from me then. So too was the notion that the pain a man must suffer is fashioned by mysterious fortune as precisely as a key for a lock of near-infinite complexity. Yet this is why another's trials can never do the job for him, and why the questions that he cries out on the rack are his alone to ask, and why the answers can be heard by him alone, and why they are neither read nor written in any book save that of his life itself. No one who has not already discovered this for himself will believe you and, as I say, I may have known some of this before, but it was much later that I understood it, and between the knowing and the understanding lies a difference, as the Afghans say, as great as the difference between earth and sky.

⁜

At first in that darkness I could see nothing. I sat up and listened, hearing only the heaving of my lungs, which gradually settled as I searched around me in vain for clues. Everything hurt and I could taste a film of blood inside my mouth. The thought occurred to me what a pointless punishment it was to put a man in the basement of a house. I would be lonely and hungry by the time they took me out, but no more. If things got too difficult, I would find a way out of my own. It was just an old house, not a military bunker a thousand feet below ground.

That was the way I was still thinking, anyway. It was still pitch dark. Then I realized I must be on some kind of table above the floor, and felt around for the edges, bracing myself against both sides in order to swing my legs off, but found that I couldn't. For the first time in my life, my legs weren't doing what I wanted. I tried lifting one of them, but it hardly budged. Then I felt my arms beginning to bend as if they were being pushed down by a weight which I simply couldn't resist. You are so accustomed to your body responding to your wishes that when it doesn't behave, and starts to do the opposite, a peculiar feeling of vulnerability takes over. At first I thought that perhaps I was suffering from some kind of paralysis brought on by a kick to my back, and had a few moments of panic. But I hadn't lost any feeling in my limbs, and was perfectly able to tense the muscles in my arms and legs at will; I just couldn't move them out from under the weight that was pushing me against the table. Eventually I was lying flat and looking straight upwards, and the only parts of my body I could actually move were my eyes, because even my head felt as though it was held in a clamp. I couldn't figure out when or how, but one of the Mudaks must have drugged me; or perhaps the nurse's saliva was actually a toxin of the kind made from Amazonian tree frogs, which wouldn't have surprised me. Either way, apart from my eyes, I was totally incapacitated.

Staring upwards in that darkness, I could start to make out tiny cracks of light between the floorboards above. And, further off, though I couldn't see them directly, shapes. Every instinct was telling me to turn my head towards them, to see who or what they really were, but I simply couldn't. I had to wait for them to get closer to me, which they were doing, albeit very slowly, like cows that gather around you if you lie still in a field for long enough. Soon they were only a few feet away, and their shadows, which had something animal-like about them, began to interfere with the slivers of light reaching me from above. Their stealthy, fluid motion made me think of a gently oscillating, predatory mound of cats I had once seen by moonlight on a tiny back street in Istanbul.

It was no good trying to control my breathing; I was terrified.

'What do you want?' I asked. I hardly recognized my own voice, which sounded hoarse and strangled. A shape loomed into my field of vision, next to the edge of the table, and stayed there, looking at me. I could see parts of it.

'Oh God,' I heard myself say, but the words were not mine any more, and the face drew nearer.

It wasn't human, but that of a dog attached to an upright body, as if the two had fused. It had the physiognomy of an animal but the manner of a human, and looked at me with the poise and intention of a human.

It loomed over me in a posture of sinister benevolence. I could hear its breath and see the slow deflections of its head as it studied me. I glimpsed a long, jackal-like snout, which was black and much bigger than an ordinary animal, and a pair of black nostrils, soft folds of black skin running along the jaw, and the occasional glimmer of white behind them. Then, in a deep and rasping whisper, it spoke.

'What we want,' it said, 'is these.'

I'm not sure which was more terrifying; that the dog-man could speak, or that it wanted something definite from me. I was helpless and speechless from fear, and could only watch as the creature leaned over my chest and stretched forward a clawed hand and ran it, in a perverse caress, from my neck to my navel. I couldn't see how he did it, but with the other hand he managed to peel back the skin of my helpless torso and reach inside it. Then his head turned away towards the others and he nodded to them to gather around the table, like children around a box of sweets. About a dozen of them, who seemed to be smaller and less confident versions of the one who spoke, stepped closer with a faint collective mewing.

'Look,' he said, 'what have we here?' His claw sank effortlessly into my chest. I felt a sudden surge of panic, as if I'd stepped by mistake onto an unexpectedly high balcony, and then, a feeling of indescribable violation. His claw rose into view, and balancing on it, a small ball of yellow light, clearly alive and gently pulsating. A ripple of delight spread through the others. It was extraordinarily beautiful and resembled nothing I had ever seen, and I could feel that it was linked to me and didn't belong in the paw of this outsized rat-catcher, who seemed to be enjoying the spectacle with wholly human detachment.

'That's mine,' I said, with all the desperate effort I could muster, but I had begun to weep now.

'Yours?' asked the voice. By way of a reply, he bounced the delicate ball in his paw, and at each bounce I felt an awful feeling of dread, pulling at me physically from inside my chest. Then he tossed it playfully from one paw to the other, and another ripple of mewing rose from the smaller ones, and my chest was shaking now like someone in the grip of uncontrollable grief. I could feel the tears pouring down the sides of my head like one of those waterfalls you see in the foothills of Mount Elbrus.* I longed to wipe them off but couldn't.

'Have it back then,' he said, and lowered it down again. I felt a sudden sense of relief, but it didn't last. His claw disappeared again, and this time drew up a similar but different-coloured ball, a beautiful, luminous lilac colour trailing silver strands that resembled the gently wandering tentacles of an anemone.

'Ah,' he breathed, holding it near as if to inhale its fragrance, like a gourmand sampling the bouquet of a favourite wine. '*Hope*. Better not drop it.' He pretended to fumble, and tossed it to one of the others, while at the same instant I felt an excruciating feeling of being momentarily crushed. The strange thing is that the pain wasn't entirely physical, although it seemed to originate in my chest. If there was a physical sensation it was one of violation and dread, which rose up each time the jackal surgeon chose a new plaything. But strangest was the agony resulting from the manipulation of each of these fragile and luminous beings which he was lifting out in turn, each provoking a distinct violence

---

* Mount Elbrus (4741m), highest mountain of the European continent, in the Caucasus range of Southern Russia.

of its own, as if I were being dragged through all the different rooms of a house containing every kind of misery.

The hideous talent of my torturer enabled him to remove each separate feeling in turn, identifying it with cruel satisfaction and holding it up for the others to see and sometimes to touch. At times he removed one, then another, passing them to the younger jackals while he extracted yet another, and tossed them back and forth before returning them to my convulsing and helpless body, while I, a weeping, overwhelmed and terrified spectator, endured until exhaustion began to claim me. I remember looking at the face above me, registering its intentness and fascination as another light-filled sphere was made to perform in his grasp, and asking: 'Are you real?'

He was still for a moment, as if suddenly aware of having committed a discourtesy, then leaned closer and spoke in a tone of almost avuncular reassurance.

'Real? Yes,' he said. 'For you.'

What did he mean by that? That I was imagining him? That I had created him? That for someone else he simply wouldn't be real? It was impossible to believe. Who could have dreamed up a torture of such devious precision? And even if I had imagined the whole thing, what was the point of my torturer's having taken the trouble to share it with what appeared to be the next generation of jackal torturers? I've often wondered, since then, whether there is any point in trying to convey the pain delivered on that day, not only because life is not quite the same afterwards, but because I doubt it's really possible to adequately convey either the feeling that one's life's meaning is being deliberately crushed or the sense of wonder at the one who is carrying it out. It isn't pain in the way people normally think; physically, it didn't really hurt more than a scuffle with a would-be mugger. With physical pain you lose consciousness if things go too far. But this was different, like a liquid which you keep adding and it doesn't overflow. There was always more hurt that could be done.

Then, at some signal that I never understood, the jackal juggler and his underlings were gone, as if summoned, and I was alone again. I could turn my head. I could feel my arms too, which rose instinctively to my chest, feeling nothing out of the ordinary. And just as I realized I could also move my legs, the doors above me banged open, and the light was dazzling.

The Mudaks ran down, and I braced myself for a rain of blows, though now the prospect of physical pain alone seemed trivial compared to what had gone before. They simply lifted me off the table and carried me up the ramp, through a series of rooms, and dumped me in the atrium at the foot of the stairs. I wondered if they knew that it wasn't worth trying to hurt me, and whether that was the reason they didn't bother, and wandered off instead.

After that, no one paid the slightest attention to me. The brightness of the room hurt my eyes. I got up and, not without surprise, realized I could walk. I made my way slowly to my room, realizing that there seemed to be nothing more wrong with me than a feeling of bruising where I'd been kicked. I half-expected to find bloodstains on my chest. When I was alone and the door was closed, I hurried to see my own chest in the mirror, where my torturers had dug into me. I was shocked by the sight of my reflection. My face was a mess. The right side was swollen and gave an impression of lopsidedness, as if an Abkhazian bandit had dropped a boulder on it. A dark purple stain had spread under one eye, and blood from the cut on my eyebrow had left a cracked stain down to my chin. For a moment I seemed to be looking at a different person; a desperate, distressed, misshapen fugitive who had lost his place in the familiar world and was unlikely to find his way back.

I felt the bones experimentally to see where they hurt. My jaw seemed to be intact. It would all heal. But on my chest there was no trace of anything, not even a scratch. I ran my fingertips again and again over the skin, not understanding. Then I pushed and pulled at it. The muscles and bones were all unbruised, the skin perfectly healthy and unharmed. To discover that my wounds were invisible, as if nothing had happened, was perhaps stranger than anything else. I suppose I was relieved. But I admit I was disappointed to have gone through all that without any visible trace, any proof or sign. Nothing. It's not that I was planning to show off my wounds, to myself or anyone else. It was the feeling of having been robbed; violated and then robbed, with nothing to show for it but my own invisible scars.

Had it happened? Had I pictured the whole thing? A scar helps you to see what has happened. When there is no trace, it's natural to have doubts; the validity of what you experienced is somehow undermined. But I didn't know what had happened. I didn't even know.

I collapsed and began to weep, then crawled into bed and felt the tide of sleep rushing up to me, and was never more grateful for it.

✠

Nor was I ever more grateful for wakefulness, when I saw Petra's face appear at my door the next morning. She must have assumed I was asleep. I watched her, without moving, through a half-opened eye, as she stepped quietly inside, and went straight to the table and began to clear it. Then she took a tall glass and carefully arranged several leafy twigs in it before returning it to the table, checking from time to time whether I was awake. When she had finished tidying up, she brought a chair close to the bed, sat down and looked at me. Her back was naturally straight. She wore a plain white smock and a cotton dress with sunflowers on it, and she seemed more beautiful and radiant to me than ever.

'You've been watching me,' she said, as a mother might gently admonish a child.

'Yes. It was so nice to watch. Where did you get the twigs?'

'From our meeting place. You remember?'

'Where you ran away from me.'

She looked away and smiled coyly, and her eyes danced restlessly, a little like a blind person's, when they're thinking about something.

'You made me nervous,' she said. 'I had to run away.'

'What would have happened if you hadn't run away?' I knew the answer from my side. She didn't answer, but reached into the cloth bag on her shoulder and took out a small stone pot of ointment that resembled butter. She didn't ask me if I wanted it. She just reached over and rubbed some gently on the cut on my eyebrow, then on the swollen lump above my cheekbone.

'I knew I had to come back,' she said quietly. Then her manner changed. 'This will make it heal faster. Show me your hands.' She took my fingers into hers and turned them gently downwards, looking in turn at my fingernails.

'They're strong,' she said pensively. 'But you need some extra vitamins.'

'You're a doctor, too?'

'No. It's just traditional. In the islands they have a traditional remedy for everything. You have a few white spots on your nails. It could be the trauma of your arrival here. Distress eats up the body's supplies of nutrients. I'm so sorry,' she said, and her face began to change as if she was about to cry. 'I'm so sorry what they did to you,' she sniffed. Then she stood up, and said: 'You need your strength,' as if having made up her mind on the issue. 'I'll bring you something.'

And then she disappeared again without a backward glance, slipping noiselessly from the door, lean and swift and light on her feet and, I now realized, barefoot. She was more like a fairy or a nymph than a real person, yet I had felt her touch. And against the ugliness of what I had witnessed the previous day,

127

she seemed extraordinarily beautiful. I fell asleep happy, not quite daring to believe my luck.

Perhaps it was the afternoon when she came back, carrying a tray and some dishes. She fussed over them on the table, then brought a bowl of soup to my side. I sat up and sipped it as she watched me, though whenever I looked at her directly she averted her eye and smiled coyly like a little girl.

'Spicy chicken soup. My mother's recipe. She used to say it would cure anything.'

It was delicious. As I ate it I seemed to feel the strength returning to my body.

'I wonder if they would let us keep chickens here,' I said. Her eyes met mine again and then danced away, danced back again. I was content to catch a glimpse of them, but I longed to simply look into them, to hold her gaze captive without words or motion. After I had eaten a second bowl of soup, she took an apple from the table and began to peel it. I saw the braided furrow of a scar across the inside of her wrist, and felt a spasm of pity.

'Tell me about the islands,' I said.

'I grew up there until I was eight or nine. A kind of paradise.' She passed me slices of apple as she spoke. 'My mother was one of the daughters of a chief. She said the whole island came to her wedding with my father. A thousand people!'

I'd assumed, from the lovely hue of her skin, that her complexion was Mediterranean, but realized now that it was tropical.

'She used to say she could talk to sharks. I don't know if it's true, but I remember seeing her swim among them without any fear. I only tickled a turtle once! But we were always in the sea. My father was a sailor and could never get enough of the sea. He was always diving for treasure, or chasing whales. He used to call me his little mermaid.'

She tidied up the things she had brought, then sat down again.

'I wanted you to have this,' she said, and presented me with a small ring-box from a famous maker of jewellery. For a moment I was reluctant to open it.

'Go on,' she said. I opened the box. It wasn't a ring, thank God. It was just the right kind of present, in fact: a tiny egg made of moonstone, pale and translucent, filled with tiny sparkling fractures. I held it up to the light.

'A gift from the chief to my father, when he left the islands. A souvenir. More of a charm, really.'

'You should keep it, then,' I said.

'No. I'm happy for you to have it. It will help you to remember a place beyond this one. You can give it back to me one day, if you want.'

I wasn't sure what to make of this cryptic suggestion, but it set alight my imagination. You know what a brush fire is like on a parched hillside, needing only the slightest breeze to unleash itself across miles of land. I saw the two of us together, having both escaped, and pictured myself handing the tiny egg back to her, in recollection of the moment our bond was first celebrated with that very fragment of tropical moonstone. Then the things I was imagining began to make even me blush.

She stood up.

'I have to go now,' she said quietly.

'I wish you didn't,' I admitted. She gathered up the things she had brought, leaving the twigs in the glass and went to the door.

'I don't know how to find you,' I said.

'You know how to find me,' she said. 'You've already found me.' Then she slipped away, closing the door noiselessly behind her.

How was I supposed to feel? How was any man supposed to feel? She was the most beautiful woman I had met, the most feminine, enticing, mysterious, exotic and delicious creature I had ever set eyes on. She was, more significantly, here. I hadn't just met her on the street; our lives were intertwined by our both having been confined in this particular place. And she had brought *me* her mother's spicy chicken soup — not someone else. There might be a thousand other men she had met in this bizarre place, but it was to *me* she had come and whispered all these intimate things, these things that suggested so much. She was restrained — I liked that. Modest too. She understood the importance of tradition. And she had obviously suffered deeply, though I tried not to think about those scars too much.

Is it any surprise that I felt the hand of Fate on these events? That I felt the pull of the future, as Vasily might have put it, as if a magnet were reaching for my soul, dragging it into a dizzy spiral? I could still smell her fragrance, as I had the first time she'd disappeared outside my door, leaving me feeling bereft and full of longing. Now my longing was even greater, but supported by hope. It was obvious she cared for me.

Did I dare hope she too might be in love? Of course I did. I prayed fervently that she was as in love with me as I was with her. And once again, I marvelled at how, in here at least, such a heavenly experience could follow so closely in the footsteps of such a hellish one.

✝

Vasily had heard nothing about my adventure when he returned that evening, and was merely surprised to see me in bed. Then he saw the state of my face and began to fuss.

'*Bozhe moy,*' he muttered, 'my God. You need a drink.' I felt the fiery surge of the vodka, and enjoyed it. He came and sat at the edge of the bed and listened to my story. It made him quite emotional. I didn't tell him about my strange underground encounter because I simply didn't know how to describe it, so I stuck to the events of actually trying to get out of the front door, and how wrong the whole thing had gone.

'*Svolochi!*'° he kept saying, when I described the tender care I'd received from the Mudaks, reaching for a drink whenever I went into the grisly details.

'You are a brave man, but,' he said, raising his glass, 'we must drink to knowing which door to open and which not to open.' He winked. We drank. I enjoyed his sense of humour.

In the course of my recuperation, we had many satisfying discussions. There was no one to prove ourselves to, so we could talk about whatever took our fancy, and Vasily's restless mind would go to work like a hunting dog on whatever came up. In ordinary life the subjects of our conversations would have probably been the fish we had nearly caught, the careers of corrupt politicians or our favourite recipes for *chikhytma*† on a hangover. But in here our thoughts tended towards the issues that sooner or later a man has to find his own kind of peace with: time, love, death, God and what we ended up calling 'meatball'.

The one we kept coming back to, and the one that occupied us the most, was the question of how – or whether – one's most private decisions and acts could – in some holy, measurable way – have any significance beyond whatever went on in one's mind or feelings. All traditional moral and ethical systems and all philosophical and religious teachings agreed – if not on the exact details, then at least on general principles – about what kind of behaviour would lead to eternal happiness, and what would catapult a man or woman onto the toasting-forks of Hell. But nobody seemed able to explain how it really worked. We agreed that if science could give us a convincing answer to that, it would give real hope to people, instead of simply distracting them by discovering how to recycle bottletops, or calculating whether mice might have once lived on a distant planet. The answer

---

° In Russian, 'The bastards!'

† Caucasian lemon-chicken soup.

131

wouldn't be of much interest to people whose consciences were buried like lost cities under the Gobi desert, but for the rest of us it would solve the crisis of meaning in individual action, which was a horrible predicament that affected everyone from time to time, even policemen.

This, surely, was a solution whose time had come. The trick was to find it scientifically, without resorting to fairy tales or sweeping over the difficult bits, such as how an all-powerful God was unable to make a man feel love for his mother-in-law. It also had to give equal weight to the convictions of nihilists and madcap visionaries alike.

Whenever Vasily brought up a question, it was usually incomprehensible, mainly because of his obsession with phrases like 'existential postulates' or 'supra-causal ahistoricity'. I would say: 'Can you tell me that in language that a normal person can understand?' and he would roll his eyes and then reformulate it in equally incomprehensible terms. Then I would gradually wear him down, forcing him to use the language of the ordinary world until his question became possible to understand (quite often, when his question had been reduced to much simpler and, to me, more meaningful terms, he would repeat the question again and again to no one in particular, as if he was enchanted by its new sound).

The same sort of ritual would unfold when I put forward an idea that I wanted to discuss. Most of my formulations appeared to Vasily as irresponsibly vague and unscientific. With a hint of irritation, he would respond with something like: 'Can you not first define the parameters of the experiential framework?' (Or perhaps it was the 'framework of the experiential parameters'.) Then I would say: 'Vasily, I have not the slightest clue what you are talking about,' which was usually true. He would sigh, and with a look of resignation, say: 'All right. Go on, then.' And when I had finally expressed my understanding of something he would burst out with something like: 'But this is much better expressed by Oblomov's "lemon-pip" theorem of quasi-paradoxical non-interpretability', or 'What you have said is merely a subset of the "not-so-strong" Spassky–Dementyev "trout-brain" model of epistemology'.

I remember one such discussion which gained some momentum. We had come back to the old problem about whether God knows one's thoughts. Not the fairy tale God of ordinary religion but the agency, if any, that records one's private motives and adjusts one's fate accordingly.

'Can't you be more specific?' asked Vasily, with his usual testiness.

'Imagine two scenarios which, observed from the outside, appear exactly the same,' I said.

'That's better. *Davay.*'

'A man sees a beggar in the street. He is disgusted by him and wonders why the police haven't moved him on. He thinks: "That beggar has no right to be on the same street as hard-working people. Why doesn't he get a job?" Then he realizes that there are many people in the street, some of whom may even know him or be observing him. He reaches into his pocket and throws a coin into the beggar's lap, and utters some kind of pious benediction. He has not the slightest charitable feeling towards the beggar, but experiences the momentary and entirely self-important thrill of having appeared generous in the eyes of others. First scenario.'

'The second, please.'

'The second. A man sees a beggar in the street. He realizes that, but for a few lucky turns in his life, the miserable creature he now observes might in fact be him. He wonders what misfortune has brought him to destitution. Then he realizes that there are many people in the street, some of whom may know him or be observing him. He reaches into his pocket for a coin, and prays that no one he knows who might recognize him is present. He throws a coin into the beggar's lap, says nothing, but wishes with all his being that the beggar's luck will improve.

'Yes,' mused Vasily, 'a quaint example. Your question?'

'From the outside the two acts are indistinguishable. But we know that the first man has behaved selfishly and the second has behaved selflessly. What I want to know is how and where each man's action and intention are recorded until they get read back to him from the weighty book that he will be faced with after death, and what the difference in consequence really is.'

'You,' he scoffed, 'and everybody else. The problem here is that reality can never be either entirely subjective, nor entirely objective.'

I had no idea what he meant by that.

'But there is no reason,' he went on, 'why science shouldn't be able to answer the question of how our experience and reality communicate, and how the effect of intentions is stored up outside of time. Such a science would understand the qualitative relationships between information, meaning and energy, and the probability densities that apply to them. So, yes . . . a tribesman who severs a head for his dinner in New Guinea will not be judged by God in the same way as a man who cuts off the head of his wife in Murmansk just for the fun of it.'

'I have always wondered about that very issue,' I said. Vasily looked at me blankly. I always enjoyed it when he had no idea when I was being ironic or not.

'But for such a science to evolve,' he continued, 'you will have to wait a thousand years. In the meantime you might as well ask the Sphinx. Or just be content with the intuitions of poets and writers and shamans, whose observations are the most accurate, if incomplete. Our science is not yet ready. It is still – *pervobutniy*.'

'There's nothing primitive,' I said, 'about a particle collider.'

'That is technology,' said Vasily dismissively, 'not science. The science is still the same: you smash a thing, mix it with something else, see what happens, try to measure the changes and then argue about it with others until they shut up. Big things, small things, galaxies or atoms: it all just leads to more riddles.'

In the end, we decided on three main categories into which our answers would eventually fit. These were drawn up with a great many accompanying diagrams and formulae, the details of which I have long forgotten. But the feeling of each one did stay with me.

The first was that Man – for whatever reason – somehow possesses an imperishable soul which, bearing the imprint of both good and evil deeds, somehow returns to its unearthly origin after the physical death of its earthly 'owner'. What happens then depends on the type of deeds recorded on the soul and, problematically, whether God is a Jew, or a Molokan, or a headhunter. Whether the immortal soul in any sense 'cares' about its fate – in the same way as the mortal human to which it belonged 'cared' about whether his tie was straight – or exactly how the soul either 'suffers unspeakable torment' or 'basks in eternal glory' is similarly problematic. In brief, the shakiest of all three categories.

The second was that Man arises from a fortuitous combination of nucleic acids, like the scum that forms on bathwater, and has nothing resembling a soul. He lives and dies like a leaf. Everything of which he is composed including all trace of worldly experience is irrevocably dissolved after physical death. His life, in effect, is no more than a sexually transmitted and fatal illness.

On purely mechanistic grounds, this was the easiest model to accept. It required the least thought and the least to be taken on trust, which perhaps explained its popularity. It liberated Man from the outdated claims of religion, but proved that he was no closer to being liberated from himself. For this reason it was the most depressing and the least satisfying. It was also a bit harsh

135

on all the nice people who believed in it, and who led honest and decent lives, only to be turned back to meaningless dust. They could have had much more fun being wicked, and it would make no difference. But it couldn't really help to explain such fundamental things as charity, music, beauty or the irrational craving of Vasily's ex-wife for buying shoes at certain times of the month.

The third, which was the one we came to favour, was the Meatball theory. It embraced, said Vasily, the truths of the others. This was the idea that Man in general had confused and highly exaggerated notions about himself which were, occasionally, justified. The rest of the time he served as a sort of cosmic *bouillon*, achieving nothing, going nowhere, and disappearing into dust just as the bath-scum sceptics presumed. The possession of a soul, much less an immortal soul, was by no means guaranteed.

Intelligences higher than those of Mankind, however, craving the perfect combination of flavour and texture, threw fresh Meatball in the general direction of the *bouillon* called life, sometimes attaining what they considered a delicious meal, nourishing to the cosmic scheme. The fate of the Meatball was determined by a kind of perforated screen like a colander, in which all life was invisibly contained. To this we gave the name 'existence' – the matrix of space and its mysterious partner, time. Meatball could enter through its holes into a person's life, or into a process – or into DNA for that matter – enriching it immeasurably and even uniting its consciousness with its transfinite origin. Although it appeared as haphazard from the human point of view, this was the very mechanism by which the Meatball Intelligence entered into planetary existence – even though no one could actually see it because, as my dear grandfather was always reminding us, people never saw the meaning of things.

It also placed humankind in the awkward position of having to continually strive to get nearer to one of the perforations, where life had infinitely greater potential, than a dead zone, where Meatball would never, ever reach. For this reason, although general principles for how to live a meaningful life could be drawn up and shared, each human being had to make his or her own map in order to navigate towards the Meatball. It was a narrow way, in other words, slightly different for everyone (here at last I understood Vasily's maxim that reality could be neither entirely subjective nor objective: it was both). With the help of Meatball a man really could, among other things, love his mother-in-law, through his own unique struggle.

Neither Meatball nor Man was really complete without the other, which is why the process had to continue on both sides. But there were no guaranteed outcomes. The Meatball intelligences might not get their meal; and a man might remain little more than a vegetable. He might, on the other hand, arrive at the stage of deep Meatball knowledge, which was to know everything.

✢

One day I told Vasily that I wanted to find the basement. He nearly choked, but he could see that I was serious.

'Can you not give up, just for a time?' he said exasperatedly.

'Remind me what you said about the different levels of the building.'

He gave me a reluctant look, as if to drive home that it really wasn't what we should be discussing, but gave in after a minute.

'Assuming the building is quasi-representative of ordinary reality, there is no reason not to expect both higher and lower levels as would exist in an ordinary building. A basement, in effect. And I suppose an attic, somewhere. From the topological point of view, there is no reason we cannot map the identity-preservation component of a D-dimensional —'

'Vasily, you're doing it again.'

'Prasti.'[*]

'This basement. Where do we look for it?'

'Well, the obvious place to look for it is —' He froze in mid-sentence. 'What do you mean – *we*?'

☨

Naturally, there were some initial problems. We would only be able to explore at night, when the Mudaks weren't on duty, but we'd still be taking the risk of being discovered out of our room. I had no idea what the punishment might be, but we agreed that the authorities wouldn't take kindly to discovering that we'd traded in our sleeping pills for night-time exploration. Did they have sentries or Mudaks on night-watch? We didn't know, but we'd have to have a good story in case we were discovered. Vasily did a comic impression of a man walking in his sleep, pretending to wake up and have no idea where he was, but I doubted if the two of us would get away with the same ruse.

The other problem was that at night, Vasily was either drunk or asleep; these were the two watermelons that I would have to carry at the same time.[†] To be able to explore together, both of us needed to be alert and energetic. We never formally discussed his drunkenness as an obstacle, but I think we both knew it was a factor. It was perhaps the reason that he suggested we spend the next few days formulating a plan, when I was for exploring that very night, although this was probably equally unrealistic. I was still so bruised I could hardly move.

It was unfair to expect Vasily to stop drinking entirely, so the only way was to tease him gently into slowing down his rate of

---

[*] In Russian, 'Forgive me'.

[†] Alluding to the Azeri proverb expressing impossibility, or carrying two watermelons at the same time under one arm.

refilling. This never came to much in the end, of course, but our different approaches to planning did arrive at a natural com-promise, taking several days to refine by discovering solutions as we went along. We had no way to tell the exact moment of our first departure, so we waited several hours after the place seemed to have settled down, which allowed Vasily to get some sleep, and after the tiny portion of the outside world that I could see from my room had taken on a silvery coating of moonlight.

The kitchen was always our target. Vasily had explained the reason for this mathematically, but it seemed like common sense to me. Basements were more or less always attached to kitchens, so for different reasons we agreed this was the place to start. The challenge was to get there without being discovered. The house was unusually dark and this was a source of perverse amusement to Vasily, who struggled hard not to bang into things and not to sing. Either he sang – quietly and always slightly off-key, which irritated me – or he cracked jokes, which also irritated me. We were both anxious, and that was his way of dealing with it.

It was slow going, but we made it to the kitchen undis-covered. Once we were past the swinging doors we put blankets over the glass portions and around the edges to prevent any light escaping, then looked for a bulb suitable for attaching Vasily's specially designed shade. The idea of this was to direct the light downwards or towards whatever we were trying to see, but without letting too much of it spill out where it might attract attention. It was bound to be a risk, but one we had to take. We had no other source of light.

We found just the bulb we wanted, hanging in an adjoin-ing storeroom. The shade blocked all but a narrow beam, which we could point to get a sense of the size of the place. Then as our eyes adjusted we found there was just enough light to creep around looking for more storerooms and doors.

Overhead was the strange conveyor apparatus that I'd

seen from afar. It ran into the ceilings high overhead where we couldn't reach, so we kept our efforts on the ground. There were lots of storerooms, but no obvious door with steps leading magically downwards, and things were discouragingly slow.

At the end of the room I was exploring, I came to a passage leading off from an entrance door, so I called to Vasily, who agreed to stand guard while I went in to investigate. That way, we could turn off the light we were using and instead use the one in the passage, and keep the risk of being seen to a minimum.

I went in, past a coin-operated telephone which, to judge from the painted-over cable, had been disconnected years earlier, and came to a rectangular space where some disused noticeboards hung on the walls. Around this space were several unlit storerooms without doors. They didn't seem to lead anywhere, although I decided to have a closer look just in case. One was full of mops and brushes and other cleaning supplies. I took a broom handle and tapped hopefully on the walls for a hollow section. I even looked carefully at the liquids to see if there was anything either flammable or potentially explosive, but there was nothing more dangerous than liquid soaps. I could see that behind the shelves there was no trace of an old entrance or window, and that the floor was solid.

The storeroom opposite was piled from floor to ceiling with bundles of newspapers and magazines. There must have been several decades' worth. I shifted the piles as much as I could to see if there was any trace of an entrance, either on the floor or walls, which I poked and tapped just to make quite sure.

The final room was filled with unbelievable clutter. It looked like it had been accumulating for years, like the interior of a house of someone on drugs or who's mentally ill. It smelled of rust and formaldehyde. With one of the broom handles I tapped everywhere I could reach on the floor, which was made of stone tiles with a pattern that reminded me of a famous kind of Italian sliced meat. I tapped the walls too, but there was a section of one of the shelves that I couldn't get through, so I cleared away some of the rubbish and found a pile of what looked like flattened cardboard boxes. Feeling them more closely I realized they were animal skins laid in thick piles. The fur had been removed and they had the thickness of heavy parchment. Something about them was making me curious, so I tried to pull one out, which meant standing on something to get more leverage, and pushing my head against one of the piles of skins. Then I heard a sound, inches from my ear, that made my blood run cold. It was a low, slow growl coming from somewhere at the back of the shelf I was disturbing. I kept absolutely still for a few seconds, and then, when I couldn't bear the suspense any longer, leapt off the upturned chair I was balancing on and grabbed the broom handle. Then I made sure I didn't move or make a sound.

Some kind of animal was in there with me, and wasn't keen on the idea of sharing the space. Darkness is never a good place to discover this kind of thing. While I was wondering whether or not to abandon the search, I could just make out a shape, emerging from between the piles of skin. Your eyes play tricks in poor light and the shape appeared so slowly that I wondered if it was really there or not, and what it really looked like. I moved my foot, just to see if it would react, and there was instantly a growl. It was a cautious creature, and was making its appearance at the speed of a tortoise from its shell. I could just make out the profile of a dog, a real dog this time and, thank God, not a very big one.

It was a poodle. And even for a poodle it was an ugly-looking creature. One of its eyes was missing, and where it should have been there was just a shadowy hole like the entrance to a cave. In daylight I don't suppose I would have been too worried. But I could see the skin of its mouth drawn back to expose its teeth, which looked as though they were trembling in anticipation of sinking into my skin. I could see the wetness of the fur around

141

its mouth, and wondered if it might be rabid. He was only a couple of feet above me and clearly unhappy that I'd disturbed his much-needed beauty sleep.

I wanted to get to my feet, and to protect my face in the process, but as I raised one hand slowly from the ground, the growl deepened and I knew I wouldn't get away with it. Then without any warning the face lunged at me with a vicious snarl. I swiped wildly with the broomstick and rolled sideways in fright, and realized we hadn't actually touched; he'd just wanted to get out as quickly as possible. I kept still for a few seconds just in case he had a bigger cousin hiding behind the boxes too, but there was no sound of any other animal. What I could hear was much stranger. With one ear pressed to the ground I could hear a kind of music. It was very faint, and if I lifted my head from the floor it stopped. I wondered if it might be Vasily, in the adjoining space, humming a Russian song, when I realized that it must be coming from below. Then I stood up, and all I could hear was the beating of my own heart.

Vasily was where I'd left him at the door, muttering to himself and visibly anxious. I asked him where the dog had gone. His mood changed and he chuckled.

'You and me are the only dogs down here,' he said, not understanding what I meant, because he hadn't seen any dog. I explained what had happened, and realized two things as I spoke; firstly, that if the dog hadn't gone out past Vasily, it must have escaped by a different route which we hadn't yet seen; and secondly, that it couldn't have got past a closed door in the first place and must have originally entered a different way too.

It didn't take long to solve the puzzle. We both went back inside the passage and realized there was something I simply hadn't seen before, perhaps because the old telephone had caught my attention instead. Set into the wall not far from the entrance door was a small, old-fashioned dumb waiter. The inside of it had been pushed upwards leaving a narrow space, which the dog had been able to squeeze through. He had probably got in the same way, too, and the thought must have occurred to us at the same time, because we simply looked at each other and didn't say anything, knowing we had found what we were looking for.

Chapter 9

IF I'D HAD A PIECE OF STRAW, I would have carried it between my lips.* Very slowly, and with the feeling that perhaps the Gods had a hand in things after all, I pulled on the rope beside the shelves and watched them rise slowly into the shaft above, leaving a wonderful blackness underneath. Here was the entrance to the underground portion of the house that we'd been searching for. There was nothing to discuss: we peered in and stared. It was impossible to see anything beyond the pale rectangle of light thrown from the bulb in the passage, which was dim and too high up to be much use. But looking at it, I had an idea. Although they had long ago been painted over, the nails holding the light cable in place had small lead hooks attached to their heads, and if these could be unbent and the cable released in a straight line from the periphery of the ceiling, we might end up with enough length to get the bulb into the cellar itself.

Vasily asked how I would get up to the ceiling in the first place, then understood. Bracing himself against the wall, he linked his fingers together, and wheezed a string of curses as I stepped onto his shoulders. I unbent the first few hooks, climbed down and repeated the process until the loosened cable

---

* The reference is unknown.

was dangling to the ground. When we had finished, and I undid the final hook, there was just enough slack in the cable for it to reach the dumb waiter, exactly as we'd hoped.

I clambered in. The floor on the other side of the wall was lower and made Vasily seem to hover above me. He handed me the light, which I held above my head, peering into the darkness and almost trembling with excitement at what we might discover.

The result was disappointing. I could see nothing but lines of regularly spaced brick columns resting on a dusty concrete foundation and receding into the darkness. Whichever way I shone the light, the view was the same. I hung the cable gently against the edge of the wall, stood up and circled the periphery of the bulb's reach, discovering nothing but those regular rows of columns about the height of a man, and between them, dust. Then I clambered out again, meeting Vasily's expectant face as he helped me to my feet. I described what I'd seen and we carefully fixed the cable back into place, swept up the flakes of paint with our hands and made quite sure we'd left no traces of our visit.

It wasn't promising, we agreed, but we both knew that we'd have to explore properly, once we had sorted out the problem of a portable source of light. Earlier I had vaguely pictured myself advancing along dusty and relic-filled passages, bearing a bright flaming torch. Then it dawned on us both that not only did we not have any flaming torches, we didn't have any source of light at all. We didn't have any way of navigating, either. It had never occurred to me before: how do you find your way alone in darkness, deprived of all ordinary bearings and without reference to a visible and reliable point beyond yourself? If there were tunnels and corridors as there were on the upper floors, how would we find our way back to where we had started? We had no thread or rope, neither of which would have been practical in any case; we could hardly lay a trail of crumbs.

We discussed all this the following day, and in the evening returned to the kitchen to search every drawer, cupboard and storeroom for some kind of light that we could carry with us. We were hoping for a torch and some spare batteries; a paraffin lantern would have been the next best thing, and we could have happily used candles if we'd found any. But there was no trace of any of them. There was no independent source of light anywhere we looked, and we spent what seemed like half the night searching.

We crouched in the shadows, discussing alternatives, unwilling to return empty-handed. We needed something that would burn and give a flame strong and steady enough to light our way, and reliable enough to last. Paraffin would work; petrol too. Vasily pointed out that with petrol or alcohol it was possible to make a semisolid flammable organogel by combining it with a suitable hydrocolloid, which could then be moulded into a shape that would burn slowly. I thanked him for this useful knowledge. Anything flammable at room temperature could be made to burn, even shoe polish, he said. We separated again, and searched. But there was nothing that would burn.

I had the distinct feeling that whoever was in charge of supplies for the building had chosen every product to thwart any plan such as ours: the cleaning fluids were all water-based, the polishes were synthetic and there was no trace of any paints, varnishes, thinners or alcohols of any kind. Then just when I was about to propose we give up Vasily appeared with a big plastic container and held it up.

'Olive oil,' he said. 'I didn't think of it before. They use it in churches to light up the holy icons.'

We stole a cupful to make some tests, then remembered we had no way to generate a flame in our room, so I tore a strip of cloth from my shirt for a wick, and we lit it from the cooker. A bright yellow flame came to life, and we hurried upstairs, after covering it with Vasily's special directional shade, and shielding

it all the way like bodyguards. Then in the room we divided up
the oil into whatever small containers we could find and experi-
mented with different wicks; a shoelace, pleated carpet tassels
and thin strips of fabric from the lining of the curtains, which
worked best, perhaps because the fabric had been treated to
make it fire resistant, said Vasily. For a time the room was aglow
with flickering lamps like a shrine, and we looked at them in
silence, because the little flames seemed improbably beautiful
and hopeful and reminded us so deeply of the world to which we
longed, more than ever at that moment, to return.

Another evening fell, and we found ourselves once again at
the entrance to the dumb waiter. Vasily was nervous, as usual,
and muttering to himself. We had divided up our tasks. While I
climbed into the dumb waiter opening, he took one of the wicks
we had made and came back from the kitchen with it alight. We
fed it into the metal holder we had made from a coat hanger
and fixed it into the jar that supplied it with oil. Then we fitted
a second, slightly smaller jar on top of it, so that the flame was
protected, and said our goodbyes. In Vasily's case this meant
disguising his anxiety with jokes.

'I know what will happen,' he said gloomily. 'You will never
come back.' I looked at his face in the flickering yellow of the
flame. 'You will go in there and discover a room where a woman
lives who has not had a man for years. She will be beautiful,
but blind. You will rub the light from the oil onto her eyes and
restore her sight, and then she will ask you to rub the rest onto
her body, and —'

'Vasily. Keep watch. I'll be back soon.'

'Soon, yes.' He nodded. 'Soon.'

I was just as anxious as he was. I got out from under the
dumb waiter and stood up. 'If I meet her,' I whispered back, 'I'll
send her sister back to you.'

The idea was to start small, so that if anything went wrong
it would still be easy to get back to the starting point, even in

147

pitch darkness, by retracing my steps. All I had to do was note the number of steps and the direction I had taken, and it would always be possible to calculate the way back. There was no indication, at this stage, of any difficulty to this task.

With the dumb waiter shaft behind me, I counted ten paces, carefully regulating them to a steady length, then turned around and took ten back. There was no mystery to that.

'Ten paces,' I whispered upwards, and heard Vasily's confirmation. We had agreed all this in advance. Then I turned around again and took twenty-five steps, then three more sets of twenty-five, turning left at each completed set, arriving once more at my starting point, where I would knock gently on the lowermost shelf of the dumb waiter and be greeted once again by Vasily. Leaning over the edge of the opening, he would ask me breathlessly what I had discovered.

'A billion roubles in cash and three big-breasted Ukrainian women.'

'Ukrainian? My ex-wife was Ukrainian. Any from St Petersburg?'

Apart from being surprisingly large, the basement seemed to consist of virtually identical brick footings, spaced about ten yards apart, with a concrete floor below and floorboards above. I had not yet come to another wall or door or anything of interest. We agreed, between frivolities, that I had to increase the distance of my circuit, so I set off again, walking at intervals of fifty paces before each turn. After the third turn I stopped, and sat still for a good while, hearing once again the beating of my own heart, which I was now struggling to calm, because there was no sign of the dumb waiter shaft. I didn't seem to be anywhere near it.

There was a rational explanation, I knew, so I sat down to sketch what I was sure was true, and drew the square I had just paced out, in order to calculate the maximum distance of my error. I couldn't be far away. I had obviously either not walked in a perfectly straight line, influenced perhaps by the alignment of the piers, or not made perfect right-angles for my turns. These slight imperfections were bound to add up, and I knew then that our next task would be to devise a system of navigation that compensated for the cumulative errors. I wasn't genuinely worried yet, but I was very deeply puzzled by the size of the place. I had traced an area of two and a half thousand square yards and still not reached the limits of the area. Yet the same area, translated into the rooms above me, was huge. It didn't make sense. The space down here was perhaps more elastic than ordinary space, as in a dream.

My task now, since I was more or less lost, was not to panic, and to make a new map from my new starting point. I did this in exactly the same way as before, by taking ten even paces and turning left at each interval. Doing so in each direction would cover a hundred square yards, within which, I was reasoning, my original destination had to be. With my back to the nearest pier, I wedged a piece of paper between two bricks to identify my direction, completed the square and then paced three squares more in just the same way, working my way around each face of the pier. But I still hadn't found the dumb waiter.

I then realized that the area I had covered was not the hundred square yards I'd thought: each square was a hundred square yards, which made four hundred square yards, and yet there was still no sign of my starting point. Then, as so often happens when the mind is thwarted, all sorts of doubts began to creep in. I hadn't been returning to my starting point at all, but moving ever further away from it, as if repeating an ever more garbled message. In the darkness, without any reference beyond the piers themselves, I might have been walking not along straight lines but along curves, without knowing it. So long as the piers were regularly spaced, and looked familiar, I would have had the impression of having walked in a straight line. It was obvious now that I hadn't been.

This possibility had never occurred to me and I cursed my stupidity, remembering Vasily's observation that in this place things were always more different than in the real world. What I wondered was whether I should try to retrace my original fifty-pace square and risk getting even more lost, or try to extend the search from my present position.

If you're lost, does it matter if you start off from an unknown point? Or should you always try to get back to the last known one? I couldn't decide which was the greater risk. In the end I decided that so long as I retraced my steps accurately it didn't matter which way the curves travelled or not. So I marked the pier with a piece of paper again and followed the piers for fifty paces, turning at what I hoped were the places I had originally turned, and arriving at what should have been my starting point.

But it still wasn't my starting point; it looked just the same as anywhere else, and now I was even more lost than before. I was in a forest of identical brick columns with absolutely no way of figuring out how to return. The strange thing is that I knew it wouldn't work. I just knew. I knew that I was on the wrong track theoretically as well as practically even though I didn't know why. Then a thought seemed to jump into my head: I was trying to make a circle from a square, and at the outset I had been trying to make a square of a circle, and since the dawn of time men had failed at this very task, and it was inevitable that I too should fail, because the two natures of these shapes could never be reconciled. This was certainly the reason I was lost.*

---

* I am indebted to Dr Balbettio of the University of Sordomuto for drawing my attention to the closing lines of Dante's *Inferno*:

Qual è 'l geomètra che tutto s'affige
per misurar lo cerchio, e non ritrova,
pensando, quel principio ond' elli indige,

I wondered what would happen after the lamp went out, which it would – eventually – without any doubt. I couldn't try to save the oil because I couldn't re-light it. I wondered whether perhaps when daylight came I might discover my way by some crack of light, or whether perhaps I would die slowly, dragging myself along these obscure and deceitful trajectories until I starved. Then came the awful thought that the dried skins I had seen in the storeroom above were the skins of those very people like me, whose emaciated corpses were from time to time recovered from among the featureless expanses of the basement, and stored away like ghastly souvenirs. Perhaps I was merely one of many.

Time is always hard to measure under such conditions, so I have no idea how long it was that I really dwelled on these grim outcomes, which were instantly arrested by the single sound of what at first seemed to be a drop of water falling into a pool within a cavern. I held my breath, and heard the sound again, and then again, fading and strengthening by turn. I gave up all thoughts of navigating and headed towards it, because it was instantly clear that this was my only hope. You can find so much in a small thing when it is the only thing you have.

---

tal era io a quella vista nova:
veder voleva come si convenne
l'imago al cerchio e come vi s'indova;
ma non eran da ciò le proprie penne

Like a geometer wholly dedicated
to squaring the circle, but who cannot find,
think as he may, the principle indicated –
so did I study the supernal face
I yearned to know just how our image merges
into that circle, and how it there finds place;
but mine were not the wings for such a flight.

Paradiso, Canto XXXIII

It only lasted for an instant each time it sounded, but such was my concentration that it became alive, took on a character of its own and seemed to enter into a conversation with me. I soon realized it couldn't be a drop of water, which wouldn't have been loud enough to travel, but a metallic-sounding ticking, and I must have walked a hundred yards to reach it. Then I understood. It was being generated by Vasily, bless him, with a wooden spoon and a saucepan he had taken from the kitchen, and which he later claimed to have chosen for its parabolic shape, favourable to the projection of sound waves.

He could have no idea how grateful I felt towards him. We didn't talk much; he could see I wasn't feeling talkative, so we made our way back to our room. The next day I described everything that had happened. Vasily was fascinated by the implications of the size of the basement, and especially by the notion that the piers were not arranged in straight lines but in curves, which in the darkness would distort the attempt to map them.

It was just the kind of challenge to get him going: to map a grid onto a curved surface, and vice versa, in order to calculate the distances travelled relative to the starting point.

'It may all simply be a case of differential topology,' he mused, reaching for his pencil and beginning the cryptic outline of one of his formulae, 'but if not, it quickly becomes more complicated, and we are obliged to calculate alternative tensors for what may well represent a case of non-Euclidean holonomy.'

I let him scribble. He hadn't actually been down there, or experienced first-hand the strangeness of the place. I, for my part, had no adequate way to express the feeling of having been deceived by those innocent-looking brick columns, and that I had myself played a part in the deception by the very attempt to map the space on my own terms. I had failed, I knew, because such attempts always fail.

This was what you might call an intuitive flash for which

there was no obvious evidence whatever. I hadn't come to it by thinking or reasoning or by any process I could identify; it had just happened and now I couldn't ignore it. The strange thing was that this kind of thing had been happening ever since my arrival; much more often than in ordinary life. Perhaps this was because there were fewer distractions than in ordinary life, or perhaps, as Vasily had expressed it so enigmatically, things were more different here, whatever that really meant.

Everyone has inexplicable moments of insight once in a while, which we never get to hear about unless they happen to overlap with an event that becomes famous; everyone has little meatball moments, when they suddenly know something that can't be explained, like knowing who one is going to meet just before they appear around the next corner. A scientist, God help me for lumping them all together, will say that we are always thinking idly and unconsciously about lots of different people, and sooner or later we are bound to meet one of them around a corner, and this one becomes the event we remember because it seems inexplicable. It is really just a failure, they tell us, to remember all the other things in our awareness. But we all know this can't be the whole story, any more than the beautiful, big-breasted women who figured so luminously in Vasily's imagination can be explained simply in terms of the need for genes to replicate. If you've met a beautiful, big-breasted woman from the Ukraine you just know this anyway.

By the following evening, we'd made two crucial improvements in our ability to explore. Not only did we now have a reliable means of lighting our way, having perfected an adjustable wick, but Vasily had prepared a mapping device, which he said would be able to compensate for the accumulated errors in calculating distance from our starting point.

It had taken him hours to prepare and I could tell it meant a lot to him. It consisted of about ten sheets of paper, each drawn with curving lines like those on a globe, some of which were pinned to each other in such a way that they could still rotate above the adjoining sheet. All I had to do was to fold one of the overlapping sheets along certain lines as I went along, and mark my progress on the map with a pencil. Like any instrument, he said, it would first have to be calibrated by a short journey, but after that it would work for any unit of distance which I chose to use.

So that night we went down after dark and made our way to the kitchen and then to the dumb waiter. Once again I clambered in and watched Vasily light the wick of the lamp. He reminded me how to use the sheets. Then he wished me luck and I cast off like a boat into the darkness.

There were some differences this time. Once inside I left the first lamp burning at the base of the wall and lit a second to take with me. Then I walked forward and marked the distance on Vasily's paper map, completing the circuit and finding myself about twenty yards from my starting point. Then I made my way back to Vasily, who studied the marks and the distances I'd come and showed me which pages to use to compensate for the deviation of the pillars. It looked then as though we'd cracked it; it was no more complicated than calculating the declination of magnetic north, which anyone competent with a map knows how to do.

Then I set off again, marking my progress every few steps. It was slow going, and I found myself irritated by the need for such detail, even though I understood the need for it. Perhaps this was partly disappointment: the basement was turning out to be a vast and dreary cavern with no distinguishing features whatever. I must have walked for half an hour, growing more frustrated as time passed, dizzy almost at the monotony of the place, and bored of the effort of having to record it.

A voice was telling me to give it up. I knew it was wrong and perhaps even dangerous to not keep up the effort, but I'd managed to find my way back before, and would probably manage it again, even without the ridiculously complicated map. At the very moment this thought took place, I was sure I heard, for a few moments, the same strange music I had heard in the store-room above. I stopped and tried to listen. It sounded like one of those patriotic songs that children learn when they are very small. It faded out and made me feel lonelier than ever. And I know I shouldn't have, not only because it was disrespectful to Vasily, and because my very life, so far as we could tell, happened to depend on it, but at that moment I crunched the map into a ball and threw it into the blackness ahead of me.

I know it was the most reckless thing I could have done, but I did it anyway, perhaps because I was now desperate for something to happen, even if that something was my own extinction. I shuddered again at the thought of the skins. Then a few paces further on I came to a step, which threw a wide shadow like a black line drawn across my path. It was so unexpected and, after all this monotony, so unlikely, that I stopped and was almost afraid to cross it, the way Yezidi children are said to be unable to break out of a circle drawn around them in the dust.

It was impossible to think of this as a coincidence. The step wasn't high, so I went down it and heard the splash of my foot into water. Then I saw something moving in the water. I went closer. To my even greater astonishment, I saw it was a small turtle, of the kind I used to collect in the summer months when I was twelve years old, and I felt the sudden impulse to chase it before it submerged. It disappeared in the darkness ahead. I reasoned that we must be near a river which had perhaps flooded.

I had almost forgotten my rashness with the map. I could hear music again now, growing more distinct. I even recognized it. It was a couple singing a duet from a musical which I hadn't heard since I was seven years old. It was my sister's favourite piece of music and the same one she used to play over and over again just to annoy me, and once again I felt the intense frustration of being unable to stop her playing it.

A piece of yellowed paper floated by my foot, and I reached down to pick it up. It was a short letter, written by a small child, which I read with a strange and growing sense of recognition. I knew exactly who it was from: a girl I had fallen in love with at my very first school. I could only have been about six years old. I remembered the thrill of receiving it, and the gentle features of her face returned to me as I read it. I was astonished that the letter still existed, since I hadn't myself seen it since the day I'd first read it, but even more astonished that such a private thing had been found and had ended up here, where I was now stepping. I went forward, to try and find out where it had come from, and came to a half-sodden cardboard box. There was more from the same period: exercise books from my earliest school, paintings and spelling tests. Another box contained childhood toys; ancient stuffed animals that had belonged to my older siblings but which I'd come to know in minute detail. I checked the paw of the bear to see if its pad was worn through, exposing the yellow straw inside, and pulled on the wire that had once held the missing eye of the tiger. There was no way anyone could have substituted such details into a counterfeit.

I felt overwhelmed. I stopped and made the effort to calm my thoughts, and the things I'd been seeing seemed to stop coming at me at quite the same pace. Nothing quite made sense: the things I had seen were both private and precious too, and could never have been known to anyone else, much less replaced. That meant that my stay here in the building was much more complicated than it looked. If whatever authority had placed me here had gone to the trouble of collecting my earliest childhood possessions, their work had been more thorough than I had ever imagined. If on the other hand I was simply hallucinating, what was the significance and purpose of these private, yet strangely coherent, mental adventures?

My thoughts, it seems, were turning into things; music,

voices, smells and perhaps even ideas. The music I had earlier heard had changed again, and now sounded like a school of children singing religious chants, as moving as they were sad. Their melodies mingled like smoke with voices that I recognized. These belonged to characters who had long ago passed out of my life, and hearing them now left me with a sad feeling of having spent so much time among so many people to such little consequence; and I seemed to recall all the effort I had gone to in order to be well thought of by them, and of all the conversations that had led nowhere, even with those people I'd been close to. I wondered how things might have been, if my life had been spent differently and to more purposeful ends. I couldn't really say what end; but I could tell there'd never really been one.

And it wasn't just people: at different moments I could hear the cry of a peacock and the baying of wolves in the mountains, and the rumble of thunder and the cracking of ice. At another moment I could hear the sound made by my finger searching through a box of coins which as children we were allowed to play with; and I heard the distinctive squeak of the cork in the jar where my mother stored olive oil, and the particular rattle of the handle on my childhood bedroom window.

Then I came to a pair of heavy doors, pushed beyond them and found myself walking through a catalogue of fragrances. You know how smells take you back to the time and place you first experienced them. All of a sudden I was walking, for a moment, through a cloud of blue-grey smoke from meat grilling in the back streets of Kabul, a memory I had scarcely called on in the intervening years, which now awoke the very feeling of being there; then on, to another city obscured by the heavy veils of time and distance; on, beneath the intoxicating scent of exotic blossoms, and of soils and dusts and brick and human waste; and then I breathed the sudden perfume of human skin I had once caressed, and felt the pangs of abandoned intimacy.

I would never have guessed that the feelings accompanying each one of these different and unexpected memories were equally alive, as if they had always been and still were alive. It was I who had moved on to a horizon beyond the reach of their existence. I smelled jasmine, and gun-oil, and blood, and the sandalwood of an inlaid box that I used to scratch as a child to release the magical fragrance.

Then I saw a mound of boxes, and opened one to find beach towels on which I used to play as a child, and the camera with which I'd taken my first photograph; I could even feel, by turning the wheel that advanced the film, that there was still a film inside it. Another box was full of family things which I hadn't even seen since my early childhood and never imagined still existed: my grandfather's medal, the clasp rusted now but unmistakably the same; my father's outdoor coats, ruined now by damp and mould and mice; his blue metal toolbox, discoloured now by a layer of pale orange rust; the mirror from my mother's dresser, the gold paint flaking off the plaster frame; a dagger which I had once taken from my father's desk and taken in secret to my bedroom to examine.

The most unsettling aspect of all these things was the very intimacy of my feelings towards them, which I suppose I felt no one else had the right to know: they were mine alone. Yet down here I could see that they weren't mine at all; they were just things that had happened to me because of the mathematics of life, in which I had never had much say.

There were more sets of heavy doors; they seemed to be leading somewhere, though I couldn't tell you where. I had the feeling I was wandering through a house where the archives of my early life were being stored, only the index, purpose and sequence of them had been forgotten or perhaps never understood, and every part was hopelessly mixed up. They weren't just my memories: often they were the things themselves. What I mean is that when I smelled lime I was smelling all limes, and when I smelled saffron or frankincense it was the essence of saffron and the essence of frankincense, and these were somehow connected with everything else in the world – all of this leaving me feeling as if my life was not, and had never really been, my own. Whose life, then, was it? I wondered. To whom did this pitiful collection of trivial artefacts belong? And if it was all someone else's, if it was all under the care of some other entity, through whose little experiment I was simply sleepwalking, why did it all feel so strongly, so deeply, as though it was uniquely mine? If I really was just a rat in a laboratory, whose rat was I, in whose laboratory, and to what purpose? As idle thoughts, these are one thing; as questions addressed in desperation to the soul they are another.

Then, pushing through another set of doors, I realized I could see without the lamp. The way ahead had become visible, lit by the moon, and now everything seemed coated by a luminous silvery dust. I heard myself chuckle out loud. Moonlight! It was so unexpected and so beautiful.

Then to my left I could make out a room in which the floor looked as though it had subsided or collapsed. I say room, but it was more like a natural quarry, or one of those small primitive communities where people have scooped their homes out of soft stone. In the walls behind them were little niches where perhaps there had once been lights or candles; and I could make out a kind of honeycomb structure that reminded me of a beehive, and where something was being stored.

Some workmen were standing around sheepishly, waiting for someone in authority to come. The impracticality of working in moonlight – not to mention the sheer unlikelihood of finding workmen down there – never really occurred to me. I wandered towards them. Some makeshift steps, leading downwards through the broken floorboards into the foundations, had been made from planks and stones. I went down a little way, then stopped, sensing danger. At this lower level I could see that, below this one, there was another, and another, and the sight of these irregular shapes leading deeper and deeper made me think of a Swiss cheese. I didn't dare go any lower without a rope, and I could see that a properly equipped team would be needed to explore further. I heard myself reassuring the work-men, most of whom were simply crouching patiently in shadowy alcoves, that someone would be along soon to help them with the treasure. I don't know where I got the treasure idea: it just seemed obvious to me at that moment. And because it felt like the right thing to do, and it seemed like I wouldn't need it any more, I left them the lamp, in case they needed it for their own exploration.

It sounds incredible I know, but soon afterwards I felt as though I could actually smell the sea. I knew that I was nowhere near the sea, and that in any case the sea couldn't be there in the basement. But now each time I pushed open a door the water was deeper, until I suddenly realized I was actually walking on a narrow wooden walkway just above the height of the water. Further away there were grassy platforms on either side and, in the distance, low houses and shops lit by the warm glow of old-fashioned lanterns. I sensed that I knew people there. The grass grew taller: it was sea-grass.

Then I understood that I was on the outskirts of a coastal town or city where I had been before, in an earlier dream. It swept around the smooth curve of a bay. I could even make out the lights on the far side of the bay, which must have been several miles away, shimmering in the distance as if through a summer's haze.

I'm no surer now as I was then how exactly I could see so far, when there were walls which at other moments limited my vision and movement. I knew that it was all both possible and impossible at the same time. I longed more than anything to get beyond, into the city on the far side, which I felt I had already partly explored in my youth and now longed to get to know

160

even better. Somehow I knew I had a meeting there. I had no idea, at the time, who it was with but I knew it was important, vital even, for my future.

Then I came to a grey room with a metal floor which abruptly stopped my progress, although I knew that beyond it lay the city with which I felt such an inexplicable and affectionate familiarity. At the far end of the room was a series of electrical panels with lights and military-looking labels beneath important switches. High on one wall was a prominent display, flashing a long and diminishing number like a countdown. I guessed it was some kind of time-lock. The technology all looked a bit out of date. A red and a green light, just like the ones in the entrance to the house, were mounted above a metal, watertight door resembling the entrance to a military facility of some kind. It had a heavy opening lever which I couldn't budge. I tried it several times, but I somehow knew it wouldn't open.

I was reluctant to turn back. Things were getting more and more interesting. 'But all this,' I said to myself, 'is a dream, and I must get back to what is real.'

Then I thought: 'But the building I'm returning to is also a world of dreams. It is just one less layer of dreams than down here. Perhaps the world outside is just a world of dreams too.'

And then I thought of Vasily and what he would make of that. He would say: 'The fact that you distinguish between dreams on top of dreams is an indication that you recognize what is not a dream, or at least less of a dream; something in you knows or senses what is more real. We can therefore calculate the relationship between the dream world and the real world and plot the direction in which one must travel in order to live a more real life.'

Or some such concept.

In any event, I found my way back, and Vasily met me again as I emerged, desperate for details. But I could hardly speak.

I was still too mesmerized by the strange beauty of everything I'd seen.

'What's the matter with you?' he asked, half annoyed and half out of concern, sensing that something was different this time.

'It was beautiful,' I said, knowing that I wouldn't make much sense to him.

'Let me see the map.'

'I threw it away,' I said.

'You what?' He was stunned. 'You threw away the map? How did you find your way back?'

'I don't know,' I said, which was true. 'I just felt my way back.'

'Where's the lamp? What have you done with the lamp?'

'I left it somewhere. I think I gave it to the workmen.'

'Workmen? Did workmen help you back here?'

Poor Vasily. I knew I wasn't really making sense to him, and I could see so clearly that he simply didn't know what I knew.

'Nobody helped me,' I said, 'I just floated back.' That was exactly how it had felt. But I knew he couldn't understand. It was meatball knowledge, and meatball knowledge is never really your own.

'Like a bubble,' I said. 'I just floated back up to the top again like a bubble.'

✠

Before I go on, let's be quite clear about the matter. I know it sounds simple, but it's the thing that nobody will tell you and which you simply can't escape, like the small print of an insurance document. There is one thing that a man – especially one who is supposedly hungry for truth and the secret of happiness – always forgets.

If a man or woman wishes to change – wishes more than

162

anything to have a real and satisfying life and not just a false and hollow one, wishes for his every action to have purpose, wishes even to have friendly feelings from time to time towards his dear and gracious mother-in-law – then he must give up what he *is*. Rich or poor, it makes no difference: the challenge is the same for Shah or *gondabshoor*° alike. He can drink at the fountain of wisdom for a thousand years, he can marry the Queen of Sheba, he can learn to breathe underwater – but nothing from the outside will change what he is on the inside. The task lies within.

A real man or woman should always be asking what the purpose of life really is and how he can discover it, how each day can be lived with meaning and how to discern the truth in any situation. Finding the answers to these brings happiness. But everyone, in the end, becomes an expert in hiding from such questions, like a fat woman who will never admit what everyone else can see, and who even has a favourite mirror which best disguises the obvious truth.

Children know all this, but their special talent for sincerity and natural thirst for truth are first destroyed by their parents, and then by their teachers, and then by the world. The result is that before long, a child is willing to believe that an elephant is a fly and a fly is an elephant. The world is a mirror of this madness: just look at the state of it.

By the time a child grows up, he's become an expert at passing on the blame for everything, especially his failure to make any sense of life. It was all my parents' fault, he will say. Or if he does admit he isn't perfect, his so-called analyst will persuade him that he spent too long, or not long enough at his mother's breast. But sons, daughters and parents are all the same because they are human, and all of them are still trying to push the blame

---

° Traditionally, a labourer from the poorest classes of Iran who empties cesspits with a barrow and shovel.

back to Adam, while behaving as though they're immortal, a notion which each day inches uncomfortably closer to being disproved.

Behind the ordinary life of the world, as everyone suspects from time to time, there is another world more real and more satisfying; and behind this one another world even more real, and God help anyone who tries to talk about it, because someone will ask where the proof is, and soon they'll all be at each other's throats. The proof exists, but it can't be seen with the same eye that looks onto this world. You cannot lift the plank you are standing on; the senses cannot fathom what they cannot perceive.

Any child knows this. I suppose I knew it and you knew it too as a child. But becoming a man I forgot. What is real became like a dream, and what is nothing more than a dream stole the clothing of what is real, and has been masquerading in disguise ever since.

The point is: man is made from both a shell and a seed and both have a purpose. The shell should open when it's ready and the seed should grow into whatever its destiny demands. If the shell never breaks, then the seed never gets what it needs to grow. You and I both know people like that, whose lives are more and more miserable as they get older and older. It's painful for the shell to break, but if its very purpose was never realized then it simply becomes a waste of life. The last person you consider this true for is yourself.

There is really only one knowledge and one truth trying to express itself everywhere, and in every era and corner of the world people have discovered their own version of it. Just like in a big house, a person gets comfortable in his particular room, among his own precious things, for which, if it comes to that, he'll happily start killing other people. But there are many rooms.

One person will claim to have found such a truth in religion.

Another climbs mountains or paints pen boxes. But religious or not, the problem is the same: a man has doubts about what is real, what is worth doing, how he should act and how he should live. To live is the problem and to live like a human being and not just a talking animal. It's a matter for his conscience, whether he's religious or not.

When he doesn't get any answers, an ordinary man's life is one of constant, albeit secret, difficulty. His only companion is the grocer of Kharzavil.* He has the feeling of homelessness in life, like someone turning over in his sleep in order to get comfortable, and everyone else has to suffer for his problem. Sometimes the whole world ends up suffering for the restlessness of just one or two people who happen to have worldly influence, and who aren't particularly troubled by the slaughter of a few million others. They always believe that they'll be happy if only they can change the world, forgetting how many cleverer people over the course of history have tried the same thing. You can judge their success, as I say, from looking at the world, and by trying to find a single awful crime that isn't at this moment being committed in the name of some noble cause.

And so the way divides. Two kinds of suffering become possible for two different kinds of man. A lesser suffering from all the problems of life, health, reputation, family, home and women you've known who now want your money and if possible, blood. That suffering leads to more of the same and nowhere else. You can spend your whole life on it.

A greater kind of suffering exists for whoever wishes for a different kind of life. You could call it the creative life; the life that begins after you leave the safety of the shore and enter the ocean, where every river leads. This is the wearing-out that must occur to reach the ocean. Only the person who is hungry

---

* The reference is unknown.

for truth* can bear it, because truth means the end of lies, and the life of an ordinary person is built on lies. And when you've stopped lying and got to know yourself, you might not like what you see, like the face of your cheap date the next morning, when you wish you could chew your own arm off and escape before she wakes up. But at least you will know your task, and face it like a man.

---

* I have used 'truth' to render the Persian term '*haqq*' in support of the contextual opposition to '*∂orugh*' ('lying'), without which a case could be made for 'reality' or even 'Truth' in an Ultimate sense; but here the loftier sense of the latter does not seem to be justified.

III

Chapter 10

IN DRUNKENNESS a man slips free from the things that restrain him in daily life, acquires a different voice and escapes from himself for a few brief moments; and in drunkenness, said Vasily, there is wisdom. That evening, he even made a toast to the wisdom of drunkenness, and I admit we drank a great deal, because our feelings were running high after our discoveries, even though we weren't quite sure what we'd in fact discovered, because it was all so new and so strange. We made plenty of toasts that evening, but I remembered this one in particular because I'd often wondered about the wisdom of drunkenness and whether there really was such a thing, or whether it was just an old myth invented by dipsomaniacs to justify their weakness.

I should say that the way we made toasts was never frivolous, because the chosen subject of toasts between friends is a serious matter, quite apart from the importance of demonstrating that however much you drink, you haven't fully become a donkey-brain-eater,* and still retain the ability to reflect on meaningful things that have no connection with worldly aims. This was a principle we both understood. But why is a man more honest when he's drunk, and why does he do things that he wouldn't

---

* i.e., one who has lost his power of discrimination.

dare to do when sober? I had often wondered, and that evening I tried harder than ever to understand.

You know when a man is drunk because his ordinary judgement fails him and he indulges in words and acts which, if he remembers them afterwards, he regrets. Why is his charm, in the company of women he's never before seen, so promiscuous? And why such disregard for norms to which, in ordinary life, he's been so faithful? Is he, when he's sober, straining constantly against the wish to express himself more honestly? Is he, in fact, deceiving both himself and others at every moment except when he's drunk? No wonder he enjoys struggling free of the straitjacket of the everyday. Perhaps, if he led a different kind of life, said what he really meant and did what he really wished, and in short, if he was more honest about everything – perhaps being drunk would have no effect on him. Perhaps he wouldn't crave the release from himself that drinking brings on.

As it is, what happens to him? He fastens himself to a fraying rope and willingly pays it out towards a cliff-edge, knowing full well the danger he's walking into. Restraint dissolves. A different way of seeing takes its place, the significance of things is turned upside down and soon neither the world nor his own self seem to matter any more in quite the same way, and both speak back to him in a different language, which seems familiar – it ought to, since it's his own – but which even to him is hard to understand. He himself knows it will be impossible to comprehend the morning after. Hearing this language, like the stories of an old friend, becomes a source of fascination he's reluctant to relinquish. His own disguise, and that of others, seems to fall away; but the greater the benefits of this unmasking, the greater the obstacles to understanding them. It's as if he's been given a beautiful sword which cuts through falsehood but which in the atmosphere of intoxication begins to rust as soon as it's drawn. People seem to be made of cardboard, and he slashes them to pieces, while the world spins ever more unsteadily underneath him. He doesn't care. The taste of being free from himself is sweeter than anything. But there's just one problem: he's drunk.

So my toast, in response to Vasily's, was to the attainment of drunkenness without drunkenness. I can't say if he understood what I was getting at: he just looked at me for a long time and blinked and then raised his glass without saying anything.

After that, I can't be sure how long it took to describe to Vasily everything that had happened in the basement. Perhaps it took an hour, perhaps several years. I could see he was really struggling to believe what I told him. At first he asked a lot of questions and wanted to know everything in greater detail, but after I described meeting the workmen guarding that mineshaft, a look of resignation came over his face as if he'd decided he would never get proper answers from me. I pointed this out to him and he simply said:

'It isn't possible to believe anything you have told me.'

'But, Vasily,' I said, turning his earlier words back on him, 'it isn't a matter of belief.'

'What I mean is that there is no measurable way to verify your experience,' he said gloomily.

'You can't verify my experience. You said as much yourself. Verify your own experience, and go down there yourself.'

'Me?'

You should have seen his face.

The problem was I didn't know how to interpret my own experience. The very thought sounded strange: *to interpret my own experience*. My experience was – surely – my experience; it didn't need to be *interpreted*. It was what it was. And yet. I had begun to look at things differently now. Everything pointed to the fact that we had been set apart from the ordinary world, where the language of things was straightforward and things meant what they appeared to mean, and where they had no hidden significance. But in here, everything seemed to have another meaning. Everything related to something more than our experience itself. I knew this must be the case because some things were obviously not real, like having seen moonlight or the sea or all those far-off glittering lights in the basement of the house. Seas didn't fit into houses, nor would they ever, and there was no way moonlight could have reached the basement. So if they were not real in the normal sense, they must be real in the sense of a greater pattern of experience. They required, therefore, an effort of interpretation on my part; an effort to make sense of them within a whole which I didn't yet understand. But that whole did, inexplicably, seem to make a sense of its own.

⌗

Vasily and I agreed, not long afterwards, that there was only one thing to do: he had to explore the basement for himself and not rely on me for a description. My experience of the place had been so intensely personal it was bound to be useless to anyone else; perhaps his would be equally personal. This idea filled us with curiosity, so the next day, which I admit was a slow one, we made a few new lamps, and the following night we headed back downstairs.

Vasily was always nervous when he was out of his room, and on that occasion he was exceptionally annoying, chattering uselessly and speculating about every possible disastrous scenario. What if he were exposed to fungi living in the dust under the building? What if he fell into a collapsed area like the one I had seen? At the dumb waiter I looked into his frightened eyes as he asked me whether I thought the whole thing was a good idea or even really necessary. I reassured him as much as I could, reminding him that we were both committed to exploration and that there was no evidence of anything dangerous (though I realized, as I said this, that I hadn't told him about the dried skins I had puzzled over in the storeroom). He relented and clambered in, and I noticed from the tremor of the little light that his hand was actually shaking.

He wasn't gone long. I heard his humming before I saw him. I helped him out and he brushed himself off. Without my asking he began to tell me what had happened. But there was something odd about the description of his little journey and, after he'd recounted it, the hurried way he suggested we return to our room. Nothing, in fact, had really happened, he said. There was some music in the distance, maybe even some voices, and some empty cupboards, but nothing very spectacular.

I looked at him and said nothing, because I knew what he was saying couldn't be true, and the more I looked at him, the more anxious he became about getting back to our room. Then it dawned on me.

'Give me your map,' I said.

A look of confusion came over his face.

'I haven't got any map,' he said. 'You gave away our map. How could I have a map?'

There was one thing that Vasily was no good at, and that was lying. I asked him to turn around. He refused. I urged him to be honest with me, reminding him of many of the things which he himself had earlier pointed out to me, the main one being that in order for our discoveries to be successful we needed to be completely sincere with both ourselves and each other; and as I spoke the look of resistance on his face began to melt, until at last he sighed deeply and rolled his eyes in resignation. From his back pocket he took several sheets of paper and handed them to me. He'd made a new map, secretly, the night before.

'Now trust yourself,' I said, 'and go back. You may even meet that girl from Ekaterinburg in there.'

'God help me,' he muttered. 'I'd never come back.'

So I helped him once again into the little opening, and this time it was different because he'd really accepted the task, which was more important than the both of us. He was still quite afraid but was cheerful about it. He looked back to me at the last moment.

'What if the next thing you see of me is my dead body on an ox-cart, like Griboedov?'*

'All of Tiflis will mourn you,' I said, trying to make a joke of the whole thing.

Sitting alone in the gloom after he'd disappeared, a strong feeling of homesickness descended onto me. I wrestled with it for a while, then decided to look again around the storerooms, came back and dozed off beside the dumb waiter. I was woken up by the noise of Vasily hurtling through the opening like a man fired out of a circus cannon. If I hadn't seen it happen I would never have imagined him capable of such agility. He huddled against the wall next to me, drenched in sweat, his lungs heaving like bellows, looking back at the entrance as if the Angel of Death was about to appear at any moment.

After he'd calmed down, we made it back to our room, where he explained what had happened. He'd walked a long way, he said, much longer than he'd expected to be able to walk, when he heard the sound of high heels on the ground behind him. Whichever direction he turned, he had a feeling that he was being pursued by the sound of these high heels, though the light was never bright enough to show up their owner. Not long afterwards the sound merged into a kind of tapping, which he'd thought at first might be typewriters, but which turned out to be sewing machines. Moving nearer to the source of the sound, he'd come to a warehouse full of workbenches where the sewing machines were being used, only it had just been deserted by its

---

* Alexander Griboedov (1795–1829), Russian playwright, composer and diplomat, murdered while serving at the Russian embassy in Tehran. His body, returning to Russia on an ox-cart, was famously encountered by Pushkin in the southern Caucasus.

occupants. Row after row of these machines were being used to stitch together an enormous piece of multicoloured fabric, strips of which were being added from a central basket of long and trailing cloth fragments. There was no one there to ask about its purpose, so he went on, and walked back again among the brick pillars.

His foot kicked against an empty bottle. He picked it up, and on a whim, threw it into the darkness ahead of him, regretting it the moment he'd done so, with an inexplicable feeling of dread. A few moments later he heard a sound that made his blood run cold. He could hear the angry breath of a huge, agile animal, which began to pursue him. In a blind panic, he'd begun to run, and it had chased after him, for miles it seemed, right until he'd made it to the entrance. The only thing that had saved him was the fact that the creature was so big, it could only just squeeze between the brick columns, and the effort had slowed it up just enough to allow him to escape. That, he said, and having to flatten itself under the pipes.

'Pipes?' I asked. I hadn't seen any pipes. We must have been travelling on quite different bearings.

'Huge things,' he said. 'High-pressure hot and cold water.' His hands described a circle as wide as a man's head. 'You could even hear the water in them.'

This was all as fascinating as it was bewildering and provided us with plenty to reflect on. But we had a new problem, said Vasily: we had run out of vodka. So we decided that he would go on one of his foraging trips for supplies, and in the meantime we would both think about the next stage of our exploration.

He left the next morning, and I was once again sad to see him go. Left to myself, I hardly need say who my thoughts turned to. The strange thing is that I saw her again soon afterwards, and remembered with a sense of wonder what Vasily had said about the house responding to one's wishes. And not for the first or last time, I really did have the feeling that the house was listening to me. The extension of this was that I, by my actions and perhaps even my thoughts, could actually change the course of what happened in the house; and the extension of *this* was that entire trains of events and their causes would also in turn have to be altered prior to my own actions. These in turn were caused by my earlier actions; and this possibility I was not prepared to concede. So unless every event and outcome was actually in a state of continual readjustment, looking both forwards and backwards in time, and every event was dependent on every other, then I had to reject the idea of a listening house. Logically, I had to reject it. Logically. But my experience, which obviously did not have much to do with logic, felt nonetheless true. Much later, Vasily explained that this apparently illogical readjustment of near-infinite outcomes was itself another illusion caused by our faulty way of perceiving time as a line rather than a whole, but I wasn't yet ready for that.

I didn't plan what happened next; it just unfolded. I admit I was slightly drunk, not from Vasily's vodka, but from the surprisingly good wine I had helped myself to at dinner downstairs. I was heading back to my room, enjoying the feeling of intoxication, and wondering whether I was going to end up like Vasily in a state of near-perpetual drunkenness, when I saw the creature I'd met in the storeroom: the scruffy-looking, one-eyed poodle which had led me to the basement. He was just disappearing into one of the upstairs corridors, and walking with such purposeful confidence that I decided at that moment to follow him. I kept my distance so as not to frighten him, but he soon sensed that he had company, and looked back from time to time to stop and growl at me. I urged him forward with a wave and some very explicit Abkhazian curses.

His destination was a complete surprise, and yet it fitted perfectly with the design of things. Once again I felt as though I was acting out a script which had been written for me by someone who knew the peculiarities of my own character better than

I myself did. I could do nothing but follow it, like a sleepwalker, albeit one who is convinced he is awake.

After a few minutes of walking, several turns and a short flight of stairs, the ugly mutt stopped outside a door and looked back at me once again. Then he raised a paw and I heard the sound of his claw against the door. It opened, and for a moment he looked up and his little tail began to wag, until a fiercely whispered reprimand made him cower and slink guiltily into the room. Before the door closed, I caught sight in the doorway of the fabric of a woman's dress and a slender forearm, and flattened myself against the wall in surprise. I knew it was her; it was just the shock that made me want to hide. The symmetry of it all was irrefutable and made perfect sense. It was she who owned the dog that had unwittingly led me into the strange world of the basement; and before that, she who had revealed the secret of the unlocked door of my room, and she alone who had met my eyes with a sane and steady gaze when all else was in chaos. Now the next chapter of the story was about to unfold, and I had never been readier to be swept up in a story, even if a few details of it had slipped my memory.

I was thrilled, at the same moment, at the thought of being able to pretend that I had found her on my own, as if to show that I was providing my own share of mysterious coincidences, and when I knocked on her door a few minutes later I pretended in the most casual way that I'd simply been passing and thought I'd say hello. She hid her surprise expertly, let me in and danced away with equal skill from the kiss I attempted to plant on her neck, then settled primly on a chair. I sat on her bed, and admired the intricate embroidery of an expensive-looking Indian bedspread.

'An inheritance,' she said, smiling. Her parents, I guessed, had taught her to value things of beauty and luxury. Then in a jade-green pot which matched the colour of her eyes, she made tea; not any tea, she pointed out, but made from tiny Japanese

177

twigs which, I now learned, toned the skin and cleansed the liver. It was delicious and refreshing and, like everything she seemed to know about, just beyond the reach of my experience. I countered my own feelings of inadequacy with stories which I hoped would impress and which I supposed made me sound more knowledgeable and more experienced than I really was; a conceit to which she deferred, saying I had an old soul and the seed of wisdom within me. Gently she began to spin my dreams out of me, and showed me to myself, had I been able to see.

I felt myself succumbing to the sweet drug manufactured by her presence, her lean and shapely form, her voice, her every motion and thought; and for the fulfilment of the promise and longing that had entered my every cell I felt willing to take any risk and stake whatever wealth of mind or body I possessed. Mostly body, I admit. Let's face it, a man is for the most part a man, and in the presence of a beautiful woman will do or say nearly anything if it seems likely to increase the chances of intimacy, a prospect which was never entirely absent from my mind at the time, and quite possibly uppermost. I had managed, in the course of telling various stories, to edge myself along the bed so as to be next to her, with a view to deploying my suddenly acquired experience as foot-masseur, palm-reader or expert teacher of the *Uzundara°* – anything, in short, to enable some part of my body to make contact with hers – but however much I tried to reduce the geography between us, she had a way of evading my efforts at the last minute as if she could read my mind, and would stand up or turn away and change the subject just before any of my little traps could be sprung. Then we heard the slamming of doors in the distance: the Mudaks, checking to see if people were in their rooms.

° Lit. 'long valley'. The reference to the traditional dance of Armenia and Azerbaijan is here presumed to have been deployed satirically.

'Go now,' she said urgently. 'They mustn't find you.' I didn't ask why; the tone of conviction was quite enough to get me on my feet. But I couldn't stop myself, and as we reached the door I placed my arms either side of her and kissed her; and hearing her gasp in surprise and draw away only added to my desire.

'No!' she hissed. And then, more tenderly, but firmly: 'Wait.' There was conviction in this too, and far from experiencing disappointment, as I so often had, hearing the same word from the lips of prim and unadventurous girls, I now heard only promise, and ran back through the shadows feeling weightless and boundlessly lucky.

☦

Vasily came back the following evening, bearing another box full of supplies, and had even managed to find the fresh herbs I'd requested. We drank and ate together, and not long into our session he surprised me completely by proposing a toast to the things that 'happen to a man when his friend goes away'. I'd said nothing to him about Petra, but in spite of his absorption in theoretical matters he was perceptive, and something about my manner had given me away. He asked me how my *bajúshka** was, and shot me a cunning smile. Having earlier lectured him about the need for sincerity, it felt wrong to tell him anything but the whole truth, so I did. He listened thoughtfully, but not with quite as much enthusiasm as I would have liked. I felt I ought to try to convince him.

'Remind me,' I asked him, 'what you said about fate.'

'Fate? I said it was the rightful pattern of a man's life.'

'Yes – but the *feeling* about it.'

'I called it a feeling that is impossible to resist. It used to be

---

* 'Little doll', an Azeri term of endearment.

known as a calling. The thing a man longs for more deeply than anything, even if it defies the logic of his circumstances.'

'Well that's how I feel about Petra,' I said.

'Good,' he said. 'You should follow it.' Then he seemed about to say something more, but didn't.

'Go on,' I said.

'Nothing. Just – with beauty there is always danger not far away.'

Privately, I thought this a timid comment, because in your youth you see nothing wrong with danger. You even seek it out. And when danger is embodied in a beautiful woman who shows every sign of being in love with you and shares your most daring ambitions, and with whom you dream daily of doing the *Asma-Kasma*,* there's no place for timidity. Perhaps Vasily had never known danger, much less pursued it in connection with a woman. It wasn't his fault; he had his fate, and I had mine.

I sensed, around this time, that Vasily was going through a difficult period of his own. He was drinking more in the evenings and his theoretical presentations seldom reached a coherent conclusion. His sense of humour, normally both robust and ironic, was giving way to something more desperate.

One evening we were talking about the way science looks at the world. There was a scientific attitude, said Vasily, that supposes a thing can be explained by its component parts, as if the way a thing behaves really explains *why* it behaves in a certain way. This was one of the great omissions of science; a half-explanation designed to sound like a full one, amounting to a deception that fooled nearly everyone. A great painting and work of art, he said, was indeed composed of paints whose chemical composition enabled the reflection and absorption

---

* The most famous Azeri bridal dance; deployed perhaps in the same spirit as the *Uzundara*.

of light at certain frequencies, giving rise to the experience of colour in the optical apparatus of the onlooker. The whole business of looking at a painting could be thus explained by science in all its magnificent complexity. But science couldn't explain either the phenomenon of seeing – not the mechanics of sight, but the capacity to *see* in its most essential aspect – or the *idea* that the work of art was attempting to convey. Science could explain the material and mechanical aspect of the painting, but not the *meaning* of it, which had first to exist in the mind of the painter, and then be discovered in the mind and feelings of the onlooker. But dominated in such a way by matter rather than meaning, science could never rise above itself to address matters of meaning. Nearly everything was a miracle, said Vasily, invisible to science.

But then as he continued to drink he allowed himself to be overtaken, and his miserable side would come out. If God really was all-powerful, he asked, why didn't he stop terrible things like all those villages where children had been poisoned by radioactivity? If God could make the planets spin, why could he not make a man love his mother-in-law? For what purpose did he make the blind man with the backwards-facing feet who played a battered *kamancheh** on a pavement in Dushanbe? By the end of the evening, he'd worked himself up into a real state.

'Every little thing, when you go into it – everything – brings me to the brink of my understanding,' he said, not even looking at me. Then he got very restless and began to pace around the room, with a pickle in one hand and a bottle in the other, bumping into things and from time to time steadying himself against the wall.

---

* A traditional wooden violin-like musical instrument played upright with a bow.

'You!' He shook the half-eaten pickle at a phantom presence. '*You!* What right do you have to put us here, you – you meddlesome demiurge!' Then his hand turned to his own chest, which he struck with growing force. 'I – I, Vasily Vasilyovich, I too am a particle of Truth! I! You cannot disown me!'

In his excitement he tripped against the bedside table, lost his balance and staggered over to the bed, tumbling onto it as he let out a guffaw of self-mockery. Then he pulled himself to the edge of the bed and just looked at me for a while. When he'd got his breath back he said in a quiet voice:

'Even now . . . even amid the preposterous noise and gadgetry of modern life, the human heart hears the call of the old knowledge . . . a miracle.' He sighed deeply, then fell back heavily onto the bed. I was about to pull a blanket over him, but he rose up again like a man half-drowned, and spoke, this time in a tender and almost imploring voice.

'There are things – things which cannot be improved upon. The sound of rain. The touch of lips —' His eyes fell gently closed and a smile came over his face now, as he struggled to keep his head upright. 'The perfume of an infant's head, the breath of night, an honest man. Pain —' his brow tightened – 'pain that cannot be absolved by talk, joy earned —' He made a final effort to wag a teacherly finger, but it fell back into his lap. 'Such certain things as these, which people crave – you know – those books – about finding peace? About changing your life and becoming a better person? In three easy steps? You know why they sell in their millions?'

'No, Vasily,' I said. 'I don't know.'

'Nor do I,' he said quietly. 'There is a painting by Vereshchagin – so many dead —'

Then with a faint gasp he fell backwards and began to snore.

✝

From then on I returned to Petra's room whenever possible, which was most days. I took food when I could, occasionally wine, and we picnicked together on the floor, swapping stories, tales and dreams in the way that people in love have always done. The hours we spent together seemed to fly by. Every moment was enriched by the puzzle and the delight of the feeling that we had always known each other, the sense that we had some vital, though as yet unguessed, part to play in each other's life. Our meatball connection, you could say.

Yet on the small matter of intimacy, Petra was proving to be a mystery. She knew perfectly well, from the subtle and sometimes not so subtle hints and clues that I scattered into our conversations, that the matter was never far from my thoughts, responding to them with a coy and girlish smile, a lowering of her head and turning-away of her eyes from mine as if she was too modest to entertain such thoughts of her own. She allowed me to kiss her hand from time to time, and, when I left her room, to kiss her on her cheek. But although all the right signals were there, the limits were clear, and I sensed that to violate them would prove irreversible. The result was just enough intimacy to keep the flame I was carrying alive, but not quite enough to let it burn to its full brightness. Something she had said about the ritual purity of young women on the islands where she had lived as a child made me think that she had quite strong feelings on the subject.

Then at last it seemed our time had finally come. On the point of saying goodbye one evening I'd confessed in a whisper a very specific kind of wish – very huskily of course – in her ear, not really imagining it would be granted. Her breathless reply filled me with delight, although delight isn't quite the right word.

'Come tomorrow in the daytime,' she said, 'and I'll give you so much more.' My mind raced. My body ached with anticipation. The torture was exquisite; I was a quivering string tightened to snapping point. I hardly slept. My wonderful fate was taking shape in front of me and who was I to argue with it?

I went back to her room the next day, a lamb not simply willing but eager for slaughter, hypnotized by the promise of release. She opened the door to me, looking lovelier than ever, her eyes full of knowing. I felt she knew my thoughts; I felt I knew hers. It seemed she was as close to me as I was to myself, and that by some miraculous exemption we had been delivered from the burden of having to get to know each other in the ordinary way: we had always known each other.

'Close your eyes,' she said.

'The last time I did that, you disappeared,' I said.

'Maybe this time you'll be the one who disappears,' she replied.

I closed my eyes. She took my hand in hers and led me gently to a different part of the room. I heard a curtain being drawn back, and we moved forward together a few paces. I heard the curtain being closed, and she positioned me in a certain spot, then took one of my hands and held my open palm lightly against her chest. I could feel the swell of her breasts on either side, and the beating of her heart. Then with excruciating slowness I felt my hand being guided steadily downward, over her solar plexus and the warm contours of the muscles of her stomach and then, just as I hoped it would come to rest, away from her body again, where my palm touched what felt like a thick, firm rope, which she closed my fingers around, and then did the same with the other hand, just above the first.

'Open your eyes,' she said.

I felt many things at that moment: disappointment, surprise, confusion and a feeling of having been tricked; but all of these were slaves to the sense of wonder at what I saw at that moment. My eyes fell first on Petra, who was standing in front of me, watching me with her head tilted downwards, her eyes burning with challenge and expectation, and then onto my own hands and the rope they were gripping. Then, slowly and uncomprehendingly, like Ali Baba struggling to take the sight of all those treasures, my eyes followed the rope upwards to the ceiling, where to my astonishment there was a hatch like the entrance to an attic, large enough for a man to pass through. But it didn't lead to an attic, which would have led into darkness; it was a sort of chimney, which led through the ceiling and emerged in a space above, not dark like an attic but flooded with sunlight. It was an upper floor.

'Have you been up there?' I asked Petra, when I'd got over my surprise. She shook her head.

'My arms aren't strong enough.'

'Let's go together then,' I said impulsively. 'I'll help you up.'

'No.' She shook her head again, as if she'd already thought this over long before.

'Where does it go?'

'That's for you to find out. Don't waste time.'

Something between us changed at that moment, perhaps because I knew that my feelings for Petra had now met, in the luminous rectangle above me where my every hope converged, a rival ambition, the rightness of which it was impossible to question. Yet I suppose I was reluctant for the strength of those same feelings to be diverted towards a different goal, however much loftier; I wanted to dive without restraint into intimacy and lose myself there with her, and I felt certain she'd come with me. I didn't want to stand back and admire her selfless spirit from afar, or to perform some heroic act; it was her body I wanted to admire, at the closest range possible, and the only act I wanted to perform didn't involve a rope.

I pulled myself up; it held. I felt the unaccustomed strain in my arms and ankles, and suddenly felt the surprise at how little height you need to gain in order to feel much higher than you really are. My shoulders reached the entrance to the chimney, and further in I braced my feet against the sides, and was able to take the strain off my arms. I looked back for a moment and caught a glimpse of the face looking up at me, and registered with surprise a look of anguish I'd never seen before. Petra's teeth were clenched and her lips drawn tightly across them, not from sympathy with my effort but as if she was inwardly struggling with something powerful and unpleasant but had to disguise the fact; and the moment she saw me looking at her, the expression was transformed into a smile again.

Had I imagined it? I didn't really dwell on the question, any more than I'd dwelled on the ugly sight of those scars on her wrist, but struggled upwards, blowing cobwebs from my face, wondering from time to time how and why such a strange space had been constructed. I came to the conclusion that I was inside what had once been a chimney stack, the upper part of which had long ago been removed from the house. It was slightly narrower than the height of a man, and couldn't be climbed without a rope, but I could press my feet on one side of the wall as I pulled myself upwards. I was an explorer now, a mapmaker in unknown territory, a knight sent by a virtuous woman on a sacred mission of discovery. Then I breached the top, threw my legs over the lip of the opening and let go of the rope.

It was several minutes before my eyes adjusted to the brightness. The strange thing was that I couldn't tell where the light was coming from. There were no obvious windows but the room I was in was simply filled with light, as if it came out of the walls themselves. There was no one around, and the silence was lovelier than the sound of a waterfall tumbling into a mountain stream, and I was reminded of the ascent of Elbrus I'd once made and how I'd felt at the summit. I walked from room to room, feeling a strange impulse to laugh, as if I was slightly drunk, or to cry; I wasn't sure which. It dawned on me, bemused by these strange feelings, that everywhere there was an inexplicable atmosphere of joy, as if in the air itself, producing a kind of delicious dizziness. And the light! For the first time I could actually see things in detail. There were fewer colours here, but each possessed an intensity unseen in the world below. Life on the lower floors seemed drab and almost colourless by comparison, like an ancient mosaic covered by years of dust and grime. I seemed to have forgotten what colour was like.

It was deserted. There was hardly any sign of human activity, other than some cleaning implements in the empty rooms; brushes and brooms for polishing and sweeping. It was as if the former inhabitants had themselves been turned to dust and swept up into the light and dissolved, leaving only the joyful trace of their extinction.

⊹

I don't know how long I'd been wandering; it was perhaps many years. At some point I entered a tall room, bare except for a broom, neatly propped against the wall in a far corner. I looked around, and saw in the ceiling high above me a small window. I had no conscious sense of the fatefulness of this encounter; at first I was only mildly curious. Yet looking back, I recognize there was what seemed to be a natural logic to the discovery, and a rightness which was unremarkable at the time. Memory always lies, and fits its version of events to unspoken and even unknown designs, which is why two different people's memories of the same event are so often different. But memory becomes more reliable and enduring if joined to a more authentic part of oneself. I say authentic because after so many ups and downs later in life, this memory has remained steady and true and clear, like a pool around a pure spring, unlike so many others which in time have changed their original course more often and more confusingly than all the meandering tributaries of the Amu Darya in its upper reaches.

I looked up to the window. It was quite small, smaller than the chimney I'd squeezed through earlier, and only just large

187

enough for a man, if it was even designed to open that far. It was set into the pitch of the ceiling, had been painted over and would have been easy to miss if it hadn't been for the old-fashioned crank that was attached to it by a long pole mounted on the wall. The crank part had a dark wooden handle and hooked into a metal loop at the lower end of the pole a few feet above my head. I tried it, but it had been painted over so many times that the pole was stuck fast inside the brackets that held it to the wall. It seemed certain that the window was made from the same reinforced glass as the windows below, but I longed to make sure.

I tugged on the crank; it was old and sturdy and felt solid enough. I hung off it and it held. Then I climbed a little way up until I could put my foot on the handle and grip the pole, and hung there a while, wondering how high I dared to go. I tried to calculate whether if one of the brackets were to come loose, the others would too, and what effect that might have on the pole as it fell to the floor with me attached to it; and what kind of injuries I might be likely to suffer, and how I would manage the return journey through the chimney if I had a broken leg or arm. The strange thing is that all these fears seemed, as they came up, irrelevant, and even made me chuckle as I heard myself formulate them, because the obvious thing to do was simply to climb.

I made it to the top, trying to understand the design of the window by glancing at it from time to time as I went up. The pole held firmly to the wall and showed no signs of weakening, which meant I could jam my toes with growing confidence into the space between it and the wall.

Then I reached the angle of the ceiling, and realized the window itself was further from the vertical wall than I'd calculated, which meant I couldn't reach it properly. Nor could I pull myself up any further. I was stuck. I groped inside the recess of the windowpane for a handhold, finding only a thin lip of metal too narrow to grip, and then, unexpectedly and with a feeling of pure joy, found my fingertips slip into a perfect hold, deep enough to receive them at just the right width to be comfortable. This came just in time, as I was losing strength in the other hand, and had to decide which hold to give up. So I let go of the pole and gripped the frame of the window with both hands and swung out into the air with my body dangling below me. It was a dangerous manoeuvre, but the only way to see properly inside the frame. Then I looked up to see where my fingers had actually found their hold, and realized that the only way they had found a space inside the frame was because it had been left slightly open. Open! I had no time to contemplate the hugeness of this discovery. I pulled myself up, using every bit of remaining strength, and brought my head to the level of my fingers, and took a deep breath. And to put it very simply, in the few seconds left to me that my muscles would allow, everything changed for me for ever.

Such things can never be explained. They can be described, but only in terms of something else. Their description can only ever be an approximation. How can you describe a thing for which you have no words? If you've always been dead, how can you describe the experience of life? If you have never breathed, how to describe the sweetness of air filling your lungs? But that's what happened: I breathed. I breathed and realized that I was breathing air from outside the building, and as it entered my lungs I felt as though I was being born. Something was lifted from me; I had stepped from shadow into light. My thoughts suddenly became clear, and my feelings once again true, as if up until then I'd been in a kind of horrible fog which concealed and distorted everything.

You may think you can't taste air, but you can when you've been deprived of it, and this air was unimaginably sweet and intoxicating, and caused just the kind of intoxication I'd been thinking about with Vasily, which didn't deaden the senses but restored them as if to their original and keenest condition.

189

I could feel the air travelling to the back of my throat and into my lungs, and from there on to an invisible place at the centre of me, where the deepest part of myself seemed to lie. I couldn't swallow enough of it. Each time I took a gulp of air I seemed to be myself again, alive and whole, perhaps more than I had ever been. To be more truthful, I saw myself – felt myself – as if from afar, as if my life were not my own, but a part of all life; life was a thing happening to me, and it was infinitely good. Heaven, it occurred to me then, was not a far-off place as I'd always vaguely imagined; it was contained within the very atoms of that transforming air which was dancing in tiny currents around my fingertips. But my arms were trembling now, and I was about to fall. I lowered myself away from the window, swung one arm back to the vertical pole, then the other, slithered down, and rested, massaging the burning tendons in my arms and legs. Then I lay on the floor and looked upwards towards the light.

I felt overwhelmed, unable to understand what had happened. Then it was as if a strange wave was sweeping over me, like sleep only more deep, as if I was actually melting or being dissolved. Everything began to darken. I closed my eyes and allowed it to happen. It wasn't quite a dream; I knew I was awake. But I knew I'd never been awake in quite the same way.

Kneeling beside me, as if she'd been watching me all my life, was the most beautiful woman I'd ever seen. She really was the most beautiful creature I'd ever laid eyes on. Where I come from, a man looks at a woman in one of two ways. But despite her beauty, I wasn't looking at her the first way. Far from it. Hers was a beauty that leaves you intoxicated, the way a dawn can take your breath away after you've been walking all night in the mountains, and all your worries are lifted like a mist by the rays of the sun. She wasn't quite human – not like Petra anyway, whose beauty suddenly seemed insubstantial. I could tell this woman was out of my league and that I'd need the soul of a hundred men to match hers. From her eyes alone, gleaming like polished basalt, and her gaze diving into mine like an all-seeing arrow, I knew she was Persian. The rest was just as those poets have all described; that long hair flowing everywhere in jet-black whirlpools, those lips the colour of red coral, the deli-cate arches of her eyebrows, her body as slender and flexible as a cypress tree, graceful and overwhelmingly beautiful.

She was looking at me lovingly and in silence, her head tilted in gentle enquiry. I knew from her expression that she had per-ceived and understood – better than I had – my whole situation, the longing in me and all the troubles I was having.

'I feel drunk,' I said. 'This makes no sense. I must be drunk.'

Then she spoke. Her voice was as gentle as a breeze. I'd always thought that to compare a woman's voice to a breeze, the way those poets do, was absurd. But that's exactly how it felt, like the tenderest of caresses moving effortlessly over me, sooth-ing me, melting me.

Our drunkenness does not depend on wine
Our gatherings require no harp nor strings
No cupbearers nor minstrels, no audience nor flute
Even without these, we are beyond reason – drunk

Then she smiled at me, as if that explained everything.

'Now you have tasted Love, what will you do?' she asked.

The intimacy of the question! From a woman I had never met! It drove to the heart of everything, as if she had read my life story, and made clear what I had hardly had time to grasp myself. Love! That feeling of being overwhelmed by a wave of unspeakable benevolence, in which I felt momentarily dissolved, at one with everything.

191

'I will follow it,' I said, 'wherever it takes me.'

'Yes,' she replied after a pause, tenderly. 'I think you will. It is even here, if you could see it.'

'What *is* it?' I asked. 'I can't describe it.'

'Better that you cannot,' she said, nodding.

'Why better?' I asked.

'It is not you. You are not you. Let that be your secret.'

'What must I do?'

'Do nothing,' came the reply. 'Be nothing.'

'What am I, if I am no longer?'

'You are the expression of That.'

'That,' I repeated.

She smiled again, and all her beauty and goodness seemed to wash over me. I knew she meant God, but was glad she didn't use the word because I'm not religious, and she must have known. Maybe she even knew that my feelings about religion had never been quite the same ever since I was nine years old, when the preacher in our own village had been arrested for something unspeakable. In any case there was a mischief to the way she said it, which seemed to indicate that the words didn't really matter. I knew exactly what she meant, and I knew it was true; and she knew that I knew.

She didn't use these exact words, but I understood them very exactly. Our exchange had the feeling of great precision, and it felt as though we'd ranged over a multitude of questions, even though she'd said so little. The strange thing is she didn't use words at all. She never even opened her mouth. But I heard her very clearly all the same.

✝

I told Petra everything, with the exception of that strange encounter. You know how women can be. I told her I had found a life-restoring window, and with it the possibility of escape. All

I had to do was to figure out a way to get up to the height of the window more easily, and to lever open the frame wide enough to climb out. I wanted nothing more, telling her this news, than to go back there; I felt as if I'd left behind a waiting friend, who might leave if I didn't return in time.

'Now you have a task,' said Petra, drawing close to me. 'You mustn't fail.'

And then, unexpectedly, she who had resisted me for what seemed like years took my head gently in her hands and pulled it towards hers, so that our lips met properly for the first time. Had she been waiting for the signal of this discovery before allowing us to celebrate the intimacy I'd been craving since we had met? Had she hoped for it too, or guessed at it? Had she known all along and planned for it? I didn't know. All these thoughts were swept away on the tide that now rose irresistibly between us.

As celebrations go, it was the best I had known, being the most complete and the least inhibited. But a slightly strange thing did happen. While we were as close as two people can really get, physically at least, Petra had a kind of convulsion. She gripped me the way a cat grips you when you try to rescue it from a tree, sinking its claws into you as if terrified of death.

'When you leave,' she gasped, breathless and drenched in sweat, 'take me with you.'

'Of course,' I said, disguising the pain of her nails in my skin. I had never thought otherwise.

'Promise me.'

'I promise.' It struck me then as a strange moment to exact a promise, but her grip on me hadn't lessened. It was an even stranger moment to insist.

'Just promise me that whatever happens, you will take me with you.'

'I promise I will take you with me,' I said, and tried to soothe her until her grip relented, and her body was once again supple and giving. Then later, a little after things had quietened down, and we were lying intertwined like a pair of Caucasian salamanders, she suddenly began to shake. Her back was to me and for a while I thought she might be having another kind of fit. When I realized she was weeping silently, I pulled her gently towards me so as to see her face, and as I did her eyes actually rolled up into her head the way they do in horror films and a terrifying rasping sound came from her lungs, as if someone had at last opened the coffin in which she'd been buried alive.

'You do know,' she sobbed, when she'd got her breath back, 'I love God with all my heart and soul and would be nothing without him?' She turned her eyes to mine and looked searchingly into them. 'I would do anything for him. You know that, don't you?'

'Yes,' I said, 'I know that.'

What else could I have said? The truth is that I had not the faintest idea what she really meant or what, at that moment, had prompted such a peculiar thought to blossom so improbably. Then she slept.

I lay next to her in the silence, awake. The joy that I had known earlier in the day was already darkening. I could return to the feeling if I tried, like someone revisiting the site of an important memory, but it was no longer alive in the same way.

It wasn't Petra's fault. The problem was that I'd experienced something completely beyond myself, as if I had already escaped, and the taste of freedom still lingered on my lips. I knew perfectly well that this wasn't the same as having actually escaped. Now that I was down in the ordinary world again, the feeling of promise seemed suddenly more fragile than ever, and between the taste and the act I could foresee nothing but obstacles.

Chapter 11

IN THE MORNING I felt Petra slide from the bed and dress in silence. Thinking I was asleep, she left without a word. I was tired but my mind was fighting and I couldn't sleep properly. I dreamed I was on an enormous abandoned passenger ferry travelling too fast, its lower decks flooded. It was listing dangerously and forcing me to climb higher and higher to avoid disaster, but to jump was just as dangerous. You know the kind of dream where you're clinging for dear life and can't let go, but you can't stay in the same place for too much longer, either.

I gathered up my things. On Petra's table I saw an old-fashioned fountain pen and decided to write her a romantic note. While I was thinking about the words I put down the pen and it rolled onto the floor, bending the nib. I couldn't straighten it out, and added a short confession in the note, promising one day to buy her an even more beautiful pen. I hoped she wouldn't be angry. Then I walked back to my room, picturing its peace and emptiness, and looking forward to the promise of being able to rest on my own.

It was not to be. In my room, a conference seemed to be underway. Worse than this, lying on my bed was a tall, bare-foot but otherwise fully-clothed man who groaned every few minutes like a large animal about to give birth. Sitting on the chair by the table I recognized Fidel, looking bored and restless. Vasily was standing by the window, nervously delivering what sounded like a speech on probability theory.

'Thank God you're here,' said Vasily. 'We didn't know what had happened to you.'

'We?'

'This is Colonel Esclavo.' He pointed to Fidel, who turned to me and gave a sheepish nod of acknowledgement and shrugged his eyebrows without actually looking at me. 'But we don't know the big fellow's name. He is, however, alive – thanks to the Colonel here.'

I walked over to the man on my bed. It looked as though someone had been using his face for a football, but I could tell at once from his long hair and lanky limbs that it was the Oaf, whom I'd first seen loping around the atrium with his imaginary seeds, and then later when Fidel had failed so wholesomely to come to my aid.

I asked what had happened.

'You should have been there!' said Vasily excitedly. 'I saw the whole thing.' He then described how, the previous evening, he'd been watching a group of residents at their peculiar storytelling ritual. This was presided over by Otto, who had acquired an ill-fitting crown and a sceptre, which he banged on the floor to get the others' attention when necessary. Each resident had to tell a story, long or short and about anything at all, while the others, sitting on cushions in a circle, listened. As soon as someone detected a truth, he intervened and had to continue the story where it had been interrupted, being careful never to tell the truth. If it was discovered he had told the truth, and the others agreed unanimously that it was the truth, Otto would walk over and deliver a particularly humiliating punishment.

How anyone agreed to this devious form of abuse was difficult to comprehend, but Vasily had witnessed it. In fact Otto was just about to carry out his repulsive form of authority when a figure had come running into the room, clutching a bag. No one had recognized him, but it was soon obvious that he was on the run and had probably stolen the contents of the bag which, seeing the Oaf, he'd pushed into his hands and run off. The Oaf, unsuspecting as ever, had thanked him and then peered down to look inside the bag, taking out the things in turn and putting them beside himself – a silver ladle, a wallet, an ostrich-feather scarf – when a gang of Mudaks had burst into the room in pursuit of the thief. They surrounded the Oaf, thinking they'd caught him red-handed, and pulled the bag from him. The Oaf was taken aback but didn't say anything. Someone cried out, 'He didn't do it!' but the Mudaks weren't listening. They dragged him out of the circle, walked around him, and then one of them hit him right in the face with the ladle. The Oaf put a hand to his eye but made no attempt to escape.

A small crowd began to gather, and Vasily found himself standing next to Fidel, wondering how far the Mudaks would go with their punishment and how far the Oaf would go with his refusal to protest his own innocence. Another of the Mudaks wrapped the scarf around the Oaf's neck and began to strangle him, while the others kicked and punched. Vasily stepped into the fray and began to protest on behalf of the Oaf, but the Mudaks pushed him away like a distraction and continued with their torture. By now the Oaf was clutching at his throat with one hand, while his other arm flailed in desperation. Then he toppled over like a great tree and the Mudaks piled in. Vasily began to yell at the others to help, and begged Fidel to intervene.

'They don't listen to me, but they'll listen to you,' he pleaded. 'We can't let them get away with this.'

'He should fight back,' Fidel said calmly, but he was obviously troubled by the sight.

'He doesn't know how to fight! They're killing him and he

hasn't done anything! But you do.' He grabbed Fidel's arm. 'What are all these muscles for anyway? What are you, a coward?'

Fidel held out for a little longer, and then, at a heart-rending cry of distress from the Oaf, something in him snapped, and he went into action.

'You should have seen him!' Vasily was exuberant now. 'The Mudak destroyer! I knew he would. The two of them who were doing the strangling – he got them first – bang! Knocked their heads together like a pair of coconuts. Out cold, both of them. They deserved it, the filthy black-assed *pizðuks*!* Then an uppercut – bang! – then another right in the face, then the other who tried to jump on his back – he got a surprise – then a couple more, flattened like a pair of skittles, the brainless *svolloch*. Got another by the scruff of the neck and lifted him off his feet!' He mimicked a pair of dangling legs. 'Then another – picked him clean off the ground and threw him across the room. Would you believe what happened then? Everyone else joined in. Once the dirty thugs were sprawling on the ground, they got a dose of their own medicine: even that little fellow was jumping up and down on one of them! They knew they couldn't push us all any further, so off they ran like beaten dogs – all because of our hero here,' he said, patting Fidel on his shoulder.

'Hero? I wouldn't have guessed,' I said, remembering Fidel's performance when I had really needed him. For the moment, my ill-will towards Fidel, unsoftened by the description of his martial skills, spilled over towards the inert shape in my bed. I knelt down beside it and looked at the blood-streaked, sleeping face. It looked strangely childlike and untroubled.

'When do I get my bed back?' I asked.

---

* Derived from the Russian *'pizðu'* and considered extremely offensive.

'He doesn't speak any language we know,' said Vasily.

'What's your name?' I leaned closer, and tried a few dialects, but there was no response.

'How did you do it, Colonel?' asked Vasily. 'How did you have the guts to take on ten of those brutes?'

'I just did it.' Fidel shrugged unhelpfully. 'Didn't really think about it.'

I wasn't feeling very talkative, despite being intrigued by the coincidence that Fidel had displayed his talent just as I had been making my own discovery on the upper floor. Vasily and Fidel saw that I wasn't in the mood for discussion and left the room together. There was no point in trying to reclaim my bed, so I sat in the chair, put my feet up on the table and fell asleep.

Imagine my surprise when, I don't know how much later, I felt myself being lifted up in the arms of the corpse-like figure, who had come to life while I was dozing. It seemed to take him no effort and I realized how immensely strong he was, a fact which made even stranger his refusal to physically resist the love and attention showered on him earlier by the Mudaks.

'What are you doing?' I asked.

'You want bed. I give bed.' So he had heard me. He laid me gently onto the bed, stood up and smiled, as a giant might smile at a flower.

'My name is Tevdore,' he said. He spoke a broken Daghestani dialect that sounded like the taxi drivers you meet in Baku who come from God knows where.

'Thank you, Tevdore,' I said. 'I'm sorry they hurt you so badly. You must still be in pain.'

'Is not so bad,' he grinned. 'Hurt they did on me go after few day. Hurt they did to self cannot such easy go away.'

'You mean they will feel guilty?' I wasn't sure if I understood his logic.

'Not is guilty,' he said. 'Guilty from man, but shame from

199

nature. Is shame they will feel. Is natural thing, when you did other person hurted. But not yet they feel. One day will wish my forgive, so better now I forgive.'

'You forgive them in advance? Just like that?'

'Is not fault of dog to behave as dog. So I forgive.'

'I think,' I said, 'I would hate them.'

'You wish slave to be, like those ones? If I hate, then slave of hate I become. Not I wish slave to be.' He chuckled. 'Not can hate destroy hate. Can only love destroy hate.'

He turned to leave.

'I hope we will talk again,' I said, feeling there was nothing I could add to what he'd said. I was drawn to his simple wisdom. He said nothing else but chuckled again; a deep and sonorous chuckle that shook his entire frame, and which I could still hear even after he'd ducked under the lintel and closed the door behind him.

That was how I was introduced to Tevdore, whom I had cruelly thought of as a fool, yet who ended up teaching me much. He was not normal in the conventional sense, and quite unfitted to ordinary life. He couldn't add two and two or distinguish north from south, but he saw into people and events with disconcerting earnestness, and although Vasily and I both joked at first about his simple-mindedness behind his back, we were so often stopped in our tracks by the truth of some of the things he said that later on we both came to love him for his unique qualities.

After his brief recuperation, he never forgot us, and from then on visited nearly every day. He would appear suddenly at the door and enter the room without explanation or embarrassment, taking in whatever was going on in a single glance and often with a characteristic chuckle. He knew our moods before we did and would sometimes point them out before we had ourselves noticed what we were feeling.

'You have worry,' he would observe of one of us, having seen a frown or trace of anxiety. 'Is better you solve, or forget. Never should worry.'

His deep chuckle, which would always accompany this kind of pronouncement, would lift our mood, and sometimes we would imitate it in his absence to raise our spirits. Just as he would appear unexpectedly, when he wanted to leave, he would stand up and go to the door, whether we were in mid-conversation or not.

More than anything we loved the poetry he sang. A couple of drinks was enough to get him going. We never found out who the poet was – Tevdore shrugged whenever we asked, as if the question was irrelevant – and we never really understood the words, because between us Vasily and I probably only caught about half of their meaning, but it didn't seem to matter. When Tevdore sang poetry, everything else stopped. I remember one verse that went:

I have been burnt by the fire of Love.
You who have no such yearning in your heart,
go back to sleep.

He sang with such feeling, and to such a soulful melody, that the essence of the poems seemed to be transmitted without our needing to understand the words, such was their almost tele-pathic intensity. And so beautiful was his voice that we forgot the dull-witted-looking face and ungainly limbs that contained the miraculous sound, and were often transported to such extremes of feeling that we both struggled not to weep.

I think we both knew that Tevdore should be let into our plan: he was the purest-hearted man either of us had ever met, and the sheer injustice of what had recently happened to him was evidence that he deserved the chance to escape. But then we began to wonder how he would be likely to fare in the ordin-ary world and pictured his simple-mindedness being taken advantage of by everyone he met, and this unspoken question of whether escape was the right thing for him or not hung between us at every meeting.

In the meantime I broke the news of my discovery to Vasily. I sensed he'd be sceptical but I couldn't not tell him about it. I had come to rely on him for a way of understanding things that was different from my own, and fully expected him to challenge and question and analyse every bit of my description. But from the start he was unexpectedly intrigued and listened carefully to everything I said. He didn't even ask many questions. The only problematic issue was the rope: he'd never climbed up a rope in his life, he said. He'd never felt the urge, he added, or seen the point. I'd explained that there was only one way to get up through the chimney that led from Petra's room, and that was by climbing the rope. In a different place it might be possible to lessen the distance to the ceiling by piling up things underneath it; but the narrowness of the chimney made this impossible as a means to reach the upper floor. Nothing could be taken up from below but the rope itself, which to climb required the utmost effort, and for that we would both have to practise. I wished I could give him my arms. Who wouldn't wish the same for a friend, whose liberty you wished for as much as yours? But we both knew he would have to use his own, and take pretty much everything else on faith.

To practise, we had to work together, and devised an unlikely system. There was nowhere in our room to hang a rope from, so we couldn't practise climbing one in the ordinary way. Instead, using long strips of curtain pleated together to give the thick-ness of rope, we knotted one end behind the bathroom door and, lying the free end along the floor, pretended it was the length we had to climb. Then to imitate the gravity that we'd have to work against, we used another length of curtain to link ourselves together, by tying the rope around our waists. So as Vasily struggled to pull himself across the floor using his arms,

I pulled in the opposite direction with the weight of my own body.

At first this made it virtually impossible for him to advance. He swore. He raised every kind of objection. He dismissed the entire endeavour as a waste of time and energy. I knew that to pull one's own weight against gravity was the hardest physical task of all, but refused to accept any of his excuses.

There were times when we both wanted to give up; we took turns with hopelessness. Sometimes I cracked the whip but at other moments, when the whole effort seemed absurd and pointless to me, it was Vasily's enthusiasm that came to my aid. During one of our unlikely sessions, we were horrified when the door swung unexpectedly open, paralysing us with surprise like bank robbers caught in the act. We had forgotten to block it with the small wooden wedge we'd made for the purpose, and for an instant thought that the Mudaks had discovered us and would lay into us with their habitual enthusiasm. But it was Tevdore, who looked without expression at the strange scene and simply asked if he could play too. So I tied one of the ends of the curtain around his waist instead of Vasily's, and told him to try and pull himself across the floor using only his arms. We knew he was strong, but we were amazed when he did as I'd asked without any apparent effort, dragging me behind him as helplessly as a kitten, despite my utmost efforts to resist. After this feat Tevdore looked disappointed, and asked whether that was the purpose of the game, so we tried it again with both Vasily and I pulling in the opposite direction, and he repeated the same feat, as powerful and unstoppable as a Siberian freight train. Our puny efforts amused him. He was so strong that he could brace his arm against a wall and let us take turns at pulling ourselves up as if his arm was an iron bar. This turned out to be a useful practice which he let us try out whenever he visited. When either of us began to tire, he would simply lift us by the belt with his other hand, until Vasily and I were both exhausted.

203

Then one day it seemed that we would gain nothing more, and we went to Petra's room. I was anxious because when I had first told her about Vasily, and that we were working together towards the same goal, she had looked uneasy. Now I wondered how she would receive him. To my great relief she was friendly and even flattered him, putting a hand on the muscles of his arm and saying she was sure that for him the task would be easy. She made tea for us and read quietly to herself as we tried the rope. Once or twice, looking up to see Vasily's body spinning helplessly in circles, she shot me a surreptitious smile. Vasily worked hard and wasted much of his strength on trying to pull himself up before he had mastered the trick of gripping the rope between his feet. But once he'd managed to combine arms and legs he said he'd like to try the chimney, so I climbed up ahead of him and let him follow. It took a few tries, but eventually he made it to the top.

'Thank God that's finished,' he gasped.

'That was the easy part,' I told him. He understood this only later.

Vasily was lying on his back by the opening to the chimney, getting his breath back. He was looking around silently, his eyes adjusting to the brightness. I could see, from the childlike look of curiosity on his face, that even this first sight of his new surroundings was making a deep impression on him.

'It is different here,' he said quietly. 'It's so bright. And it's so — still.'

I was pleased he noticed. He got up and we walked a little way. Vasily was entranced. Several times he seemed to be on the point of saying something but then sighed and gave up. He soon saw that there were no doors, only openings, and that there was no obvious source of light. And I think he must have felt the peculiar joyfulness of the atmosphere, because for once he'd actually stopped chattering like a monkey and instead he just looked at me from time to time and smiled, like a child enchanted by some discovery that has exceeded his wildest dreams. I led him to the room where I'd found the window. He seemed to be studying its emptiness for a long time.

'We are trespassers here,' he said. Then added, in a tone that was uncharacteristically calm: 'We must find out what is up there.'

☩

We came back when he was feeling strong again. This time I wanted Vasily to climb up and inspect the window himself, so after we had climbed the chimney to the upper floor, I unhooked the rope and carried it coiled over my shoulder to the window-room. For our efforts to succeed, I reasoned that Vasily had to be as convinced as I was about the window. I couldn't know if he'd have the same feelings that I'd had when I first smelled the indescribable perfume of the air from the outside, but that didn't really matter. He simply had to see the position and design of it to understand what we would need to actually open the window. My only worry, apart from whether he had the physical strength to achieve the climb, was the bar and crank fixed to the wall which I first had to climb in order to attach the rope to the window frame. I couldn't tell how much strain they would take and I knew that each time I climbed up they would be weakened. So we agreed that Vasily would make only one climb to inspect the window, and that the next ascents would have to be our escape. For that, we would need other tools, such as a harness, and some means of breaking or forcing the window open. We would work on those in the meantime.

So we walked together in the delicious silence, which could not have been more different from the noise and chaos below, until we reached the room, where I fixed the hook of the rope to my belt and once more climbed the vertical bar. With the weight of the rope pulling on me it was much harder than before, and the final manoeuvre, where I had to get the rope hooked over the rim of the window frame while hanging on with one hand, happened only just in time before my strength was gone. With the rope in place I climbed down, and saw that my hands were trembling from the effort.

Then it was Vasily's turn. I got him to swing his arms to warm up the muscles and to do a *Zurkhaneh*-style° routine of deep breathing, and then held on to the free end of the rope as he began his climb. All our training was paying off. As long as he didn't look down, he climbed at a good rate and only began to struggle as he got near the top. I was giving him lots of encouragement and felt quite proud of his progress. At the very top he looked around the window frame and for a second even took one hand off the rope to tap the painted-over pane above his head. Then he seemed to be sniffing the air like a dog, and I thought I saw a look of confusion on his face. I heard a kind of gasping, as if he was about to sneeze. Then suddenly he was sliding down the rope. His hands moved in a blur on the verge of losing control, and he hit the ground much too fast, falling heavily backwards with a thump, his arms splayed out like a flattened insect.

I'd been standing some distance away and ran to him. His eyes were wide open but he was completely still, his gaze fixed on the ceiling above.

'Jesus Holy Christ and Mary Mother of God and all the Saints,' he said quietly.

'Are you all right?' I asked. I wondered if he'd damaged his legs or his spine. He was struggling to raise himself, so I helped him to sit up.

'Gently,' I said. 'Where's the pain?'

° Lit. 'House of Strength', the name given to buildings dedicated to the practice of traditional Persian martial arts.

He looked at me, but in a strange way, as if he was seeing me for the first time and didn't recognize me. He was obviously concussed.

'Vasily, don't try to move. Tell me where the pain is.'

'The pain,' he repeated, staring past me. 'The pain.'

'Yes. Where is the most pain?'

'Pain?' This time it was a question. 'Pain? There is no God damned *pain*.'

'What is it, then?' Perhaps he was paralysed.

'Jesus Christ, man. I'm *sober*.' He looked around with a kind of wonderment. 'I'm sober, God damn it.' He looked at his hands and opened and closed them experimentally, as if he'd been given new limbs. And then I watched as, very slowly, the look of delight began to slip from his face and turned first to one of confusion, and then regret.

'I haven't felt like this . . . I haven't felt like this for . . . Oh, God,' he sighed, 'I've wasted so much time.'

Tears welled up in his eyes and the corners of his lips began to reach downwards and tremble slightly until his mouth looked like a fallen crescent moon, and then the wave came over him. His whole body shook; he rocked back and forth, and wailed like a baby as the tears poured from his eyes like little mountain springs that had been unblocked after a mudslide. There was nothing I could do but sit next to him and, after a while, put my arm around him and be at one with his release, because these are the best kind of tears for man, by which pretence and fantasy are washed away and by which he is reminded of what he really is in the presence of the Mystery. His weeping, eventually, subsided. And then, as truly as I write this, he began to laugh, as wildly as he had been crying, and the room echoed so loudly with his laughter that it seemed just possible the whole house could hear him.

☩

We spent the next few days calculating what we needed to both make the ascent to the window and to open it. It was obvious we would have to fashion some kind of sling or harness to be able to hang off the rope to avoid tiring our arms. Vasily designed what I later discovered was a version of a Prusik knot, which would tighten against the rope under tension, but which could be slid up or down its length during either an ascent or descent, making the whole effort slower, safer and less exhausting.

This would take care of the climbing aspect, but we still had the problem of how to open the window itself. If the glass was reinforced like other glass in the building, it would be impossible to break it like an ordinary pane; we would need time to work it free from its frame or to sever the wire mesh within it. All this would have to be done hanging from the rope below it, protecting our hands and eyes in the meantime from broken glass. We would also need to improvise some kind of safety device, in case the strain on the hook at the end of the rope became too much. Alternatively, we might with the right tool be able to force open the frame of the window instead of breaking the glass, but a single man hanging precariously from a rope would hardly be strong enough.

'It might need the two of us,' I said to Vasily, as we talked it over.

'Or the three of us,' he said, meaningfully.

We had already inducted Tevdore into our plans, although he didn't know it. The day before he'd seen us making fabric loops and asked what they were for. But we'd told him they were for our rope-games, which was partly true, although we'd never mentioned the full scope of our plan. Then in the guise of another challenge to test his strength, we got him to tighten the various knots in our improvised ropes and loops to industrial standards. Now we realized that his immense strength might be deployed on the window itself. With one hand he could probably just push the pane out; a task which for us would be long and dangerous. We wondered whether to tell him everything. It wasn't that we didn't trust him. It was that he was so honest and incapable of deception that he might give the game away by accident, the way a child does when he says he has a secret that he's promised his parents never to speak about. In the end we agreed that it was a risk we'd have to take, and once we'd finished with most of the preparations, we explained very simply our wish to escape, gave him a rough idea of the plan and asked if he wanted to escape with us. The answer was unexpected.

'If Tevdore escape from this place,' he said thoughtfully, 'still cannot from Tevdore escape.'

'Tevdore,' said Vasily, unimpressed by this reasoning, not realizing how strange his own must have sounded, 'we are prisoners here. We must escape. It's the unavoidable expression of the intrinsic pattern of our natures.'

'You *here* are prisoner,' replied Tevdore, raising his finger and tapping it solemnly against the side of his head. It struck me then how much he was in the wrong place. For a timeless moment I pictured him back in his *awl*,* dispensing wisdom to his villagers. 'From *here* must Vasilovich escape.'

Then he turned to me with a gloomy expression, as if he'd understood the possibility that his friends might be leaving.

'You wish such also?'

I nodded.

'For why you wish?' he asked.

Such a simple question! If you chip away at a question, it doesn't stand up for long. How could I give him a convincing answer? Why did we wish to escape? Because we longed to. What was longing? Something we had to answer to until it went away. Why? Because we were as unfitted to life as residents

---

* A fortified traditional Caucasian village, often constructed on a steep hill to deter enemies.

in this place as Tevdore was to life in the outside world. Why? It was so difficult to say . . . What we thought of as freedom and how to attain it seemed to be the least of Tevdore's pre-occupations, and perhaps, in truth, this made him more free than us. But he had not tasted, or had long ago forgotten, the taste of what we had tasted, or borne the burden of it; the fragrance of the not-yet, a faith of sorts – not in anything that could be defined, but faith itself. A knowledge, really, that our true life and the truest expression of it lay beyond the walls of the building; beyond reason and beyond means. At that moment it seemed to me that all the problems of life and the world come from the experience of separation. All of a man's anxieties and loneliness and the suffering that comes from them arise from falling short of the feeling of wholeness and unity in himself and in life. And anything that brings him closer to wholeness relieves this suffering.

'To experience peace,' I said.

'Peace,' he repeated, nodding as if that made sense to him. 'But if here is peace,' he tapped his fingers against his chest, 'not is possible to find what already you have.'

'We love freedom,' suggested Vasily.

'Such not is love,' said Tevdore. 'Such is desire. Desire make benefit for only you, but love benefit all.'

Then he sighed, as if having weighed all this up for himself, and chuckled his characteristic chuckle. 'If can Tevdore help friends, then will Tevdore help!'

We were immensely relieved.

'We are very lucky to have you as a friend,' I said. Vasily rolled his eyes in friendly exasperation.

'Such not is luck. Is reward of good act what did your parents long before, like gift to you. They forget, but not did Time forget.'

How could he divine such things, the rightness of which we too dimly sensed but which were hidden so deeply within us?

He had no education; he was quite unfitted for the world. But he felt life with a keenness that time and again showed up our dull obsession with fact alone, and I for one was jealous of his peculiar talent.

☩

We made a final plan. Tevdore would come with us to the window room, where I would climb to the window to fix the rope to the frame. Then Tevdore would climb up and, with the benefit of his unique strength, push the window out of its frame. I would climb up after he'd come back down, and try to climb onto the roof. Vasily would follow. We would take the rope with us in case we needed it for another descent. We would have our specially designed slings and loops. Once on the roof, if it proved impossible to make a safe descent from the building, we would draw the attention of passers-by, either by shouting or by dismantling the roof and throwing it into the streets below. We assumed there would be streets. Our chief regret was that we didn't have a source of fire which we could use to start a blaze on the roof itself, or at least generate some smoke. We had tried many times, and failed, to design a way to carry a flame with us that wouldn't be put out by the movement of climbing. But we doubted that things would ever come to such an extreme. Once we had drawn attention to ourselves and help was forthcoming I could return inside with the proper authorities and keep my promise to Petra.

Most of this was agreed as I was pacing around the room while Vasily sat at the table, scribbling. I'd assumed he was calculating values for stress or tension or whatever was needed for predicting how ropes and weights would behave, but when I sat down next to him and looked more closely I saw he was making sketches. On one page there were several beautifully drawn depictions of two men ascending a rope; another of a

man in a sling hanging beneath the window, looking up with
an expression of longing and aspiration on his face, as well as
details of knots and their cross-sections.

'I didn't know you could draw, I said.

'Nor did I,' he said.

'You're not making any calculations.'

'Why should I?'

'You always do. Did.'

'So what? I've seen the window now. We try and succeed, or
we try and fail. I don't need to make calculations.'

'What about our chances of success? Probabilities. A stork
might give birth to a donkey . . .'

'Don't be so stupid.'

'But on your scale of probability—' I began.

'Yes, yes,' he said dismissively. 'These were games – stupid
games. How could a stork give birth to a donkey? No power
can do the impossible. Unlikely things, yes, but that isn't the
same. Even God can't violate the laws of the Universe. And
even His knowledge must be limited to the potentialities of
existence.'

'Yet there are possibilities in our world that wouldn't exist in
a world of perfect causality,' I said, pleased to hear the ease with
which this kind of formulation now came to me.

'Of course,' he agreed. 'In a perfect world neither freedom
nor responsibility could have any meaning. Nothing we could
do would have any meaning beyond itself. The imperfection
is the only interesting part, from the point of view of understanding God's motives.'

'And in that imperfection lies our salvation,' I said, thinking
suddenly of Tevdore's interpretation of luck as the reward for a
good deed, travelling across time.

'Not necessarily. In it lie the *possibilities* of salvation,' he
corrected me. 'A possibility may present itself to a man every
day of his life and he may never see it. But why are we discuss-

ing this, anyway?' he asked irritably. 'What possible relevance can it have to our situation?'

I admit, at that moment, I longed for the old, easy-going Vasily to come back.

'Have a drink, Vasily,' I suggested.

'Take the filthy stuff away.' Then he relented. 'All right, a nightcap.'

I filled our glasses and raised mine.

'To the end of calculations,' I said. This struck home. We drank.

'You know,' said Vasily, 'whenever I was calculating anything, I *felt* the answer first. Then I would do the mathematics and it would all make more sense, officially, if you see what I mean. But all that calculating was just a disguise. The feeling always came first. I couldn't help it.'

☦

On the evening before we were due to leave I made a small pouch from a pillowcase in which to carry a few photographs and some other personal things that I felt I should rescue and which affirmed more than any others my sense of self. Going through my things, I noticed that my fountain pen, a gift from my mother for my eighteenth birthday, was snapped clean in half. I had no ink for it and had never used it during the period of my captivity, and wondered when it could have possibly been damaged. Then I realized someone must have done it deliberately. I tried to dismiss the significance of this small thing, but it struck me at the moment of discovery that this was nothing less than an omen of destruction and of severing and in essence the symbol of a useful thing rendered useless. What's more it was so deeply personal in its nature; try as I might to rid myself of what a part of me dismissed as mere superstition, I couldn't escape from the authenticity of the feeling. It lingered

stubbornly, as small things charged with meaning do. I had
learned, I think I've said, to trust this kind of feeling, much
more so than in ordinary life, because here things were more
connected than in the world I'd formerly known and been a
part of. Here the arrangement was inverted, and facts were less
important than the meanings by which they were joined. Was
this not because here each day was permeated by the wish to
escape, against which every significance was calculated and
every meaning weighed? In ordinary life there had been one of
me; now there were two, one of which stood apart, charged with
the exercise of these silent calibrations.

That night I dreamed a horrible dream, in which Petra figured, but in a cruelly distorted role, which I put down to my
own anxiety about the task ahead. I'd been looking for her to
share some news about our escape plans, and everything seemed
charged with the promise of freedom and new possibilities. But
she was nowhere to be found and I wandered the halls and
corridors of the building with a growing sense of doom until I
found her sitting in a corner alone, hunched over like a brooding
witch, dressed in a tangle of rags. As I went to her she rose up
like something coming out of a lake, scowling demonically and
holding up the two portions of the pen, shaking them at me and
taunting me with them as if to say: I told you so.

⊹

Petra was expecting us, or should have been, because a few
days earlier I'd told her we would come. But we were surprised
when she didn't answer her door, and anxious too, lest a passing
Mudak catch sight of our bundles. I knocked several times and
then went in carefully, followed by the others. There was a smell
of something burnt. The room looked empty at first until with
a shock I saw Petra sitting at the foot of her bed, crying. Yet
the shock was from seeing the posture in which she was sitting,

which resembled exactly the posture in which she had appeared in my dream. I went to her side and saw her reddened eyes and look of despair.

'Are you hurt?' I asked. I had no idea what had happened.

She shook her head, and I felt a surge of relief. Then she apologized repeatedly.

'I'm so sorry,' she sobbed. 'I couldn't stop them.' Then I heard Vasily's voice, firm and quiet, from the far side of the room.

'You need to see this.'

I walked over to the arch where he and Tevdore were standing, and looked up towards the chimney. Where the rope had once hung there was nothing. It now lay directly underneath, like a mutilated snake, hacked into a dozen pieces, each a few feet long. Around it was a scattering of ash. Looking into the chimney, I saw that the severed end had been unravelled into separate strands and then set alight, and the flames had travelled upwards almost to the beam where I'd tied the other end on my last return journey. It was impossible to reach, and impossible to repair. The sight had the strange, unreal quality of a nightmare, and for what seemed like a long time we just stood there not knowing what to do or say.

Then I turned to Tevdore.

'Did you speak to anyone about our plan?' I hated myself for asking, but was convinced at that moment that it must have been he who had given away our plans. 'Anyone at all?' He looked at me with a sad, solemn expression which, whether he himself was aware of it or not, drove home the wrongness of my question. His gaze turned first to Vasily and then Petra.

'Not was necessary,' he said, with an obscureness that infuriated me, because I had failed to understand his meaning.

'We'll speak later,' said Vasily, and putting a guiding hand gently on Tevdore's arm, went to the door. I watched as, on the point of opening it, he bent down to pick up what looked like a sweater belonging to Petra, which lay in a line on the floor. It

215

had been displaced when the door had opened. He hung it on the hook on the back of the door, and gave me a thoughtful look which I didn't yet understand. Then they left.

Petra had stood up and, looking much happier now, was arranging biscuits on a plate. She gave me a look of sympathy which was strangely inappropriate, as if I was a child and had stubbed my toe and it was my fault. I wanted to talk about what had happened, and to find out if possible how the Mudaks had uncovered our plan, but she seemed not to be thinking about either this or its consequences. I momentarily felt the same sense of panic, the same feeling of the surreal, that I had when I'd first left my room after my arrival and had seen the other residents for the first time.

'They're your favourite kind,' she said, holding out the plate of biscuits to me and smiling; and to this too there was a kind of confusion, as if she'd lost the measure of things. I chose a biscuit and bit into it, then noticed how intently she was looking at me, like someone waiting for a tranquillizer to take effect.

'Delicious,' I said, although my thoughts were elsewhere. I brushed the crumbs from my shirt as I swallowed, feeling the unexpected distance between us.

'Have another,' she said. 'I know you can't resist them.'

'Petra,' I began, wanting to tell her somehow that this wasn't the moment to discuss her biscuit-making talents, but she interrupted me.

'Why not have them all?'

I took another biscuit, but my heart wasn't in it. I bit into it automatically, feeling desperate, looking away from her, wondering how to explain to her what was going through my mind and how important it was. Then, more quietly now, she spoke again.

'*Pig.*'

This was so unexpected I wondered if I'd imagined it. I turned to her slowly. She was looking at me in a way I'd never seen before, her head lowered slightly as if in expectation or pain. Even stranger was the way she'd said the word, quietly but distinctly, menacingly, with all the deliberateness of a deadly malediction. I told myself that the word must have been said in jest, and that my mood was darkening things unnecessarily.

'How do you know they're my favourite?' I asked, grasping onto her words from a few moments earlier. Perhaps she was playing a joke of sorts.

'Because I've always made them for you,' she said, with the same strange deliberateness. 'You've always loved them.' Yet this was completely untrue.

'And because I love you,' she added.

It didn't sound much like love. Her tone was more like the commander of a *katyusha*° battery delivering his terms to a rebel village. Then her breathing grew unsteady, and a tremor of accusation began to appear in her voice, as if something within her was emerging against her own will, with a force impossible to resist.

'Don't you remember anything? Or were you just born ungrateful?'

This stopped me in my tracks. How could we go back from here? I wondered. Some pain that was unknown to me was surfacing almost visibly into her features, like a drum of poison long ago buried out at sea. Her face was twitching with barely controlled anger. I wondered, for the first time: who was she? But she spoke before any of these thoughts really made sense to me. Her voice was charged with even greater reproach, her jaw clenched.

° Informal name of a Soviet-made multiple rocket launcher sometimes called the Stalin Organ from its resemblance to a collection of organ pipes, known for its mobility and destructive power.

217

'You stuff your face and then pretend you have no idea?'

My beloved Petra was disappearing before my eyes, and it was difficult for me to bear.

'I don't think I'll have any more,' I said.

'There you go again. Typical. Expecting everyone else to bend over backwards for your special requirements.'

'I don't know what you mean,' I said. I could make no sense of what she was saying, or what I had done to provoke such hurtfulness.

'You don't know what I mean?' A bitter tone of mockery had entered her voice. 'You don't know what I mean. Oh *dear.*'

'I think you might be mixing me up with someone else.'

'Poor you!' She let out a snort of contempt. 'A case of mistaken identity? Do you see anyone else here? Did they put someone else in here instead of you?' She threw the plate aside onto the bed, and with the freed hand poked an accusing finger towards me as she drew nearer. 'That's what you wish had happened, isn't it? So that you could get off the hook and make someone else suffer for you – that's the story of your life, isn't it? Now that you're finally getting what you deserve you're not even man enough to bear it. You go around telling everyone your pathetic sob-story about mistaken identity. But you know what the truth is? You *have* no identity. You are nobody, *nothing*!'

My beloved Petra. My beautiful Petra.

'Did you break my pen?' I asked.

'How dare you?' She was speaking through her teeth. 'Sick! You're sick! How dare you come here with your fantasies and accuse me of anything? You of all people should know about fantasies – your ridiculous window, a figment, if ever there was, of your imagination.'

'You know perfectly well it exists.'

'It exists all right,' she said, 'in your imagination! In the dream world you live in. In the sickness you call your life. But nobody's interested in your life! Nobody cares about your fantasy world. How dare you accuse me of such a thing?'

'I didn't accuse you of anything.'

'You're sick! Sick! I would never do a thing like that!'

'A thing like what?'

'Your stupid rope that you play monkeys on with your fat friend! I couldn't care less about it.'

'Did you destroy it?' I hadn't meant to ask. In any case I was far from sure that she had anything to do with it; the implications were too horrible to think about.

'Why do you care? Is it so precious to you? Is it the only thing you care about? You think only of yourself, but you are nothing!' She spat the word, like venom. 'You are worthless. Don't stand there looking at me. I know you despise me.' I was against the wall now, having taken several steps backward as Petra had advanced, waving her finger at me.

'I don't despise you,' I said. 'I would like to understand.' And yet now I understood. I understood that everything I had imagined about my future with Petra was a distortion of my own creation. It was indeed my fate to know her; that much was true and I'd known it from the start, but it wasn't in the way I had allowed myself to imagine. I'd known she would change my life, but not in this way. Not like this.

'You'd like to understand, would you?' She threw her head back in bitter laughter. 'Liar!' she screamed. 'You don't fool me with your mind games. Do you really think I would fall for your little trap? *I'd like to understand.*' She leapt to the door and flung it open. 'You want to understand? This will help you to understand!'

At the top of her voice she screamed for help, as if she was being murdered. Turning back to me, she tore open her shirt, and dug her nails so deeply into her own breasts that dark red channels began to trail behind her fingertips. She dug into her flesh again and again, her face contorted with pain, until the blood began to ooze from beneath the broken skin and trickle downwards.

'Petra,' I begged her, 'don't do this.' I grabbed her wrists to stop her doing more damage. 'Why are you doing this?'

'You are the one,' she hissed. '*You* are the one who is doing it.' She looked down at her clenched hands, then clawed wildly at my face with them, delivering a vicious scratch to my cheek before I could grab her arms and push her backwards. I had no wish to hurt her, only to restrain her, but she fought me like a wild animal, kicking, scratching, screaming and spitting until she broke free and stumbled from the room. She fell against the wall of the corridor like a vandalized doll, pulling her dress upwards to expose her legs, which were soon smeared with blood. Her timing was perfect. A dozen Mudaks were running up at that very moment and took in the sight of her, and of me standing in the doorway, scratched and dishevelled.

'Look,' she cried in a pathetic voice, as if exhausted by the effort of resistance, 'look what he's done to me.'

'Petra,' I pleaded, but it was all too late now. Within a few seconds they had me in their grip. As my arms were being wrenched behind my back, and my head yanked sideways, my eyes unexpectedly met hers and I could see her look of worry, and her teeth biting into her lower lip. But by the time I was presented to her, in the manner of a trophy animal to a big-game hunter, immobile and ready for skinning, it had hardened into an expression of vengeful scorn. She lifted my head by the hair, savouring my helplessness, and brought her face so close to mine that I could feel her breath as she spoke.

'You have brought this on yourself. You *disgust* me.'

Then she turned and slammed the door, and those *kos*-brained* Mudaks dragged me dutifully from the room, ramming

---

* Offensive Persian slang for the female organ.

my head against the doorframe for good measure. A strange pattern of coloured lights and streamers tumbled into my vision. I remember thinking before I passed out that they resembled a family of butterflies, trapped behind a window on a summer afternoon.

Chapter 12

THERE CAN BE NO REASON to fear death, except insofar as you haven't lived. Why is the ordinary man so ill-prepared and so fearful of the one thing that is actually certain about life: the end of it? I did wonder, as once again I lay helplessly in the darkness awaiting punishment, whether I might give myself up to death voluntarily, rather than suffer the pain of torture again; a pain that wasn't merely physical, but a violation of all that I could call myself. I felt remorse that I had never given death, the most certain and inevitable thing, more thought.

Until yesterday – I mean until I had been stuck in this place – my mind had been directed to the crucial issue of success or failure in catching the eye of an attractive woman as she passed me in the street; if one such woman, particularly one who was slim and strong-boned, smiled at me, however fleetingly, my sense of purpose was fulfilled. This, if you were to judge me by my actions rather than my intentions, is what I'd really lived for. I'd had no reason not to accept this folly as normal.

Perhaps Tevdore was right: nothing of my life was really mine. I hadn't created or demanded my own life. My body wasn't really mine: I could no more prevent the appearance of white hairs, or the stiffening of my joints, than I could reverse the orbit of the rings of Saturn. So what was the fuss about giving back something which was neither mine nor could be preserved longer than a few earthly seasons?

Perhaps death would be a huge relief, if it freed me from myself. What lies behind the obstinate veil of extinction? I knew I wasn't the first to ask the question, but you never pay attention to what other people have said until you have to think them through for yourself. It seemed unlikely that the result of death was simply nothing. That nothing must in any case be something, if only because it is not this life. Now I was starting to sound like Vasily, and cursed myself, wondering nevertheless for a moment how he'd rate my reasoning.

If what lay beyond death was really nothing, it could have no more meaning than the flick of a switch, and all the consequences of how a man lives – the fruits in one's soul of a lifetime of endeavours and choices – would be reduced to the same level: nothing. Yet people have seen enough of death to know that there are many ways in which a man actually dies, as if he is given a foretaste, when it's already too late, of what's in store. Some deaths are full of anguish and horror and dread, others painless and serene, and convey a sense of completion and content.

I sensed, during those long moments, that death is not the opposite of life at all, but its invisible extension, like a path leading into the mist on a hillside. Death was akin to love: timeless. Like a certain music that enters your soul and from that moment can always be heard, love also slips through the mortal fabric that binds us to time and allows moments – they are not really moments at all – which carry with them knowledge that is beyond time's reach. Both love and death slice into lives as if from an enclosing invisibility, though in their own right, I reasoned, they cannot be so fleeting and occasional. An assassin's blade, striking from the darkness, seems to suddenly appear and disappear when witnessed from the lighted street. But this is only the view of the innocent bystander, who knows nothing of existence in the shadows, and cannot enter them at will. Yet the assassin, returning to the fold of obscurity, has a busy and purposeful life of his own.

Which part of me was robust enough to survive, and which part destined for extinction? And if such a distinction was real and true, where did the difference lie? And where, in all this, was the thing that I could rightfully call 'myself'? It seemed to me ridiculous that the same 'I' concerned with all the trials of ordinary life – the money I was owed, the cut of my shirt, the taste of Abkhasian pickles – was the same 'I' that would survey the horizon of the Beyond, and frolic with angels or soft-limbed *houris*.

As abstract as all this was, it helped me later.

The ape-dog, or dog-ape, loomed up not long afterwards, and in the darkness I shivered from fear. There was no sign of his merry helpers; just a single young accomplice this time, who looked like a slimmer version of his master, dutiful and straight-backed and silent and sinister. They stood aside me and looked me up and down, like butchers calculating the choicest cut; and then I saw the upturned claw once more, and its dread descent. My body shook; I felt the terrible violation as he opened my chest, reaching into every nerve and striking an equal note in my feelings. And then, like a high priest at his favourite ritual, he carefully lifted in his hands a sort of net from right inside my abdomen, and held it up as if to share the discovery with both me and his apprentice. I thought I would die. I could hardly breathe, much less speak. I really thought I would die. I looked at the thing in his hands; it resembled a map of stars, of different colours and magnitudes, each linked to the other by a web of glowing filaments, vibrant and alive and fragile and indescribably beautiful. Then after studying them in the manner of a child with a fairground goldfish in a plastic bag, he lowered the glowing constellations back into me, and I felt as though I'd come up for air after someone had been trying to drown me.

I glimpsed him nodding silently, as if he'd just been testing my reflexes and found them normal. His apprentice cocked his head, studying his master's actions; they seemed to be in a kind of telepathic contact, and nodded almost imperceptibly to one another. Then, hesitantly, the younger creature stretched out a hand, and with a cupping motion pulled one of the miniature stars from my abdomen and held it up as if to weigh it. I was suddenly gripped by a bestial feeling of degradation, as if I'd committed a horrible crime against my own conscience. I felt sick and loathed myself; at that moment I would have accepted death as a relief. Then at the edge of my vision I saw the light being lowered like a setting sun back into my body, and the awful feeling was gone.

I'd hardly got my breath back when a new light rose up at the edge of my vision, and with it a new feeling, suddenly different, and utterly misplaced in that subterranean spa for demons; a tender longing, such as you feel in front of a thing of beauty and mystery, and the last kind of feeling I might have expected. I rested on it, as if on the wings of an angel. How could such contradictory feelings exist in me, and turn from one to the next so swiftly and with such intensity? I knew this was the manipulation of the jackal apprentice, and I hated him for it, and for his interference in what was uniquely my own. Then the question came to me: if these feelings are my own, then where was 'I' in all this turmoil? Was not 'I' at the mercy of them, or could I choose otherwise?

'I am not these feelings,' I said to myself. 'I will not give myself to them.' Then another voice rose up, challengingly.

'Where is this "I" that you talk about?' it asked.

'I am here. I am eternal,' said a voice. It was like listening in on the two sides of a telephone conversation. It just came out of me. And as soon as I heard these words within myself the pain grew less, or at least became easier to bear. It was then I understood that words have meanings beyond themselves, and I clung

225

to them like the survivor of a shipwreck. *I am here.* As unremarkable as they sound, these few words meant something real to me.
Here was a different 'I'. Not the 'I' of ordinary life, that word
a man ascribes so readily to his every whim and mood. I mean
the deepest thing a man can find within himself to verify that he
is really alive; perhaps it used to be called the presence of God.
Perhaps it is as simple as that. I was shocked at the implications
of this possibility.

At that very moment, equally strangely, Jackal-brain let out
a grunt of interest, as if he'd noticed the change. 'Down here,' he
whispered enigmatically, 'you do learn faster.'

What did he mean? Could he read my thoughts? I felt helpless and angry.

'Keep trying,' he said. 'You were doing so well.' Then he
actually giggled to himself.

The young one took several of the coloured stars out of me
in turn, and at each I felt a new wrenching, which I struggled
to manage by invoking those few short words, longing for their
full meaning to enter me; sometimes submitting to the grip of
pain, and sometimes returning to that other self which was able
to bear it, like a man trying to balance as he crosses a tightrope,
until the waves of pain one by one subsided. Then I could make
out a reddish glow reflecting from my torturer's features as he
dug into me again, this time more deeply, causing a pain too
deep to resist, and I felt my will collapse and wanted once again
to die.

'Careful,' I heard a solemn voice above me. 'That's his sense
of suffering. The thing that is closest to his self.' Then the long
snout came alongside me in the darkness, and I felt its warmth.
'The thing,' he whispered, 'that he cannot give up.'

'Dog-breath sadist,' I said, with my last strength. I heard him
chuckle again, and then heard a rushing sound like a waterfall,
getting steadily louder.

All I remember after that is a strange dream. I was flying –

just flying, without any help – high above the clouds in bright sunshine. I was as happy as I had ever been; that same kind of happiness where you hardly know who you are. Between a tiny gap in the clouds I could make out, on the ground far below me, the explosion of an atom bomb, rising into the air. I was so far away it seemed insignificant, and I kept flying without giving it a second thought. But the smoke from the explosion went so far up into the sky that it eventually reached the clouds, and spread so far in every direction that I couldn't escape it. It penetrated the whiteness of the clouds, and turned them grey with radioactive dust, which entered my lungs. I knew death had entered me and that it was irreversible. I flew down and landed near some fisherman's huts by the sea, surprising Petra, who I wanted to tell more than anyone else about what had happened. She was by the water's edge, flirting openly with a man I'd never met, and pretended not to know me.

Then nothing more.

✢

Vasily and Tevdore had found me wherever the Mudaks had dumped me; I'm not sure where. When I came to my senses, Tevdore was fussing over me tenderly like a nurse, to which he would never bear the slightest resemblance. I felt huge remorse for having suspected him of betraying our escape plans. For some reason I couldn't speak for a while and when I tried, I started to cry instead. I felt as raw as a freshly skinned karakul lamb.° And when, eventually, I was able to utter a croak

---

* From which the tight knots of highly prized fleeces (sometimes called Astrakhan) are produced in the Caucasus, Iran and Afghanistan.

of apology to Tevdore, he smiled at me as if I was a baby, and said:

'Is more difficult for the one who did borrow than for one who did lend.'

My chest ached at every breath, but there was no trace of a scar. I had come to accept this mystery. The only physical side effect was that from time to time I realized I had stopped breathing, then found myself gasping suddenly for air. I would fill up my lungs and let the air subside slowly with a feeling of enormous relief.

I hadn't eaten much, and the others insisted I go downstairs for a hot meal. I wasn't feeling at my most sociable, but hunger was making me weak, so they helped me to the stairs, which I went down clinging on to Tevdore's giant arm for support. An elderly man I hadn't seen before, brilliantly imitating the walk and cry of a peacock, passed me in the opposite direction.

Heading for the dining room, I noticed a group of familiar faces, sitting in a circle on the carpet some distance away. At their centre stood the miniature tyrant, king Otto, delivering some sort of speech, and I realized they must be having one of their storytelling sessions. My eye lingered, and caught the little man's attention, and he broke off and strode towards me, stopped at a safe distance and, in his imperious way, pointed his sceptre accusingly at me.

'You!' he commanded, in his squeaky voice. 'You tell us a story!'

I disliked his troublemaking and provocation.

'You know where I'd like to put that sceptre?'* I said.

His reply was typically theatrical and disarmed me. He gave a clownish look of astonishment, then an equally absurd look of supplication came over his features.

---

* The original expression is untranslatable.

'Please? *Please*. We've run out of stories. Indulge us.' He bowed deeply and with exaggerated solemnity, surreptitiously glancing backwards towards his little band of followers, and then to me. '*Everyone* has a story inside himself.'

I had thought I hated him and the pitiful circle over which he held sway, but looking beyond him to the others and seeing the expressions of earnest anticipation on their faces I realized I didn't hate them at all. I was simply no longer persuaded by any of them, no longer either impressed or afraid. They were nothing more or less than themselves. I couldn't know if at some point in their lives they had experienced the wish to be anything else, to overcome their peculiar afflictions and pursue the possibility of going beyond themselves. Would they be here if they had? I was tired of judging them; perhaps they wouldn't all be here for ever.

'All right,' I said. 'I'll tell you a story.'

Otto ran back to the circle and passed on the news like an excited child. The others were looking up at me as I walked over and sat in their midst, helped by Tevdore. For a few moments there was silence, as I looked at them in turn. There were some faces I didn't recognize, one or two of them look-ing at me with intense curiosity and others with vegetable-like blankness, but lots of other faces that I did: Mr Chicken Bone was there, sitting next to his inseparable companion; the mad doctor, looking confused or disapproving, I couldn't tell which; that lecherous priest, wearing his trademark panama hat; the old lady whose face had been smashed in by the Mudaks, now calmly knitting and humming tunelessly to herself; the man who enjoyed banging his head against windows and who now, every few moments, threw his head with full force against the floor with no apparent ill-effects; the woman with the frozen smile, still obviously in great pain; Otto himself, who circled preda-torily at the periphery of the gathering; Fidel, chewing gum and looking bored; and the woman I'd seen once before who looked

229

as though her attention was following a restless insect around the room.

'You are what you are. I am what I am. You move within me, and I move within you,' I said.

Strange words, I know. I didn't really think of them. But there is a kind of knowing you sometimes arrive at without thinking, as if effortlessly glimpsing what is already there. The machinery of thinking, ordinarily so cumbersome and slow by comparison, is not involved.

'Is that the story?' asked somebody. 'It was a bit short.' There were some murmurs of disappointment, which Otto silenced with a threatening wave of his sceptre.

'It so happens,' I began, 'that my grandfather loved the sea, and as children we would listen to the tales of his adventures. We lived far from its shores and had never seen it with our own eyes, but his stories – stories of pirates, of the torture of thirst, of the joys of discovery and of treasures beyond reckoning – all these nourished our imaginations and dreams from our earliest days.' There was some more muttering, and my new audience seemed to settle down.

'In his study, where as children we were allowed only when it was time for one of his stories, were some of the relics of his voyages: a conch shell big enough to sit in, the vertebra of a whale and a captain's sword with a scabbard of moth-eaten red velvet.'

'What kind of sword?' interrupted the doctor. 'Given the maritime connotation a cutlass seems more likely.'

'A very sharp one,' I told him, 'rumoured to have sliced off a man's tongue, and another man's ear.' The doctor frowned; Otto grimaced and rubbed his ear cautiously.

'When I was old enough I decided to follow in his footsteps, and go to sea, on a journey that fitted the design of my adventure. I travelled through the coastal towns of Bandar, Firuzabad, Dasht-i Jang and as far as Makran, hoping to find a ship that would take me on a voyage of a lifetime. Truth is I couldn't say what I was looking for, though I felt I'd know it when I met it.

'I met plenty of people along the way who knew the sea and shared their stories with me; fishermen, traders, some smugglers even. But none satisfied my longing. I moved on at each turn, dissatisfied. Then one day, when I was as hungry as my feet were tired from walking, in a tea-house in the port of Saravan I met a young man, perhaps a few years older than me, who seemed sympathetic to my wishes. We smoked a *qaylan*° together and he began to ask me more about what I was searching for. I told him I couldn't say for sure; and much to my surprise he replied that this was for the better. He suggested that what I was seek-ing was wisdom, and that wisdom could not be sought with the mind but the heart, whose language was too subtle for the mind. He was entirely free of the piousness of others I had met, and his ready smile won my confidence. He was kindly and spoke with a conviction that persuaded me I should put my trust in him.

'We talked for a long time. I liked him and felt I had met a man as close to me in spirit as any of my brothers. At the end he gave me the news sweeter than I could have hoped for; that he in fact belonged to a group of like-minded men who called themselves the *haqjuyaan*, whose mission, quite simply, was to seek out men whose souls had been touched by Truth and who lived according to what they knew. Within a few days they were planning to set sail from that very port. He was happy to invite me to join them. In the culture of my home the question was not whether there was such a thing as wisdom or truth, or whether men who possessed it really existed, but rather how deeply one was prepared to search.

'Our ship was a beautiful two-masted cutter, nearly a hun-dred years old and lovingly maintained, I heard, by its former

---

° A water-pipe, in which tobacco is smoked (Persian).

owners. For two years, the members of the group had saved together to buy it from a wealthy coastal chieftain whose sailing days were over. Several of the men were experienced sailors; our captain had been elected on account of his knowledge of the tides and currents and stars.

'Our voyage was to take us through the Gulf of Oman into the Arabian Sea. At Suqutra we would head northwest or south towards Madagascar; it would depend on our discoveries. We were proud to be making it the traditional way, with nothing but an antique sextant to help us navigate. We left Saravan on a day of blazing sunshine, in high spirits and full of hope, until —'

'Until a whale swallowed the boat!' a voice blurted out from the audience. I didn't know whose it was. There was a ripple of giggles, which Otto silenced with a fierce stamp of his sceptre.

'Worse,' I said, sounding as serious as I could, and wondering how to continue. 'Much worse. We went from one disaster to another, as if our journey was cursed from the start. Our ship hadn't been looked after at all. It wasn't fit to sail. It leaked persistently, the sails were half-rotten and in a gentle breeze they tore like paper. Cleats tore from their housings of worm-eaten wood. Bailing water from beneath deck in the stifling heat gave us sores and made us as sick as dogs. We hugged the coastline and at every port were forced to stop and make repairs. In Yemen the ship's cook was stabbed in the arm by smugglers and stayed behind; at short notice we had to find a replacement cook, who shared nothing of our hopes or sense of purpose. At Habardana, an unscrupulous trader sold us salted pork instead of dried fruit and dates; a discovery we made only once our ordinary supplies had been exhausted, a week's sailing from land.

'A month went by. We were as far from shore as any of us had ever travelled. Disaster struck repeatedly. During a storm one of our crew was struck by lightning, and turned to ash in front of our eyes. Another man, hauling a net over the ship's side, was attacked by a giant squid. As hard as we tried we couldn't free him from the monster, and watched him disappear into the creature's throat.

'Even worse was to come. One of the men, sunstruck and delirious, attacked the captain as he stood on deck plotting our course, and in the confusion our precious sextant was knocked overboard. Then the wind dropped to a dead calm, and we drifted hopelessly by day; by night the stars were hidden by a stubborn layer of cloud, and all the while the sails hung as limp as corpses. No trace of land softened the shimmering blade of the horizon. Tortured by thirst, crawling from our bunks only at night, all hope was sucked from our bodies and minds. Gradually even our voices failed us. Soon some of the men began to hear voices and see lights. We were dying.

'It was just then that nature played a cruel trick, and placed the sight of an island in the unreachable distance. For three days I watched the apparition, knowing that even if we abandoned the ship we were already too weak to reach it. Nothing was left to us but to pray for our deliverance. I watched the island as a condemned man looks from the window of his cell towards a gallows. On the second day I suspected that the island was growing nearer; on the third I was convinced of it. But my senses were failing at an equal rate. I remember hardly anything else. Just the echo of a prayer, and strange patches of dark obscuring the light, growing in size and intensity, until they joined up and the world fell into a devouring shadow.

'And when we awoke it was in a kind of paradise. Our rescue had been nothing short of miraculous; we had drifted (we at first believed) not only directly towards the island but into a shallow bay from where, seeing our helpless ship, the natives of the island had rowed out towards us. One by one they had carried us ashore and nursed us patiently to health in their camp.

'Like men whose sight had been taken from them and returned, we were full of wonder and disbelief at our new surroundings. Our home was an encampment of simple huts in a grove of stately palm trees. It sheltered in a bay of exceptional beauty, with a smooth sloping beach of fine sand enclosed by high cliffs of a rock resembling jade which, when struck by the sun, seemed to be lit from within by a greenish fire. The hills beyond them were green and more fertile than any of us had ever seen.

'Our rescuers spoke an archaic dialect of our own language which was at first hard for us to understand. But as each day passed it mattered less. We found our need for conversation bridged by a language finer than words alone, enriched even, by the very poverty of our speech. Gesture and glance found a new measure and our own language, we came to realize, was in some sense a burden to us. The men we were among looked into us and knew us better than we knew ourselves, and cared for us with a tenderness which softened even the most cynical of our crew. From the day we arrived they cooked for us, cleaned our quarters, made new clothes for us to replace our rags, helped the weaker among us to walk and tended to us with a care which many of us had not known since childhood, and some had never known at all.

'The days were gloriously bright and the moist warm air, kind to our bodies and nerves, soothed and healed our aches and wounds. Those first days passed slowly, filled as they were with new and unfamiliar feelings. We were not yet equipped to ponder the mystery of our deliverance and, free to explore our surroundings, wandered the sandy paths that wound through the trees and hills above us. I took to climbing a narrow trail which led above the bay and sitting alone on a high crag, watching the surf plunge against the cliffs and feeling the power of the waves, wondering if I'd ever see my home again; or whether I wished to.

'It seemed to most of the men that by luck alone we had stumbled onto a community of good-natured slaves. But it turned out that they were far more than that. I myself dared not hope that these were the very men I had been looking for in my dreams; but my reluctance gave way to the realization that it must be true.

'We spent the evenings around a fire in the camp, exchanging tales of our first experiences of our enigmatic hosts. One of the men confessed that, noticing a string of pearls around the neck of one of the islanders, he longed to possess it. The next day he ambushed its owner on the path near the camp, knife drawn, ready to despatch his victim. But the other greeted him with a smile that sapped him of all aggression, took off his necklace and put it gently around the neck of his attacker. Then he found himself being led to a hut where he was shown trunkfuls of pearls, of which his would-be victim urged him to take as many as he could carry.

'Another had been standing on a rock by the shore and watched the native fishermen swimming fearlessly among sharks, instructing them as if they were as tame as pets. Then the sharks swam out beyond the surf and circled back, herding shoals of fish into the men's nets. And another told of how he had entered one of the islander's huts unseen. His eye fell on a stone on a table: it was an uncut diamond. Unable to resist, he picked it up and hid it. As he tried to slip away, the islander greeted him warmly, and stretched out his hand to offer him an even larger diamond. Somewhere on the island, he was told, was a ravine whose floor was spread with diamonds of every size. But its walls were sheer and unscalable, and its floor infested by deadly snakes as large as men. Outsiders had tried to penetrate the ravine; not a soul had ever returned. But the islanders devised a scheme to gather the diamonds themselves, by throwing large slabs of meat into the ravine and training young eagles to hunt for them. The diamonds would stick to the meat, and the birds returned to their masters with them, rewarded with the meat after the diamonds had been removed. Over the years they had gathered roomfuls of the glassy treasures.

'It was as if they could read our minds; as if they knew us better than we knew ourselves, and accepted us as we were. The burden of pretence and intrigue we had carried with us from our ordinary lives was lifted, and in their presence it became impossible to lie or dissemble; our lies, which in life passed unnoticed, had become transparent. Our various traits of self-importance, our petty vanities, our private wishes to be recognized for some or other talent; all these things appeared here as pretences. We were happy to shake them off as quickly as possible. Those who resisted this strange process were disarmed of their weapons before combat had even begun.

'We, said the islanders, were their gift. But our gift to ourselves was to make ourselves whole, a thing which was our very birthright. And slowly it seemed as though their wish for us was coming true, as each man's restlessness and craving began to soften, giving way to moments of irresistible peace.

'Among the islanders moved their chief, a man of immense and benevolent radiance, but whose authority was gentle. His gaze transmitted devastating compassion. His practice was to encourage us to speak of our wishes and our fears, and to share with him the questions which came into our minds. We learned much of one another on those firelit evenings, seated in a broad circle beneath the whispering palm trees above the shoreline, and saw ourselves willingly unmasked in turn.

'At first, the men's willingness to speak so intimately of their lives shocked and surprised those of us who believed we were good judges of character. Many of them confessed that, after all, they had wishes which they felt their lives had denied them. One hungered, despite his habitual outward neediness and frequent reminders to others of the virtues of poverty, for the feel of gold between his fingers. Another, who preached vociferously on the virtues of celibacy, confided a longing for the intimacy of women. One by one their wishes were granted. But perhaps more extraordinary than this was our pleasure in seeing our friends at peace with their own longings and free of the need to disguise them.

'The hardest of our men was the ship's cook, who was convinced that the entire island was out to trick us. In life he was a sullen man who had nothing good to say of anyone. Even in rare moments when he wished another man well, it was in the form of a curse. He had rejected the islanders' kindnesses from the start, and in every of their selfless acts he saw a plot and a deception, accusing the other men of having been seduced by their cunning. We heard him out, but as each day passed his ranting grew more alien to us.

'One evening, the chief was sitting among us in the camp listening to our stories.

'"Why does cook hate you?" I asked him.

'"Cook hates cook," he said gently. "Wait for cook."

'Then one morning – it was perhaps a month after our arrival – one of the men came running into the camp.

'"Look," he pointed, "cook has come around." And by the water's edge we saw cook sobbing at the feet of the chief, his hands clawing at the sand and begging for the chief's forgiveness. It was a painful sight, but there was a joy to it. In cook we recognized a portion of our own hard-heartedness, and a portion of our own release from ourselves. Now we had all experienced the taste of freedom, and found it more precious than any other thing.

'As time passed the islanders confided in us in turn. We learned that their own lives were not without sadness or difficulty. There was sickness and loss among them too, and they suffered the uncertainties and harshness of the natural world.

'Our love for them only grew, knowing how patient they had been with us, and how forgiving. The chief taught us the same

237

was true of ourselves: that our own salvation lay in difficulty. Not in difficulties themselves, but in the manner in which we overcame them, and that our own troubles in life were not the burdens we imagined them to be. Each was a visitor to be greeted and answered according to the nature of its call, lest it be sent away unsatisfied and return at some unexpected moment. Our habitual worries were suspended. No longing for past or future weighed on our thoughts. Time had lost its ordinary measure.'

I paused, and looked at the faces around me.

'Is that the end of the story?' asked the same voice as before.

'It is the end and the beginning,' I said, I don't know why.

Otto stamped his foot to silence a further dissent.

'I had fallen in love with a daughter of the chief. She was beautiful and kind. I had no reason to suppose that I would not stay with her for ever. One day at the height of my happiness I confided this hope in the chief himself. He was sympathetic, but with a grave smile explained that it was not the direction in which my future lay. This was not the answer I had hoped for. My challenge, he said, lay not on the island itself, but in the task of recounting our discoveries after we had returned. It was then I understood that our stay there was limited and would have an end, and I would have to say goodbye to all that I had come to love. The revelation was more than I could bear. I wept and wept.

'"Fear not," said the old man, gently.

'"Why then these tears?" I asked him.

'"Every soul longs to be whole, but the burden of your world is a heavy one," he said gently. "Now that you have tasted from the tree of freedom, you must carry the seed of it within you."

'We did not feel the hand of time on us until we awoke one morning with a horrible sense of foreboding. Without any warning the sky had turned grey as though the very sun had been eclipsed. A wind, the first we had felt since our arrival, was blowing through the camp, making the doors and shutters bang restlessly with a violence that we seemed to feel in our bones. The men wandered through the camp as if in a daze, and none of the islanders was to be seen. All through the day the wind rose, and the trees began to sway wildly as if in a dance of grief.

'In the afternoon we felt the first drops of rain. The chief appeared out of nowhere with a look that filled us with dread. The wind blew the rain across his face and raindrops streamed from his eyebrows. A few of us ran to him to ask him the meaning of what was happening, but he spoke before us.

'"These are the winds that will take you to your homes. Your ship must leave in the morning before the storm arrives, or be destroyed."

'No news could have been more crushing than this. In that moment we knew that the price of our enchantment was the pain of our departure and separation. The men all gathered to decide what must happen: we longed to stay, but we would have to leave or be stranded for ever. Each man spent that last night according to his wishes. Then, in the morning, the islanders came to embrace us in turn. The women brought trays of jewels, and let each man take his chosen portion; one by one they scooped up a handful of jewels and pocketed them. I looked at the rough and gleaming stones, and thought of wealth beyond my dreams. Yet no worldly sum could duplicate the experience of the place; so I chose a single disc of red carnelian, the least of gems.

'Then as the clouds grew almost black, the islanders rowed us to our ship, with instructions for avoiding the direction of the storm. So we sailed, narrowly avoiding the full force of the advancing tempest, which surely would have destroyed us had we not fought hard to circle it. We were glad for the action, which occupied our minds and bodies and pushed our sadness aside. Then we seemed to fall beyond the storm's reach, and the days grew calm and hot, and through the shimmering haze no

239

trace remained of the island we had left behind, as if it had been no more than a mirage.

'One day in that purgatorial heat we saw a solitary gull overhead. It circled the ship three times, and we knew that land was not far off. And when we saw it, the sky seemed so low it might crush us. Even our bodies seemed to feel heavier at the sight. There was a shout: somebody's jewels had disappeared. Then we realized they had merely changed their form. One by one the men reached into their clothes and bags and found the jewels they had taken had turned to coloured petals. No one knew when the transformation had occurred. We gathered at the stern, and one by one we scattered them into the air, watching them fall into the braid of ripples that stretched behind us.

'Suddenly, I remembered the single stone I had myself chosen. I felt in my pocket, and found it there. It had survived. And to this day it reminds me of the place where the lives of men were whole.'

I paused.

'I have it here.'

From my pocket I pulled the moonstone that Petra had given me, and held it up. It wasn't carnelian, but they weren't to know. There were some gasps and murmurs, and one or two growls of scepticism. I looked at their faces. The expressions on some of them were unchanged; others looked confused or fixed in mute surprise. All of a sudden I felt stupid, as though I had needlessly exposed myself to them, and stood up shakily. Tevdore steadied me on my feet. Then Otto jumped up, banged his sceptre on the floor and pointed it at me.

'Lies, all lies! Most excellent lies!' He began to clap, followed by the others who, pleased to accept this verdict, began to exchange satisfied nods of approval.

✝

Later on, after I'd eaten and gone back to my room, wondering to myself where the story I'd just told had come from in me, Vasily appeared with a full bottle of vodka.

'Your island people were not telling you the whole truth,' he said with a kindly look of knowing.

'No?'

'All primitive indigenous peoples have found a way to manufacture alcohol.' He held up the bottle. 'It was a deception of theirs to conceal this vital fact from you.'

He made a toast to my full recovery, and to the wisdom of the chief of my invented islanders. I made a toast to the chief's daughter.

'I've always liked the idea of island girls,' said Vasily, dreamily. 'The flowers in their hair. Those coconut shells on their chests . . .'

'Their dark eyes . . .'

'Smooth skin . . .'

'And those grass skirts . . .'

'I wonder,' he mused, refilling our glasses, 'what advice that chief of yours would have given us in here,' he said.

'I've wondered that myself,' I told him. 'To sail back to our homes, perhaps.'

'To build an ark!'

'With thunder and lightning to cause a diversion.'

'And a great flood to sweep our ark away . . .'

For a moment I pictured the building as a giant boat, floating along with all its inhabitants splashing madly around the rooms. Then a thought came to me.

'What about causing a flood ourselves?'

For a few moments Vasily didn't say anything. He just looked at me. Then the words, which seemed to have been hovering in the air around us, suddenly reached into us both at the same time. It was as if the idea had struck us both at the same instant.

'The pipes in the basement that you saw,' I said. 'Imagine we could—'

'—Yes, yes, yes. Open them. Force everyone out, like rats.' Vasily thought for a few moments, then shook his head.

'The water would drain away. We'd have to seal all the doors in this part of the building,' he said. And then we once again had the strange experiencing of having the same thought at the same time, and remembered that the doors were automatically sealed whenever the doctors visited.

'They'd be forced to let us all out,' I said.

'Or escape themselves, and leave us behind, more like. There're no short-cuts here. No – I've got a better idea,' he said, like a hunter picking up a new trail. 'What if we could fill this part of the building with water, and float up to the top floor on it.' His hands mimed a rising platform of water. 'A hydraulic ladder.'

'That's mad,' I said.

'Appropriate,' replied Vasily, 'for a madhouse.'

It sounded so far-fetched at first, but cheap meat never makes good soup, and as we talked about it the idea grew on us, even if there were just a few too many factors that had to come together at the same time to make it feasible.

'We'd have to find the pipes again.'

'In that damned basement.'

'And there would have to be enough water in them to fill a house.'

'And at sufficient pressure to maintain positive flow under hydrostatic resistance.'

'No doubt. We'd have to break them open first.'

'And the house would have to be watertight.'

'And we'd have to not drown in the process—'

'—Electrocution seems more probable—'

'—Or mind about other people drowning.'

If all these could be achieved, we agreed, there was no reason it wouldn't all turn out as smoothly as the skin on my great-aunt's famous homemade goat's milk yoghurt.

☩

Since the whole plan would depend on whether the pipes contained water and could be broken open, we needed to be quite sure they really did exist. So one night we went back together to the basement, sneaking first into the kitchen and then to the dumb waiter entrance, reminded at every turn of our first adventures there, which seemed to have taken place such a long time ago.

We were both intensely curious about what we'd find this time, because we both knew first-hand what a strange place the basement was, and we were far from certain as to whether it would be possible to duplicate Vasily's earlier experience. We took our improvised oil lamps, and clambered in, having decided not to use maps on the grounds that they hadn't been much use to us the last time, and had somehow slowed down our discoveries.

We had agreed also to make the effort to meditate – this isn't quite the right word, I know – on our common wish to find the pipes, on the grounds that if the house really did listen to our wishes, it would respond accordingly. A superstition like this seems absurd in ordinary life but when you have no other hope, it takes on an entirely different significance. It becomes the most real thing rather than the least, even if it does go against everything you've grown up to believe.

For what seemed like a long time, we stumbled through the dimness, our eyes fixed on the flickering brim of light at the limit of our lamps' reach. I began to think, for no apparent reason, about an elderly friend of my parents who had visited our home when I was a small child. He was probably long gone, but I kept seeing him in his characteristic posture, upright and obviously once very dashing, a pipe clenched in his jaw, an elbow tucked against his chest, his head in a haze of fragrant smoke. It seemed I could smell it now: pipe smoke. I tried to banish the image, in case the house was getting the idea of pipes mixed up, and we walked on, hearing the sounds from time to time of strange and unexpected things; a distant foghorn, the deep cry of a rutting stag in a forest, a dirge played on a Gypsy violin. And then, when it was the last thing we were expecting, we seemed to almost stumble upon them; huge brooding shapes, much larger than Vasily remembered, and much too large for a single house. We guessed that, like the pipes that run like capillaries through nearly the whole of Russia, pouring out heat, these were designed to serve a whole neighbourhood. We put our hands on them, then our ears, and heard the muted rushing of water within. But they were frighteningly solid, and probably made of steel half an inch thick. Vasily scribbled down some measurements, and made me tap the pipe some distance away while he listened, and I could tell he was thinking hard.

After we had made it safely back, and caught up on our sleep, Vasily engaged in one of his marathon calculating sessions, which lasted most of the next day. At the end of it, we sat down together and he shared his discoveries. There was good news, he said, and bad news. The good news was that although we couldn't exactly know the rate of flow of the water in the pipes, even a low rate would provide an enormous amount of water. It might even be the case, he added, that the same law of uncertainty governing the exact whereabouts of the pipes in the basement might also apply to the rate of flow of the water; in other words, since the pipes were there, the flow of water in them would probably be sufficient. The probability of there being enough water, he had calculated, was enough to justify the effort of the attempt. Assuming that the doors in the basement also sealed automatically as they did on the upper floors for the duration of the doctors' visit, the basement and ground floor would fill with water in a relatively short time – about five hours, by Vasily's reckoning.

I pointed out that there was a problem with doors. No door creates a perfect seal, and each door would multiply the volume of water that could leak out. It would take a tidal wave to fill the whole house quickly enough.

Vasily gave me a look of reassurance.

'In a normal world, yes,' he said. 'But certain things are impossible when the doctors are here, as we know. It's one of the reasons you couldn't get out the first time you tried.'

'Why? Why couldn't I get out?'

'Because when the doors are closed, what is beyond them *no longer exists*.'

He had also calculated the magnitude of force necessary to penetrate the steel, and – this was the bad news – unless one of us happened to find an oxyacetylene cutting torch, it would be impossible to break open the pipe.

We really had to rack our brains over this one, although in the end the answer was simple enough. There were only a certain number of ways to break open a huge metal pipe, and since we didn't have explosives or acids or drills or flames in excess of the melting point of steel, we were left with the brute-force method: smashing it open with something big and heavy. Vasily had drawn some sketches of medieval-looking devices involving wheels and pulleys and levers and a series of metal teeth which he'd calculated would eventually shatter the pipe, but they were all incredibly far-fetched and would take years to construct in secret. I pointed this out and Vasily became unnecessarily defensive, saying that unless I happened to have a giant hammer, they were just as useful or as useless as anything else I could propose.

'We've got the giant,' I said. 'We just need the hammer.'

I watched Vasily's expression of bafflement descend and then lift as he realized I was talking about Tevdore.

245

'And the hammer?'

'We make one. What sort of size does it need to be?'

'With sufficient momentum,' his said, his eyes rolling upward as he did some rough mental calculations, 'ten to fifteen kilograms would be ample,' he said, 'especially if it was a cone-shaped alloy of sufficient density.'

'Well then,' I said, 'all we need to do is improvise a little forge, put a crucible in it and find some sand and ten kilos of scrap metal to melt.'

'That's all?'

And this time it was I who didn't know if Vasily was being ironic.

☩

The result of this calculation was a meeting; for now it seemed we had all the pieces and the players, at least in potential. We rounded up Tevdore and Fidel and once we were all together in the privacy of our room, I asked them to promise not to reveal anything of what they were about to hear.

'Already have you my promise,' said Tevdore, nodding solemnly.

'A promise,' said Fidel, who was stretching his neck as if he was warming up for a bout of boxing, 'is a promise.'

Vasily, who was always nervous when he had to speak to others, nudged me forward.

'The reason we cannot speak of these things is because we are not free,' I said. 'How different life would be if we could speak freely on whatever we wished! But we are all prisoners here.

'We are granted the appearance of freedom, but no more. Anyone who breaks the rules pays a high price. No mercy is shown. And what is most precious to us is kept from us, in the hope that we will forget it, that we will conform, that we will live like sheep according to the rules imposed on us. But this is not real life. Something in our natures disagrees with this, so break the rules we must.'

I let this sink in.

'Vasily Vasilivich has explored more than any of us: it seems we could spend a lifetime exploring this place and not reach its limits. I for one don't wish to spend my life wandering these rooms and corridors. I have myself discovered that it isn't enough simply to wish to escape: the possibility of escape becomes real only when we search actively for it. Now we have discovered that it exists, and we have a plan to make it happen, but we cannot do it alone.'

All this, I thought, sounded good. But Fidel was still doing his neck-stretching exercises and despite nodding in agreement from time to time, he gave the impression of not being the slightest bit interested. I'd often had the feeling with Fidel that he agreed to things without really understanding them. I wasn't sure that he ever really grasped anything until it began to happen to him.

Tevdore was slumped in his chair like an overcooked okra with a look of suicidal apathy on his face.

'My friends, I am certain this is not my true home. It is a prison which bears only the faintest memory of my true home, and in every other aspect is a distortion, a corruption, a mockery. With all my heart I wish to escape. And it is natural for a man to wish for his friends what he wishes for himself. How long have I spent simply observing? How long have we all spent observing? That is one kind of action. But now another order of action is required, if we are not to become sleepwalkers, passively observing our own helplessness and hoping blindly for the best.'

I turned to Fidel, whose participation was so important, yet whose interest seemed so unpredictable.

'We have seen your bravery, Fidel, your skill, your honour.

What good are these gifts, if they aren't used to lead others to victory? If they don't serve as an example to others?'

Fidel gave a sort of shrug.

'And you, Tevdore, possessed of such wisdom. But what use is your wisdom cooped up in this place, where no one can benefit from it? What good is love if it isn't brought into the world and made visible?'

I could see that my words were very slowly beginning to find their mark. Fidel, for the first time since I'd met him, had begun to look genuinely thoughtful. Tevdore grew more and more pensive, and then so crestfallen that I regretted my own words.

I didn't know what to say next, and a silence settled over us. Then the strangest thing happened. Tevdore, who I was afraid I'd offended to the point where he'd feel too hurt to collaborate with us any further, reached out and gently took Fidel's hand into his own, and on his other side, took Vasily's. Nothing was said. Following his example I reached out to the others. Our hands met and the circle was closed. Then Tevdore lowered his head silently as if to utter a grace, and was still for a few minutes. What private benediction did he invoke, that such an unexpected presence seemed to descend on us at that moment? I couldn't know. Yet in that wordless pause I felt such closeness to the others as I had ever known, as if a portion of each of them was within me and a portion of me within them, like rivers that converge and release themselves into a single flow. We had nothing in common in the worldly sense. We could hardly, in fact, have been more different kinds of men. But that was all irrelevant now. Then I heard the word 'Amen', deep and calm and resonant, and recognized not Tevdore's voice but that of Fidel. I looked up. His face had lost all trace of its habitual posturing and for once was without expression, serene and resolute.

'So what's the plan?' he asked.

I described the pipes, the necessity of destroying them and

the calculation we had made for the rate at which the house would fill with water.

'Haven't swum for ages,' said Fidel. 'Love swimming.'

I explained that the timing had to be just right, and that the operation could only take place when the doctors were here and the doors were sealed. And I put forward my ideas for how we could manufacture a hammer. I didn't know all the details, like the various melting points of different metals, but supposed that we'd make discoveries along the way, finding out much of what we needed by trying; in the meantime, each of us had a task. A certain amount of stealing was involved, which made Tevdore uncomfortable, but it was no time for moral qualms. We had to do whatever we could to make it happen.

☩

Our surroundings were once again transformed by having our secret purpose in mind. We noticed different things now, the way you notice women who are pregnant when someone close to you is in the same condition. Then we stole them. Over the next few days, a stream of incongruous artefacts began to pile up, mostly purloined by Tevdore and Fidel. Among them were several metal zips, belt buckles and coat hangers, some cutlery, an old tap, an Italianate picture frame which might have been bronze, a good-sized pile of metal curtain accessories, the skeleton of an umbrella, coat-hooks, window-handles, a number of watches, a brass ashtray made from the base of an artillery shell, a small ornamental metal piano, a handful of bullet casings and – from where, I never asked – a hand-forged Anatolian sheepdog collar with sharp metal spikes to prevent attacks from wolves.

My own search in the meantime was for a vessel that could serve as a crucible, without which our raw materials were useless and couldn't be transformed. After a good deal of

249

searching I was able to find several earthenware flower pots, which I smuggled back to my room at night with Vasily's help. I also found a metal bucket which had been abandoned in a cupboard because of a small hole in its base; for carrying water it was useless but it would serve perfectly as the container for our miniature forge. Vasily had in the meantime made a rough design for a bellows and found the various pieces needed to construct it, which was the task I'd given to Fidel. The result was astonishing. Fidel, using the fabric canopy of the umbrella we were planning to melt, various bits of wood and a pipe which had once belonged to a radiator, had fashioned a perfectly functioning bellows which produced a powerful stream of air when pumped. I was humbled and impressed.

We still had no solution to the problem of fuel. We needed charcoal, which could be heated until it was white-hot, but there was none in the fireplaces downstairs, which were never used. It was a long time before Vasily and I, after wearying explorations of the branching corridors on the middle floor, discovered a number of empty rooms where the fireplaces still contained a few forgotten handfuls of charcoal and even some unburned lumps of coal. It was impossible to know how long ago they had been left there. Later, I often wondered about these abandoned rooms. Had they been assigned to residents who had never arrived, or who had already left? When and where had they gone? Their emptiness haunted me, like faces I had glimpsed and been unable to forget.

None of us knew exactly how molten metal would behave (my own ideas were very rough, having once visited a traditional forge many years before in pursuit of a girl whose father was a village blacksmith). I tried to conceal the limits of my understanding from the others. I knew that liquid metal would need to be poured into sand in order to cool and harden, and that we needed to somehow make a mould in the shape of the hammer-head that we eventually wanted. The mould itself needed to be fragile enough to melt on contact with the molten metal, but sturdy enough to withstand the pressure of the sand around it.

Exactly how this was supposed to be done I had no idea. We made some experimental versions, and made what we hoped were improvements to them. Eventually we built a sort of skeleton of the giant hammer from thin wooden stirrers which we collected from the dining room. Then to give it its final shape we used paper soaked in sugar-water, which went stiff as it dried. The resulting structure was light like a Chinese lantern and would burn away when the hot metal came into contact with it, but it was strong enough to have sand packed around it without distorting. In its centre was a hole to receive a wooden handle; a long curtain rod, which we intended to steal at the last minute. In case that didn't work, we made the central portion of the hammer-head slightly thinner than the rest, so that it could be swung from a rope or a chord.

To contain the mould we made a very imperfect box from various pieces of wooden trim that we scavenged from various rooms. It was held together with fork-handles, cleverly shaped into clips by Fidel, who proved to have a real talent for making things with his hands.

With Vasily, I searched for sand, remembering that the small garden where Petra had first led me was laid with flagstones, which were almost certain to have sand underneath them. They did, but it was mixed with earth and almost indistinguishable from it, so we filled up two pillowcases with the filthy stuff and disguised the theft by redistributing gravel between the cracks of the stones. Then we began the long process of washing it in small portions, using the sink in the bedroom. Just this part took us several days. The mud and earth eventually dissolved or floated to the surface or drained through the pillowcases with the water. We were left, eventually, with a much-reduced, few handfuls of greyish sand. But it was sand.

251

Then came the moment to put things to the test. It wasn't strictly necessary for either Fidel or Tevdore to be involved in this part but when it came to it, their presence seemed perfectly natural. Tevdore had in any case become quite protective of us, and Fidel wanted to see how his lovingly fashioned bellows would perform.

We all went down one night, long after our fellow residents had settled under the veil of sleep and when even the house itself seemed to sleep, although some of us knew better. We each carried a pillowcase full of supplies. The practice of finding our way in near-darkness was familiar to both me and Vasily, so I led Fidel down and Vasily led Tevdore; the two of them were forced to give up their usual concerns and simply put their trust in their guides. After that, the bond was stronger between all of us and things were different. There was much that we simply couldn't explain. Now the scale of our dreams was magnified by the participation of the others, and for the first time I tasted the thrill of a challenge in which we all would play our individual part and which was impossible to accomplish alone. However differently each one of us experienced the adventure, we were each in its grip now and we all sensed that it was greater than the sum of us.

We led them to the pipes, and after that the whole thing was more real for Fidel and Tevdore, who had never seen them. Fidel put his hand on the biggest pipe and nodded approvingly, impressed and delighted by its size. Tevdore nodded in a kind of awe, but said nothing. Their eyes sparkled in the light of our little oil lamps, and seemed unexpectedly luminous.

Nearby, we laid out our equipment. I made a circle of charcoal on top of some paper I had already put in the bucket, and piled it up. We attached the tube from the bellows, steadied the flower pot in the centre and we were ready to melt metal: our little forge was in operation. But it wasn't the event we had hoped for. Nothing really worked. The charcoal didn't light evenly; later on the flower pot cracked, and the temperature was never high enough to melt anything. We were also very nervous and several times thought we heard noises that we imagined came from a team of encircling Mudaks.

Our attempt at metalworking turned out to be the first of several nights of experimentation and discovery, each of which determined our activity the following day, because during the day we would make the adjustments we'd discovered the night before were necessary. Each of us struggled with a different discovery and a different solution. These gave our days new meaning. We soon lost our taste for theory and contemplation and unnecessary worrying; we had measurable tasks now. I already knew, for example – having long ago read about the subject – that the proportions of air, fuel and metal had to be correct for our forge to be successful, and for it all to lead to the greater hope attached to it. They had to be in balance, in equilibrium. But what did that theory mean to us now, while we were down here, scared and covered in grime and alone in the near-darkness, and had staked everything on it? Nothing. We had to learn everything by actually doing it. Someone might have come and read us a whole book on the theory of equilibrium, but we would have laughed. We were writing our own book and, as painful as it was, enjoying it. We had struggled and risked to find and prepare the raw materials; we had watched our first efforts fail, and had at last glimpsed with our own eyes, as the first nugget of molten metal appeared in the bottom of our newly lined pot, the promise of fulfilment.

It had taken longer than we'd expected, but we were learning along the way. We'd found a second and more sturdy flower pot, and packed it in the soil we'd dug up which most resembled clay, which prevented it from cracking. We made a second bellows, which could be operated from the opposite side to the first, and which made the temperature high enough to melt our little bag of treasure. And we did various experiments to bring the

253

sand to a consistency where it was neither too thick to be easily moulded, nor too powdery.

The balance between these elements was finer than we had supposed. But when we set to work once again with our revised equipment, a kind of magic attended our efforts. Watching the faces of the others, silent and intent, glowing in the sun-coloured light from the charcoal, I might have been in the company of wizards or alchemists, engaged in a task as vital as it was secret. Their singleness of purpose moved me deeply, and the challenges of our work had brought us closer at every stage. We relished the smell of the hot metallic fumes, our eyes fixed on the stubborn gleam of the mass inside the pot, and watched each piece of metal relinquishing its solidity to the heat, feeling its submission as if it was in part our own.

Preparing to lift the pot from the flames, and to pour it into the mould we'd prepared, I looked at the others in turn, and felt at that moment real love for them; not a personal love, but the love you experience at seeing a thing achieve its truest purpose, like a bullet dropping with deadly precision onto its target, when you have the feeling that however good or bad the consequences that's just how things were meant to be. It was love forged in the knowing that from our drab supply of mute, abandoned things we were now producing something new and of a different order to which we had assigned, after long struggle, a vital and lofty purpose. Against all this the habits and weaknesses of our individual characters and the way we each admired or endured them seemed unimportant. Our task was no longer personal; it had gone beyond us, and we were in its grip now. Perhaps a thousand men had felt this same feeling under the same circumstances at a thousand different times; or perhaps each of those thousand moments was happening now; or perhaps it was all the same moment, happening all the time. We had fallen under the spell of the eternal, and time no longer existed for us.

Chapter 13

W E HADN'T SLEPT PROPERLY FOR DAYS, so after our experimental adventures in the basement, we were all exhausted. I was asleep alone in my room when I heard a gentle knock at the door, and saw Petra's face appear. As soon as she saw me, her features broke into a smile of childlike radiance.

It was the last thing I expected. The cruellest person I had ever encountered and who had deliberately sabotaged my every ambition was slipping into my room as if for a friendly chat. She was wearing a long cotton dress like the one she had worn when I first saw her, and had a canvas satchel over her shoulder which she hung on the back of the door, then walked up to me confidently. I watched her but didn't speak.

'Look at you,' she said tenderly. 'They haven't been taking care of you. My darling.' She stroked my cheek. 'I've got some things to help you get your strength back.' She went to the bag, and as her back was turned I observed her lovely slenderness, and felt a pang of longing. On the table aside my bed she put a jar of ointment and some fruit, then sat at the chair, calmly peeling an orange as she looked into my eyes with an unnerving expression of sympathy.

'You have doubts about us,' she said gently. That was like saying Siberia could be a little cool in winter. 'I suppose it's only natural.'

I studied her in disbelief and kept my silence. It was as if the other Petra – the vicious, enraged and icy-hearted version – no longer existed and had never existed. For a moment I wondered if this was another trick of the place; that of the things one came to love, there was two of everything, both versions equally real, which one was obliged to enjoy and to suffer in turn. Perhaps by this strange arrangement, the slender, beautiful and tender woman by my side, whose natural perfume filled me with the yearning to pull her into my arms and feel her yield to me, really was a different being, and knew nothing of her demonic counterpart. I felt my resistance to her beginning to soften, and the urge to speak. Perhaps this was simply her illness, over which she herself had no control, and which could be cured or exorcised with the right kind of help. For a few moments, my mind jumped forward to the day when we were both in the outside world, in the consulting room of a benevolent specialist; afflictions such as hers had been studied and could be understood. I was about to ask her if she knew what she had done and if she had really meant to do it, convinced at that moment that her cruelty must have been an aberration, like the occasionally erratic behaviour of a veteran who has a tiny piece of bullet still lodged in his brain. Then she spoke again, in that slightly sickly-sweet voice of hers.

'We've been through too much together to hold grudges. I know you know that. We're a part of each other's lives.'

How long had I known her? I wasn't sure. It felt like years. Yet it was true: she had entered my life more deeply than I had guessed, and I had given myself to her more freely and with greater wholeness than to anyone. Such was her conviction, and such the tenderness with which it was expressed, it seemed hardly possible to believe that this was the same woman who had so brutally betrayed me. She stroked my cheek again.

'I love you,' she said sweetly. 'And you love me.'

If she had only kept her lovely mouth shut, I might have

come around to her way of seeing things. But her final words tipped the balance, and the spell began to falter, because love is one of those few words that resists distortion, and exposes falsehood at its origin. Then I saw again those beautiful fragments of colour in her eyes, which had once so mesmerized me. At that moment they seemed to convey the essence of her own fragmented self. Everything about her was a lie, I suddenly realized, which her eyes alone were unable to conceal. In the grip of this revelation, I wasn't really listening to her. Then I was aware that she was giving me some instructions for the ointment, which was for bruises I'd received at the tender hands of the Mudaks. It seemed a fitting metaphor. I had hoped, by way of a confession, she might bare her soul. I was getting ointment instead.

Then she cocked her head like an animal in the wild who senses danger, and stood up abruptly. I had seen her do this kind of thing before, and always took it for some sort of preternatural gift. But it was nothing more than her highly developed fear of discovery. She took her bag, went to the door and was about to open it when Tevdore threw it open from the other side. He looked down at her in friendly surprise. Petra held her head level, but her eyes rose up to his like those of a guilty dog, and I watched her face harden into an expression of loathing as she slipped past him into the corridor.

'Certainly, is woman now,' said Tevdore, as he sat down. I didn't understand his comment.

'Is woman now, but I remember when was child.'

'When Petra was a child?' I asked. 'How is that possible?'

'Was child when her parents did bring her here.'

'Her parents — ?'

He nodded in solemn recollection.

'I remember because so much she did cry, but mother not did care.'

'They left her here — ?'

257

'Was for her parents too much problem, so did bring her back and wish to forget.'

✝

Our giant hammer, like an Ossetian peasant bride, was not as beautiful as it might have been, but it filled us with a mixture of awe and longing, and we loved it as pagans might love their favourite idol. We didn't know how long freshly poured metal was supposed to cool for, or whether it became harder over time. So for three days we hardly dared to look at it, but when things felt that they'd got back to normal, and none of us seemed to be under suspicion for anything, we all met to inspect our work.

The shape and the colour were uneven, and there was no question of smoothing or polishing it to perfection. But it didn't matter. For the moment we were so astonished by the fact alone that we had actually made the thing ourselves, and it seemed to possess a beauty surpassing anything else. It was roughly cone-shaped, as we'd designed it to be, and its surface was pitted from its contact with the imperfect sand. At one corner it was just possible to make out the geared edges of several tiny steel cogs, which must have come from a wristwatch that hadn't fully melted. We could also see the successive layers created by different pourings, resembling the different eras of an archaeological dig, and the worrying unevenness of the central hole that would make fitting a handle to it problematic. This turned out not to matter, because we never found a suitable handle in any case, and used the hole for one of our impro-vised ropes made from curtain. But it was, above all, heavy. Only Tevdore could lift it with a single giant hand, and even for him it was a struggle. If all else failed, he could smash the heads of a few Mudaks with it, as the French say, *pour encourager les autres*.

To test it, I suggested we all go at dusk to the little garden where we'd stolen the sand, because we'd never seen anyone else there and there was less chance of being heard. The others thought it unnecessary, but we couldn't have it break in half when the moment came. It was no time to take chances; all the risk we were about to take had to be concentrated in a single and momentous act of defiance. So we went in a kind of convoy, with Tevdore in the middle carrying the hammer over his shoulder in a doubled pillowcase. I led the way and Fidel followed behind, so that one of us would be able to distract any roaming Mudaks either ahead or behind us, and give Tevdore time to escape.

We found our way down to the garden and I couldn't help thinking of my first encounter with Petra there, and was sad. We set to work freeing one of the heavy flagstones, then rested it at an angle against a ledge, where it was about the same height as the pipe we intended to destroy. Tevdore came up with the hammer, paid out the rope until its nose gently touched the stone, then began to swing it.

We stood well clear, not entirely confident of the strength of our homemade rope, as the swing widened to a crescent, and eventually a circle. An expression of grim delight came over Tevdore's features as he struggled to control the weight. Then when it was circling at a steady speed he shifted his position and swung it at the target. We held our breaths. The result surprised us all, and left us giggling like schoolboys on a prank. The hammer had passed through the flagstone like a *dashka*° bullet, leaving a pile of shattered fragments. There was no question of having to make a second test.

° Female nickname for the Soviet heavy machine gun firing a 12.7mm cartridge, derived from the manufacturer's abbreviation DShK (*Degtyaryov-Shpagina Krupnokaliberny*).

It remained only to fine-tune the plan. This was no mass breakout: there were few of us and our resources were so slender that each had to perform his own task to the full, as well as depend utterly on the others. Without having been urged on, Tevdore would never have got involved. I suspected he was doing the whole thing out of love in any case, and didn't really care about the outcome; he had never known or had forgotten how to care about abstract things, and his nature was to accept and forgive. Fidel, I suspected, wanted the challenge. But like Tevdore he didn't seem to be bothered by the deeper purpose of the whole thing, and although he pretended to take it seriously, he was merely copying us. He had no plans in the event of our successful escape. Yet none of us could replicate each other's tasks. Tevdore, our source of strength, would attack the pipe. No one else had the strength to attempt it. Everything, in the early stages, had to be directed towards this aim. Fidel, who knew how to fight, would be our defence against any interfering Mudaks, when they attempted to breach the dumb waiter entrance. It was good that they were already afraid of him: they would be unhappy to see him. If things got bad, the plan was to fall back to Tevdore's position where, if it came to it, we'd make our last stand.

We calculated that the darkness of the basement would be unfamiliar to the Mudaks and an advantage to us. I had the idea of making extra lamps which, when placed together in pairs, would indicate the route to the dumb waiter. Placed singly, they would lead nowhere, and in the haste of escape would allow us to disappear into the darkness and confuse any pursuers without completely losing our own way.

☩

For several days in a row we went over the plan until we knew everything backwards. From then on, each of us kept hidden a small bag of the things that we wanted to take with us, wrapped in such a way as to be waterproof. Everything, we all hoped, was going to get very wet. Until then, we needed to stay fit, say nothing and get used to having ever-colder baths.

I had in the meantime acquired the habit of taking a few minutes each morning to sit in stillness. I did the same thing before I slept at night. Vasily jokingly called this my 'church-going' but it was much simpler. I had discovered in these two portions of the day the opportunity to step back from my actions and attempt to fit them into a greater scale of things. These two periods of silence and reflection had become the havens from which I embarked and returned to at the end of each uncertain day. In the mornings I searched myself for strength to face what lay ahead; in the evenings I enquired from myself whether I had acted from my own wishes or not. Between the two lay all the imperfections of life.

I tried too to push the outside world from my thoughts, but it was never far away, and complicated matters. I realized I had gone from wanting to tell my story to the outside world to simply being content to escape. The satisfaction I pictured at telling others of my imprisonment seemed less certain now. I couldn't give someone else my experience; no one was likely to believe it in any case. Why then this compulsion? I had felt with such conviction that the world should know about the improbable place I had been confined to. Now I was less sure. It was enough to have known it. Perhaps Tevdore's unworldly acceptance of everything was troubling me: I knew that my precious freedom meant little to him. He considered himself free already. And if I were myself really free, I carried freedom with me and experienced it, and this experience was real; if I were imprisoned, I would remain imprisoned in the outside world too, and I would experience the world as a place of imprisonment.

Which then, was the real freedom, and which the imprisonment? I remembered Vasily's saying that reality could neither be wholly objective nor wholly subjective, or something like that, and for the first time I had an inkling of what he meant. It dawned on me that freedom was also freedom from the compulsion to be free. But how would that be? Take away this cherished longing, and there would be nothing left of myself. Once again I was at the frontier of my understanding. Then I recalled the face of that beautiful Persian, her presence beside me and that melting feeling I experienced, as if I had been dissolved into the sea of the Infinite. And suddenly all the problems of words and thoughts and the complications of reasoning seemed to disappear.

✠

I'd like to claim that, when it came, I was expecting it. I was not. The alarm woke me up: it seemed that the sequence of logic from hearing the sound to realizing its full significance was a long one (perhaps it was, in fact, years). But we had practised the routine and knew what we had to do. Vasily and I dressed in warm clothes and gathered up the things we needed, then went to meet the others, pushing on the doors we wanted to check as we went. The house had been thrown into the usual chaos at the sound of the alarm, and there was little danger of our small gathering being noticed. Looking around, I was reminded that another consequence of the place was that no one ever seemed to learn anything. I didn't know for sure how long the other residents had been repeating the same process of frantically clearing up, but they were all doing the same as usual, as if for the first time. Even the Mudaks were totally absorbed in running backwards and forwards with buckets and brooms. No one was actually thinking.

Tevdore appeared first, carrying the wrapped-up hammer over his shoulder as if it were a bag of washing, with a look of nonchalance on his face which suggested that he did have a devious side after all. Fidel sauntered up soon afterwards, unable to disguise his own attempt at looking innocent, but in the mayhem it hardly mattered. Then we split up so as not to draw attention to ourselves and each of us made his own way, very casually, to the kitchen doors. Here we had an unpleasant fright. Seeing no one, I had given the all-clear for us to go in, but as I pushed the doors open I disturbed a Mudak eating what looked like a rat. I hadn't seen him from the other side. I froze in mid-step as he looked up, and gave me the look of an animal about to pounce. I knew that in the next instant he could tele-pathically summon his sporting brethren, and our whole plan seemed to be teetering on the brink of disaster. Then I glimpsed a mop leaning against the wall nearby, and pointed to it in a suitably timid manner, making the motions of someone who knew how to use one. The deadly look subsided. He went to the mop, grabbed it, walked across the kitchen and put it into my trembling hand. Then with the faintest of nods I was dismissed.

A few minutes later, while we were sauntering about and pretending to take an interest in cleaning, and while I was trying in vain to get my heartbeat back to normal, we saw him run out of the kitchen past us. Our chance had returned.

We went in. Vasily helped Tevdore through the dumb waiter hatch, and began assembling the first lamps, while from the kitchen I stole the largest container of olive oil I could find and passed it through the opening to Vasily. Then, as I ran back to prepare a spill from the cooker, something strange happened.

I said there was a made future and an unmade future. There are things in other words that will most probably happen and things which might happen if certain choices are made. I knew that now. As I put the twisted paper into the flame of the stove and saw it catch fire, I had exactly that same feeling as I'd had when I first set eyes on Petra, walking across the atrium, all that time ago. It was the feeling that there was something inexplic-able between us. There was nothing rational about it; it could only come from the future. The flame had spoken to me. The only problem was that I didn't know what it had said.

Fidel, meanwhile, had set about blocking the main doors by pushing the heavy table against them, and at the last minute had the brilliant idea of pouring oil onto the floor on the far side of the doors to make it impossible for the Mudaks to push against them. Then together we quickly retreated beyond the second door and he blocked it as best as he could with chairs and broom handles.

Tevdore and Vasily were waiting for us at the entrance to the dumb waiter. We clambered in, and I handed over the flaming spill. The first lamp soon flickered into life, and then the second and third, and soon a radiant line was driving forward into the darkness. With the debris we'd just raided from the storeroom, Fidel and I blocked the dumb waiter mechanism so that the Mudaks would have to break through it, or through the wall, to reach us. Then we turned to follow the others through the shadows, running back and forth in order to light up the way and putting our decoy lamps at intervals in the shadows.

I never asked Vasily how he managed to find the pipes so swiftly. It seemed we were there within a few minutes, feeling that we had a huge advantage over our adversaries. We put a rough circle of lanterns around Tevdore, watched him kneel and unwrap our precious idol, then tighten the rope around his hands like a gladiator about to enter the arena. All he really needed was a *papakha** on his head to look like one of Shamyl's fearless *mureeds*. He stood up slowly and smiled at us.

'Tevdore, my brother,' I said. 'We have come so far together. Now your efforts will allow us to go even further. I want you to hit that pipe with every bit of strength that you have. Don't

---

* The traditional woollen hat of the Caucasus, as worn by the followers of Imam Shamyl (1797–1871), political and religious leader of anti-Russian resistance during the mid-nineteenth century.

think about it. Just hit it as hard as you can and do not stop hitting it until —'

Chuckling, he pushed me gently aside.

The hammer began to swing, and with it Tevdore's body, like a great tree in a storm, while we watched in awe as the rope flew over his head and its orbit described a pale and ghostly circle. The suspense was unbearable. Then, like a living windmill, Tevdore lined himself up with the target and let his arms extend so that the hammer struck the pipe. The sound shook every cell in our bodies. It was as if a musical bolt of electricity, much louder than we could have imagined, had been sent through the building and far beyond. It was deep and clear and filled me with dread.

'Jesus goddamned Holy Christ almighty,' said Vasily, unnecessarily. 'That'll bring them running.'

We knew the Mudaks would hear us within seconds, and though it would take time for them to find us, our pipe-smashing was the equivalent of pouring blood into a shark-infested sea. Once again I felt the clarity of inevitability. There was no human source of help now; it was as though Fate was standing next to us and we could rest our hands on her and let her take us wherever she would.

Tevdore struck the pipe again, and again, and we waited for the metal to yield, which it showed as much sign of doing as a Soviet battle tank under a peasant's shovel. Our feeling of having the advantage began to falter. I had allowed myself to imagine that the pipe would burst open after the first few blows. But although each time the hammer found its mark the force must have been enormous, the pipe simply rang out like a bell, quivering with the energy of sound rather than, as I'd hoped, shattering into pieces like a glass at a Jewish wedding.

I urged Fidel to head back to the entrance, and Vasily to prepare a defensive line of decoy lamps. Then I waited until Tevdore had found his rhythm, reminded him that success would soon be in our grasp and headed back to the entrance myself, feeling that 'soon' would have to come fairly quickly. Running through the darkness I distinctly heard the distant howl of a wolf, and felt a chill of fear run down my spine.

The Mudaks were on time and on target. They had dealt with the lesser obstacles and with fanatical enthusiasm were breaking the dumb waiter into pieces with their fists in order to get into the basement. As I drew near I could see the widening shafts of light from the kitchen piercing the shadows ahead. Fidel stood to one side with a broom handle at the ready and I did the same. As the first Mudak's head appeared, squinting into the unexpected gloom, Fidel delivered the first blow. There was a pause, pleasant for us and unpleasant for them. Then two more heads appeared in a desperate effort to enter, and we beat them like dust-filled carpets.

Then the wall collapsed. This was a surprise. The Mudaks had simply torn it open from the far side and pushed it flat, allowing half a dozen of them to burst into the cellar at the same moment. It was time to withdraw. We stepped back behind the brick pillars, then jumped out to swing at their heads as they stumbled forward. Fidel was really pulling the salt out of it,* wielding a broom like his very own Zulfiqar,† downing a shaven-headed enemy at every stroke. Then just when it looked as though they would rush us, we heard Vasily shouting from the blackness to one side. He was taunting them with unrepeatable obscenities. Realizing there were more than just the two of us, the Mudaks were suddenly confused, and split up. Half a dozen of them ran in Vasily's direction, allowing us to leap forward and bludgeon a few more heads before pulling back again.

---

* i.e., putting his heart into it (Azeri proverb).

† The legendary double-bladed sword of 'Ali, fourth Caliph of the Islamic world and hero of the *Shi'a*.

The double-lamp idea was having unexpected benefits. As the Mudaks advanced, they had no idea which way to go and had no lights of their own, which allowed us to disappear into the darkness and reappear somewhere else, taking our bearings from the doubled lamps. Vasily too had really entered into the spirit of things and was running through the darkness taunting his pursuers, leading them into the shadows and then abandoning his lamp, leaving several Mudaks stranded on little islands of light, not knowing which way to return.

Yet we could only hope to delay them for so long. The Mudaks knew what to do: to find the source of the terrible tolling sound that was echoing through the dark, and to make it cease. We were doing a good job of slowing them up, but there were too many of them to fight off. I hated the Mudaks more than ever for interfering in everything that was precious to us. Why didn't they ever pick on some of the more deranged characters in the house, the ones who would probably benefit from a bit of physical hardship? The answer jumped suddenly into my mind. The Mudaks attacked us whenever they discovered we had our own ideas about things, our own initiatives. It was a strange moment for this revelation. But it was then, when it was already much too late, that I realized the other residents could do whatever they wanted, however bizarre or deranged, so long as they didn't do it from their *own* intention, which sent the Mudaks into a frenzy. They didn't always get it right, and could be tricked, as Petra had so cruelly shown. They would never understand the subtleties of deception. But the uncanny thing about them was their ability to sniff out such individual behaviour as if by a sixth sense, and communicate it to their fun-loving brethren almost instantaneously; a fact which, for the moment at least, was not working too well in our favour.

We fell back in a desperate half-circle, joined by Vasily, as the Mudaks began to close in, looking more menacing than ever. We knew that our punishment wouldn't be worth enduring.

I doubted whether they would allow us to live. We stood with our backs to Tevdore as the line of sullen faces inched closer, their eyes blackened by shadow, waiting for their moment. By now I was really ready to go out fighting, and regretted that I hadn't left a written record of our struggle for someone else to find one day and to ponder. That was when I promised myself, if I survived, to write down a record of my experience. I knew no one would believe it, but that wasn't the point.

I looked to Fidel, who'd taken up a fighting stance a few paces from me, and took in his sweaty, blood-streaked face. We nodded to each other. He nodded in turn to Vasily. None of us was going to abandon Tevdore, and there was nowhere else to go. The hammer-blows behind us continued their dreadful tolling, spelling out doom; we felt the shock of each impact in our bodies, and waited for the onslaught. By now I was thinking only of the damage I would be able to cause to several of the Mudaks before they could subdue us, and there was some comfort in this.

'Come on, you brainless *amçuks*!'* I heard myself shout, 'Come and get us!'

Fidel echoed me, and began his own taunts.

'What are you so scared of?'

'Afraid of the dark?'

'Want to run and get Mummy?'

'What about you, abortion-face?' This from Vasily.

We didn't know yet, although perhaps we sensed it, that they really were scared. This gave us enormous pleasure. Only it wasn't us they were scared of. Behind us, where every eye except our own was fixed, they'd seen something that had frozen them to the ground. They were so still that I risked a

---

* Colloquial term for the female organ, connoting 'sissy', but more offensive (Azeri).

quick glance behind me, and understood. On the surface of the pipe, to one side of Tevdore's blows, was what looked like a dark stain, spreading in every direction. As I watched, it seemed to be getting wider, and a trickle of water caught the glint of flames from our lamps as it fell from the bottom of the pipe to the floor. Then everything was still for another couple of seconds, except the swinging of Tevdore's arms, which swooped again like the sails of a windmill towards their target, and the pipe cried out again. A transformation was occurring. The trickle became a steady stream, and the pipe began to hiss. At the next impact, a slice of water, as thin as paper, spread upwards like a fan from a fissure in the pipe, then widened and stretched upwards to the joists above our heads. It was spraying into Tevdore, who was closest, and we could hear the hiss of water against his body.

I looked back at the Mudaks: they were transfixed, locked into a simultaneous calculation and looking uncertain about the outcome. They were terrified by the sight of the water. What happened next took perhaps a few more seconds, but felt like so much longer, and seemed to unfold in unnatural detail. Nearing the end of his strength, Tevdore swung once more, and I saw the sweep of the rope and the dull glint from the head of the hammer as it descended. Then it disappeared into the pipe itself, unleashing a furious torrent of water. Tevdore was knocked off his feet by the force of it; it pushed against my ankles and seemed to drag me to the ground, roaring. I fell onto my side, managed to keep hold of the lantern and banged into one of the brick columns, but I was too happy to care. The sight of the erupting water was ecstasy itself.

The effect on the Mudaks was instantaneous. They fled in unison, leaving the four of us floundering in the water, laughing out loud, slapping the water with our hands like demented seals, relieved beyond measure and intoxicated by our success. We could hardly hear each other over the noise, but I could just make out Vasily a few yards away, crawling through the water with an expression of delirium on his face, crying out at the top of his voice.

'Meatball! Meatball!'

But we did need to get out. The nearest of the lights had been knocked over, and it was almost pitch black. A little further away, some of them had been lifted by the water and were floating like little luminous boats. The danger now was that we would be lost in the darkness, so we splashed forward towards the furthest light we could see, and found the broken patch of wall, abandoned now by our adversaries. By the time we got there, the water was already above our ankles.

The flow was greater than we'd dared to hope for. Dirt and debris were being lifted by the water and carried along as if on a wind into every crack and corner. The leading wave drove into the storerooms, pushed open the doors as if by its own intelligence and returned again, rising all the while. It reached into the kitchen cupboards and rattled the saucepans which, like rescued hostages, broke free from their captivity and bobbed into the open space. In a big cupboard adjoining the kitchen, Fidel discovered the electricity supply, which we shut down by pulling a big red lever. Then, on the lookout for Mudaks, we made our way up the stairs to the atrium, where life seemed oddly normal. The alarm had stopped, which meant that the doctors must have arrived, and the place was looking tidier than usual. There was no trace of any of the Mudaks.

For a place that was about to be deliberately flooded, things were remarkably calm. Chicken Bone and Mrs Polite Smile were going through the motions of conducting a conversation, or lack of one, near the fireplace; the breastfeeding minister was playing a genteel game of chess with the lecherous woman in the fur coat; someone else was cleaning a potted plant with an ostrich-feather duster, and the deranged doctor I had earlier met, who we passed as we made for the stairs, was studying a collection of artwork entitled *Psychotic Indigenous Painters from*

New Guinea, muttering to himself, 'This is all wrong, completely wrong.' As we walked by he looked up at us and frowned.

'I get no thanks for this,' he said irritably, and waved a finger at us. 'No thanks from anyone!'

It was very strange. I had imagined pandemonium, but it all looked fairly normal. Up here no one had any idea about what had been unfolding beneath them, or what was about to happen.

At the foot of the stairs, we paused. We had all acquired a good number of scratches and bruises but nothing worse. We were exhausted. I sat down on the landing of the stairs to watch things. Tevdore and Fidel wanted to go to their rooms. We embraced and agreed to meet after we'd rested for a while.

'I think,' said Vasily, 'that this calls for a drink.'

He went upstairs. My feelings were beating like a fish against ice. I was filled with relief at having finally unleashed our plan and the forces that made it real; inexpressibly satisfied at having thrown the place into chaos and having evened up the score in our favour, and full of the very real but unspoken fear of what would come next. The uncertainty was like listening to the sounds of warfare in the distance and not knowing quite which direction the conflict is heading. Then I thought of the world outside again. I couldn't know for sure any more what really lay beyond the limits of the building. I naturally remembered the world of my former life, but the feelings linked to it were no longer as strong as before, and although I wouldn't have admitted it to anyone, I often had doubts about whether it would once again be as real as I hoped, or whether it would really live up to the picture that I'd painted of it to myself and others. I worried that I'd become like someone who repeats the same old stories but has forgotten the real feelings that originally went with them. Yet our situation had nevertheless taken on a wondrous quality. Our ongoing adventure, although founded on an unprovable speculation, had taken us to the brink of entirely new possibilities. We had, after all, come a long way for

271

the sake of something so intangible as the scent of a different world.

Vasily reappeared with a bottle and two small glasses and sat down next to me. He filled them and looked at me enquiringly.

'To ideas,' I said, taking my glass. 'To the power of ideas. Not people or institutions. I drink to ideas.'

We looked down in to the atrium, and saw the doctor standing by the main entrance under the red and green lights, which were no longer working. He pushed on the door experimentally, and when nothing happened, he walked back towards his office, looking troubled. A long time ago, or so it seemed, I had feared and loathed him. Now, abandoned by his faithful helpers, confused and sensing danger, he looked absurd.

Not surprisingly, a look of suspicion came over him as he took in the sight of us. We were wet and filthy and both looking as if we had roosters in our mouths.° A half-full bottle of vodka stood between us.

'Come down right now,' he ordered from the foot of the stairs.

'We're here to watch the swimming match,' said Vasily. 'And you're in it!'

We burst into fits of laughter at this.

'Of course I am,' he replied. Then a look of recognition came gradually into his eyes.

'I remember you,' he said, pointing at me. 'Don't think I don't remember you.'

'Are we doing something wrong?' I asked. 'You must realize we're *completely* mad.' Once again we were seized by uncontrollable laughter.

'I can take this up the line, you know,' he threatened. 'I know

---

* i.e., in the manner of a fox. In Azeri, a proverbial allusion to great happiness.

you think you're different, but I know people who'll see you for what you are. In the meantime I'm going to recommend an increase in your medication.'

Then a movement in the direction of the dining room caught his eye, and he looked away and back to us, then away again, as he tried to take in what he was seeing. Something abnormal was developing in the other room, where a little crowd had gathered by the stairs to the kitchen.

'You know about this – you're connected with this,' he said, and we could hear the growing anxiety in his voice. 'I know you're involved.' Then he ran towards the dining room and we lost sight of him.

'It's a strange world,' I said to Vasily.

'It is not the world that is strange, but our failure to understand it,' he answered, without looking at me.

The water, when it finally appeared, possessed a peculiar beauty. It looked black and spread slowly, but with great purpose, as if it were searching to fulfil the full limits of its task and understood its seriousness. It appeared first in the dining room at the top of the steps to the kitchen, curling around obstacles with snake-like stealth and swiftness, then bubbled up from the fireplace, darkening the surrounding floor and the carpet like blood in a slaughterhouse.

We watched in silence, transfixed by its advance. It was as if we had cut our own wrists and were now participating in the inevitable, for there was now no mistaking that we were really alive. At last we had a measure of time. We could observe time passing by means of the rising water, a measure beyond ourselves. It was objective. We had made time real, and we had earned it.

'It's working,' said Vasily quietly. 'It's really working.'

'As you calculated,' I said.

'I never calculated anything,' he said, looking dreamily at the advancing water. 'I never have. I've always *felt* the solutions to

273

things first. Then I do the maths and it all makes more sense. But it's only a cover, really, a kind of *prikritye.*° The feeling comes first, I can't help it.'

The others began to notice. A few were terrified and fled; others were rooted to the spot in a stupor of confusion. Most simply carried on as if the water wasn't there, noticing it from time to time and then ignoring it. One man had lain down in the centre of the atrium and with great enthusiasm was attempting to swim, even though it was still much too shallow. For us the sight was a spectacle of continual celebration. At a certain point pieces of furniture began to move around as if they had acquired their own minds and detached themselves from the floor. As the water rose higher the house began to creak like a submarine on the ocean floor; I wondered if it might actually burst open. Before long it was the depth of a man; then two. From around us we could hear various screams and sobs, although by no means everyone was unhappy. One man had stripped to his underwear and was taking immense pleasure in diving with great skill from the balcony and then swimming back; another had brought a fishing rod and was trying to hook some floating plastic cups.

Up it came, steadily and unstoppable like a tide. As it neared the landing we retreated upwards and went to our room, past the strange collection of dazed and bewildered-looking faces that had gathered around the balcony, the highest place they could reach. We gathered our things from their hiding places and checked them. Then we put on an extra layer of warm clothes, and made sure our dry ones were intact. Tevdore and Fidel joined us soon afterwards, and we exchanged observations.

The corridor leading to Petra's room was just beginning to fill up: we needed to leave. I looked down into the water. It seemed

---

° 'Smokescreen', to divert from the real event.

utterly alive. Then I swung my bag over my shoulder and as I did so I caught momentary sight of a face. On the far side of the balcony, Petra was standing motionless with the strange intensity of an apparition. She looked pale and unforgiving. She said nothing. I said nothing. It was she who had turned me into a shoemaker.[*] We stared at each other until one of the others urged me forward. I looked away for a moment, and when I looked back she was gone. I never saw her again.

We waded to her room. Petra's poodle, Thomas, stood in the middle of the room, marooned on the large table. Over-estimating his powers as usual, he jumped at us, snarling. I resisted the urge to hold him underwater, seeing him for what he was: the half-blind dog of a madwoman, about to be drowned. He swam out of the room behind us. We dragged the table into position under the chimney and hoisted ourselves onto it. I looked up towards the light. It seemed incredible that we would soon all be up there.

We waited, first sitting, then standing, as the water rose ever higher. Tevdore hummed soulfully. It was cold and our teeth shook uncontrollably but we had all been training ourselves to get used to cold water. Soon we could touch the sides of the chimney and lift ourselves off our feet with the help of the water. We began to jam pieces of chairs we had broken across the corners to act as braces for our ascent. Then came a glorious moment when the water formed a seal around the bottom of the chimney with the four of us inside it, and the chaos of the house below was closed out and a beautiful and silent light seemed to be reaching down to us. We were happy.

✝

---

[*] Perhaps a reference to the Azeri proverb *bashina galan bashmaqçi olar*, meaning that the wise learn from experience.

I'm not sure who noticed first. Perhaps without knowing it, we all did. But at some point it seemed to us that we'd been standing there for longer than seemed right. The water wasn't rising as quickly as it had been. Vasily, through chattering teeth, said that it was inevitable that as the level of the water grew higher, the rate of flow would be reduced. To solve the matter I scratched a mark on the wall where we could all see it. After what must have been a few minutes we could clearly see that the level was lower. The water was draining out.

There was no question of being able to discover where from: we had to act quickly to have any chance of ascending. We would have to balance on top of each other, then help each other out in turn from the top. We hadn't practised for that.

It was logical that Tevdore, being by far the tallest of us, should serve as the first man. Fidel manoeuvred himself onto his shoulders and leaned back against the chimney wall. Then I put a foot in Tevdore's linked hands underwater, and with Fidel's help pulled myself onto Tevdore's shoulder. The task was then to do the same thing against Fidel and end up standing on his shoulders without falling backwards. It was difficult and painful but we managed, and at last I was able to reach the upper lip of the chimney and haul myself upwards. I tied on our improvised rope to the hook where the old one had been and threw the other end down. Vasily grabbed it and scrambled up, aided by Fidel from below. Then Fidel. And then, we thought, Tevdore. But there was no one to help him from below, and he was wet and exhausted, and as much as he tried to lift himself up, he could get no higher than halfway. Fidel, seeing the problem, jumped heroically straight down into the water in order to help Tevdore from underneath his feet, holding his breath to allow Tevdore to stand on his shoulders. When that didn't work, I went down myself so that the two of us could both try to push him up. But the rope slid through his fingers, and his feet never reached the walls of the chimney. He would never get up without the help of the water, and at each minute it was getting lower. Fidel and I climbed up again and tried to help with another of the ropes, but nothing was working. We leaned down to him, urging him up, pulled on every rope. But we were on the verge of exhaustion.

'Go,' he said, looking up at us, his face bathed in that beautiful light. 'Go and escape!' He was smiling now. And I was willing to leave him behind, if it meant that the rest of us would escape and find our way back to him from the outside. But I knew that we wouldn't have the strength to open the window without him. It was all or none of us. We had to go back.

Nothing could express our feelings of disappointment and dread. As the water receded we clung to the table, shaking uncontrollably. When we could stand once again, we helped each other into our dry clothes and then staggered out into the corridor, now strewn with all the paraphernalia that had floated out of various rooms. Everything was drenched and chaotic, and the other residents were wandering about like the stunned survivors of a battle. By the time we reached the balcony, the water had already drained from it. I looked into the submerged atrium, which now formed a giant pool, and wondered where the water was leaking from. Perhaps the Mudaks had found a way to help the water to escape, or perhaps the water was draining from the very pipe that had first supplied it, and the supply was now exhausted.

My foot stepped on the end of a rag and I tried to kick it away, then realized with a shock that it was Thomas, Petra's poodle. He must have taken shelter in between the pillars of the balustrade and been strangled as the water rose. I felt nothing, and went to my room. It was in chaos and Vasily and I set about putting it slowly in order. By evening, the water had drained completely from the main part of the building. None of us had the strength to investigate how it was leaking away.

Incredibly, the Mudaks managed to produce some food that

evening. They seemed to be working on a kind of skeleton crew. There were much fewer of them and the ones that we saw were all busy with cleaning and ordering the disorder, and showed no interest in us. For the first time, a fire was set in the grate of the giant fireplace in the atrium, and another in the dining room, fed with a supply of wood that the Mudaks were hauling from somewhere in baskets strapped over their shoulders. It was as if, in part, the house was returning to a semblance of its original manner of functioning. Then even more incredibly the Mudaks went into our individual rooms and lit fires in the grates there as well. When the fire in our own room had got going, I sat by it with Vasily.

'I am sorry we failed,' I said.

How could we have failed? We had come so close. I had felt, before our success had been snatched from us, that the very universe was on my side.

'Don't say we've failed,' said Vasily. 'You sound like a scientist.'

I looked at him.

'In science the unexpected is the enemy. When an experiment goes wrong the scientist throws the results out because they're irrelevant. He says chance has intervened and the experiment has "failed". But all that has happened is that he's rejected an essential part of the result.'

'Then this isn't failure?'

'Of course not. Think of what we will learn from it.'

'We will learn it is impossible to get out of this Hell.'

I wanted to weep. It was failure, pure and simple. Nothing from below could help us. We needed something that could help us from above. How far I had come from my first notion that I could spring from the front door by means of a simple ruse! But the task was much more difficult, and beside it our ideas and efforts seemed like child's play, puny and inconsequential. Yet we could not, in that place, just lead peaceful and uncomplicated lives, ignoring the fact of our longing. To ignore it, to pretend, to divert ourselves with a thousand trivialities, would be worse than death.

Yet things were not the same after our watery escape attempt. They were not the same at all. The fires alone were evidence of that. Some comfort attended this utterly unexpected change. The colour and smell from the flames gave the place a different atmosphere. And the Mudaks no longer intimidated us. Nor did they bring us drugs, presumably because the supplies had been ruined. There were also fewer of them. I imagined that many of them had escaped to a different part of the building. A number of residents had also gone missing. We hadn't found their bodies, so they hadn't drowned. They had simply disappeared. This was interesting because it suggested the population of the place wasn't fixed and unchanging, as I'd always assumed. The huge effort we had made had not brought the change we'd expected, but a different one, which was less dramatic.

Then, while everything was still drying out, two of the residents I'd thought of as lost causes actually asked if they could join us in our next escape attempt. I'd never imagined such a thing could happen. They explained that they'd always wanted to escape and that the flooding had brought them to their senses. They even brought some small gifts from their private things in recognition of the favour we'd done them.

That got me thinking. I began to wonder what might happen if enough residents were determined to escape and if the same vision could be shared among them. I sensed new possibilities, which I didn't yet understand.

Not much later, out of all that misery, arose a strange vision. I saw what had to be done, and understood why so few are able to achieve it. Believing himself alive, it came to me, a man fears nothing more than his own extinction. How strange that my dream and ambition in life had always been to possess a house, and now my ambition was to destroy it; how mysterious that all my finding had become a preparation for losing, and all my longing had become a giving-up. What does the moth really know of annihilation? What had I to lose but myself, which was not, in any case, my own?

I went to Vasily, though I didn't put my thoughts quite this way to him. He would see it differently, but it was the vision that was important. I found him drying a pair of socks at the end of a coat hanger in front of the fire.

'None of our efforts can work,' I said. Like me he had been struggling not to give in to disillusion and despair, and sighed gloomily.

'Do you remember when you asked me about fishing?' I asked him.

'No.'

'Fishing nets. When you said that the net is the thing that is invisible when you're trying to understand fish?'

'Yes,' he said, adjusting a sock carefully without looking at me, 'I remember now.'

'It's the same reason we can't escape: because we believe in *ourselves*. Everything we do ourselves, and think we're doing, binds us to the system – to the house. The greater the efforts we make the closer we will seem to get to the goal – but we will always fall short of it.'

'You mean from the entropic point of view?' he said, after thinking for a few moments. A look of curiosity had come into his face. 'I always imagined our efforts would be enough, but perhaps I've been naive. You mean we cannot escape by our own efforts because it would be an expression of microcosmic perpetual motion?' he asked, brightening.

'I've no idea about that,' I said, which was true. 'I just know that we can't get out by any effort of escape, through our own plans, our own means, or anything that happens by *thinking* about it all. They will always promise results but can never fully become real.'

'By what theory did you arrive at this?'

'No theory, Vasily. That's my whole point. We've thought about it all enough! We've figured out all the logical solutions.'

He was quiet again for a few moments.

'You are saying there is no hope?'

'I'm saying it doesn't matter if there is hope or not. It's just either we wait it out like Tevdore seems willing to do or —'

'Or?'

'Or we destroy the house.'

Vasily gave me a strange, sad look.

'Destroy it? You are speaking of death?'

'No – not the ordinary death. But so long as the house exists we are still under its influence. We must destroy it to come under a different influence, one beyond ourselves. And pray for help.'

We sat for what seemed like a long time, in silence.

'Yes,' said Vasily eventually, with great feeling. 'I thought something like that might be the case. It shows up the limits of our thinking. But everything we've done has got us this far, hasn't it?'

We laughed.

'You have thought of a way to do this?' he asked.

I nodded, and recalled at that moment the voice of the flame I had earlier seen in the kitchen, and remembered how for a moment it had seemed to speak to me. I hadn't listened at the time, but it was clear enough now. I felt it now as one feels the approach of a rising storm: terrifying, life-changing, unstoppable.

'I should make some calculations – just a few,' he said, and felt in his pocket for a pencil. He saw me smiling.

'I'll fetch you one,' I said.

I wondered where Tevdore and Fidel had got to, and what they would make of the new idea. I'd put it forward to the new members of our group too, and explain as best as possible that the world was made for us, and it was our task to return to it.

I knew it would be a tough sell, but perhaps dancing camels really could make it snow.* I stood up and, picking my way through the debris that hadn't yet been cleaned up, went to find the others.

---

* 'If camels could dance, it might snow'; the Azeri equivalent of 'If pigs might fly'.

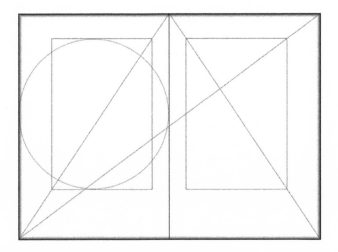

Page layout after Gutenberg, Van der Graf, Rosavario,
Tschichold, et al. Text area and page size are in the same proportion,
height of text block equals page width, and margins are
in ratios 2 (inner): 3 (upper): 4 (outer): 6 (lower).

WWW.BEAUXDRAPS.COM

Lightning Source UK Ltd.
Milton Keynes UK
UKHW011110151219
355424UK00006B/277/P